MURDER
IN
VENICE

MURDER IN VENICE

MARIA LUISA MINARELLI

TRANSLATED BY LUCINDA BYATT

Text copyright © 2015 by Maria Luisa Minarelli
Translation copyright © 2019 by Lucinda Byatt
All rights reserved.

Previously published as *Scarlatto Veneziano* by Amazon Publishing in Luxembourg in 2015. Translated from Italian by Lucinda Byatt. First published in English by Thomas & Mercer in collaboration with Amazon Crossing in 2019.

Published by Thomas & Mercer, in collaboration with Amazon Crossing, Seattle

www.apub.com

Amazon, the Amazon logo, Thomas & Mercer and Amazon Crossing are trademarks of Amazon.com, Inc., or its affiliates.

ISBN-13: 9781542094184
ISBN-10: 1542094186

Cover design by @blacksheep-uk.com

Printed in the United States of America

First edition

For my beloved Martina and Luca

DRAMATIS PERSONAE

Marco Pisani, *an avogadore (a high magistrate of Venice)*

Daniele Zen, *a lawyer, Marco's friend*

Nani, *Marco's gondolier*

Rosetta, *Marco's housekeeper*

Jacopo Tiralli, *Marco's secretary*

Chiara Renier, *a businesswoman and clairvoyant*

Tommaso Grassino, *aka* Maso, *Chiara's apprentice*

Alvise Cappello, *Patrono of the Arsenale*

Marino Barbaro, *an impoverished noble*

Lucia Piumazzo, *Marino's maid*

Lucrezia Scalfi, *a courtesan, Marino's lover*

Piero Corner, *a young aristocrat*

Dario Corner, *Piero's brother*

Francesca Corner, *Piero and Dario's mother*

Biagio Domenici, *Piero's former gondolier*

Maria Domenici, *Biagio's mother*

Lucietta Segati, *a former maidservant in the Corner household*

Paolo Labia, *a dissolute noble*

Zanetta, *owner of a second-hand clothing shop*

Marianna Biondini, *a fine-linen seamstress*

Menico Biondini, *Marianna's father*

Giannina Biondini, *Marianna's aunt*

Angela Sporti, *Marianna's friend*

Giorgio Sporti, *Angela's brother and Marianna's fiancé*

Baldo Vannucci, *an informant working for the inquisitors*

Francesco Loredan, *Doge of Venice*

CHAPTER 1

It was poor young Tommaso Grassino, whom everyone called Maso, who literally stumbled into the first dead body.

It had been a freezing night in early December, one of those Venetian nights when it feels as if icy droplets have risen from the canals by some process of sublimation, filling the *calli* with damp air and drenching the clothes of passers-by. It was still dark when Maso reluctantly dragged himself out of the warm bed in his parents' house behind Campo San Polo. Then, in the half-darkness, he walked down Ruga del Ravano and over the Rialto Bridge, hands deep in his pockets as he headed towards the heart of the Cannaregio district, to the silk-weaving workshop in Calle Venier where he worked as an apprentice.

Hardly anyone was about, just the occasional baker on the way home from work, wrapped in a heavy cloak, and a couple of tipsy patricians who had spent the night gambling at the Casin dei Nobili in Campo San Barnaba, now drawing into sight just a little further ahead.

He could hear the calls of the youngsters who worked in the drinking houses and taverns, sent ahead by the landlords to remove the shutters on to the street and light a blaze in the fireplace. They were waiting for the first vegetable sellers and fishermen who would soon start to arrive and would come in to warm themselves with a nip of wine before they started work offloading the boats around the Rialto Market.

Maso hurried along the street, whistling a jaunty tune as he went, when, perhaps because of the biting cold, or maybe because he'd left the house too soon, he felt a sudden and urgent need to urinate.

He swung right and headed into the maze of alleyways behind San Silvestro, ducked under a portico lit by the guttering flames of a candle-end below a shrine to the Virgin, and took a few steps into the pitch-darkness of a small courtyard. He had relieved himself quietly and gone back towards the street when his foot came into contact with something he couldn't readily identify. Someone must have left it lying there. He bent down to pick it up, curious to see what it was, and in the flickering candlelight from the shrine found himself staring at the wide-open eyes and protruding tongue of a face twisted into a grimace of terror. It was unquestionably the terror of death.

'*Aiuto!*' Maso croaked. Then, more loudly and with growing fear: 'Help! A man's dead! Someone, help!' His legs had turned to jelly, and he went on holding the lolling head in his hands and didn't even hear the rush of footsteps in the *calle*.

Two hands grasped his shoulders and pinned him against the wall. A gravelly voice shouted, 'What have you done, you scoundrel?' Another answered in shrill tones, 'He's killed him.'

A knot of people gathered in no time at all. The young men from the nearby taverns arrived, one of them carrying a lantern. The nosier ones bent down to look at the dead man. 'The poor sod's been strangled!' cried one.

'The guards! Call the guards!' shouted a man's voice. He was tall and well built, perhaps a porter from the market.

All around now the inhabitants were wide awake. Shutters clattered overhead, candles were lit, women wrapped in shawls peered out of the windows.

'Are you sure he's dead?' asked an old woman from above.

'He's strangled him,' someone answered. 'He's going to pay for this.'

In the midst of this uproar, Maso stuttered, his voice edged with terror, 'But I didn't . . . it wasn't me . . . I found him . . .' No one listened.

He became increasingly frightened as he was manhandled by a group of youths who thought it was their job to hand him over to justice. Around the corpse, the crowd swelled as hastily dressed men and women crowded into the courtyard and inquisitive passers-by in the calle were attracted by the shouting.

'Make way! Move aside!' The shouts announced the arrival of four agents in uniform, complete with bandoleers, high boots and lanterns. Maso heaved a sigh of relief at the sight but was then seized by two of them, while the others moved the corpse into the calle and examined it carefully. The sky was now filled by a milky dawn, and it was light enough to assess the situation.

'It's a patrician,' commented one of the guards. 'Look at his jacket and cloak, and his silk stockings.'

'But one of those impoverished types,' added his colleague. 'The shirt's darned and that wig looks moth-eaten.' It was true. The victim's clothing looked unkempt.

'He's been strangled,' the first went on. 'The rope's still around his neck. And he tried to defend himself with that dagger, see?' He pointed to the dagger clasped in the man's hand. 'It's got blood on it, so he must have wounded his attacker.'

The guards needed to disperse the crowd and decide what to do. But they were baffled. It wasn't every day that a corpse was found in the street. In fact, for all four of them, it was the first time something like this had happened in Venice, and the event had already made quite an impression on them.

'It's really up to the soldiers from the criminal court,' noted the youngest one wisely. His name was Antonio.

'But given that we're here now, we can't lose face over this,' replied another. 'Let's move the crowd on, for starters.'

It was not easy to convince the overexcited onlookers to return home or go about their affairs, but in the end the guards found themselves alone with Maso and the corpse.

'Who are you?' asked the oldest guard, one Luigi Biasio. 'Why did you kill him? Were you trying to rob him?'

'I haven't killed anyone,' said the young man defensively. He was deathly pale. 'I've never even set eyes on this gentleman before!'

'So why did they find you holding the body?'

'I was on my way to work and needed to take a leak, so I ducked under this portico. It was then that I stumbled over the body, but he was already dead.'

It had to be said that the young man, tall and scrawny, with a round face and ears that stuck out, did not look like a criminal as he stood there shaking with fear and indignation, dressed in his honest workday clothes. Nonetheless, he would have to be handed over to a magistrate.

And what should be done with the body? Before displaying it in public on the Ponte della Paglia in front of the prison, as was customary when the identity was not known, it would be just as well to make a few enquiries.

One of the guards took it upon himself to call a few of the local shopkeepers over to see if they could identify the man. And indeed a certain Zorzòn, the owner of a small general store, knew him. 'It's Marino Barbaro,' he said. 'He's one of those *barnabotti* and he lives behind Ca' Rezzonico, not far from here. He never had a copper on him, and he's gone and left me a pile of debts. I'll be lucky if I ever see my money again! But what a way to go . . .'

So, he was a barnabotto, the guards nodded. One of those impoverished nobles who would do anything and everything to make ends meet while living in the cramped apartments paid for by the Republic in the nearby parish of San Barnaba. That accounted for his shabby clothing.

For the time being, they could do nothing except carry him home, so two of the officers, Luigi Biasio and young Antonio, who had rustled up a sheet and a stretcher, began the necessary preparations. The other two, Giuseppe and Momo Serpieri, tied Maso's hands together and headed for Rialto, and then through the elegant streets of the Mercerie towards the ducal palace and the New Prisons.

The city was waking up. In front of the Erbaria, below the palace of the Camerlenghi, the Grand Canal was bustling with crafts of all types – rafts, *burchi* and *caorline* – piled high with fruit and vegetables from the islands. The fresh produce was gradually being unloaded on to the market stalls by tradesmen wearing heavy aprons. The icy air was filled with shouts of encouragement in a variety of local dialects, occasionally accompanied by the snatch of a tune or a hoarse cry of warning.

A little further on, the fishing boats from Chioggia and Pellestrina, rowed by well-muscled fishermen wearing coats and woollen hats, arrived with supplies for the fish market. A silvery stream of sardines, sole and scad poured from their baskets and lay, still quivering, on the stalls, surrounded by brilliant red prawns and mullet and black eels. Garrulous voices rose up to blend with the cries of the gulls.

Early customers had begun to arrive: working-class women with their shopping baskets on their arms, old men impatient to meet someone with whom to pass the time of day, a couple of mendicant friars.

Beyond the bridge, on Riva del Vin, the porters unloading barrels tried to avoid the small groups of young patricians wrapped in their cloaks who lurched rather unsteadily back from a night of partying, many wearing glazed expressions or still in the embrace of heavily made-up women.

For Maso, slouched between the two guards, it was a nightmare: the relief of having escaped a lynching by the crowd had evaporated and now nothing made sense. How could this possibly be happening to him, an honest apprentice who had never hurt anyone? How could he be accused of murder? It was all a misunderstanding and surely he would soon be freed.

Having passed the bridge beside the church of San Salvador, Giuseppe suddenly tugged sharply at the rope and Maso nearly fell over. 'Look there, Momo,' he said, stopping outside a drinking house. 'The Gatto Nero's open. What do you say to a quick glass of white wine?' Not waiting for an answer, he opened the door.

The three of them advanced into the room, which was lit only by the flames in the huge fireplace. In the dim light it was just possible to make out the counter in the middle and the hams and salami hanging from a heavy beam above it. The few customers seated at the tables were little more than shadows. Maso was relieved because he would have been humiliated to be seen trussed up like this.

'Will you have a glass too?' Giuseppe asked him.

Maso shook his head. The lump in his throat prevented him from swallowing. While the officers took evident pleasure in consuming a jug of wine and a plate of fried whitebait, which smelled delicious, the young man brooded over what had happened. Who would tell his parents? he wondered. They would never believe the accusation, but what could ordinary folk like them do about it? Nothing much, he thought. But surely Signorina Renier would come to his defence. She was the proprietor of the silk manufactory where he worked and she knew him well. Moreover, she was educated and a businesswoman. She would know the right people.

Back on the street, the three of them went on down the Mercerie. The fashionable clothes shops were still shut, but the crowds were growing: clerks on their way to the office, craftsmen heading to their workshops, women selling hot fritters, maidservants walking to the market followed by off-duty gondoliers. Maso saw none of them. He kept his head down, frightened of running into someone he knew and all the time wondering how it was all going to end. Yes, he was sure that Signorina Chiara Renier would help him; she was so clever, so well informed.

The thought of his employer reassured Maso, until, as they neared the end of Piazza San Marco, Giuseppe gave another tug on the rope and, with a macabre sense of humour, pointed at the columns where public executions took place. 'That's where you'll end up!' he laughed. 'Between Marco and Todaro.' For Maso, this was too much. He broke down and sobbed like a child.

CHAPTER 2

'Nani, where are you? It's time to go.' Marco Pisani was in the garden below his palace and, as he spoke, he looked up at a window on the mezzanine floor. In that instant, a handsome young man with a smiling face looked out. 'I'm coming, paròn. Just putting my jacket on, and I'll jump in the gondola!'

'And where did you spend the night, Plato, you scoundrel?' Marco smiled affectionately as he stroked a large grey cat stretched full length on the metal plate covering the wellhead. 'Be careful, Plato. If you go on annoying the lady cats of the parish, I'll be forced to call in the barber.' Plato looked unconcerned and jumped off the cover and on to the ground, where he started to rub against his master's legs. 'Off you go into the kitchen,' advised Marco. 'I happen to know that Rosetta has kept you a tidbit or two.'

Marco walked to the small jetty at the bottom of the garden and stepped into the gondola, where Nani was now waiting. The boat slipped through the watergate that opened in the thick wall on the right and glided along the short stretch of the canal by Campo San Vio, not far from the church of La Salute.

Nani stood on the stern, as usual, while he steered through the heavy traffic that already thronged the Grand Canal first thing in the morning, and every now and then he thought to himself that his master had many merits, but also the defect of being too modest. He would have liked to see the Pisani coat of arms on the gondola, since that would have sent the *bragozzi* and smaller boats scuttling. But his master liked to go unnoticed.

The young man believed that, in Venice, elegance was a civic duty. As he rowed, he mulled over the fact that no patrician would ever go out without a wig. None, that is, except his master, who insisted on going around bareheaded. He had very nice chestnut hair, of course, and it was always neatly tied. He also dressed well and his clothes were good quality, albeit sober and correct. But you only needed to look at him, with his elegant posture and penetrating gaze, to see that he was a born aristocrat.

Weaving the gondola skilfully around the other vessels that now thronged the canal, Nani pondered something else that he didn't understand about his master: his mania for work. Nani knew that he was one of the most highly trained magistrates, but ever since he had been elected *avogadore*, his master hadn't had a moment's peace; if the truth be told, he worked as hard as any bourgeois. Nani craned his neck to get a better view of the plunging neckline of a gentlewoman seated in a nearby gondola, and once again regretted the fact that he was always being sent on errands by his master. The servants in other patrician houses spent the day lying on their backs and sleeping in the antechambers. However, Nani had to admit that he enjoyed himself and was also well paid. It was just that a little more flamboyance from his master would not go amiss.

'Meet me here at the usual time,' Marco said as he stepped off the gondola in the Piazzetta and headed for the Procuratie Vecchie, which housed the administrative offices of the Serenissima Republic of Venice and served as the seat of the powerful Procurators of Saint Mark's. Heading under an archway, he climbed the staircase to the mezzanine floor, where he opened a painted door and entered a small room where he kept his official robes. Many of his fellow magistrates did the same in other small rooms around the square.

'Now, let's dress up as an avogadore,' he muttered, donning the white wig with ringlets down to his chest and the floor-length black state gown complete with train. He looked at himself in the large mirror and was not particularly impressed by the solemn figure he saw there. *Who knows why we have to administer justice in this get-up?* he wondered. *It's a different matter when we have to accompany the doge in processions or attend the Senate, but what possible good is a robe and wig on ordinary days when we have to question the suspect and the witnesses before a trial?*

Taking care not to trip on his way out, Marco crossed the square, which was already busy, given the time of day. He nodded to his acquaintances and glanced wistfully at the coffee shops, but he knew it was too late to stop. He entered the ducal palace through the Porta della Carta, which was surrounded as always by the desks of public notaries waiting for clients, then climbed the Giant's Staircase and crossed the loggia to the second floor and the clerks' offices.

The offices of the Avogaria were in the block of rooms between the mezzanine and the second floor, together with those of the other high magistracies, such as the criminal court of the Quarantìa. They stood between the basin and the New Prisons, to which they were linked by a covered bridge.

Neatly dressed in black, in keeping with his office, his secretary, Jacopo Tiralli, was waiting for him. 'Today, 7 December 1752, at dawn,' began Tiralli in his official voice, 'the body of the patrician Marino Barbaro was found close to Rialto. Death seems to have been by strangulation. The murderer was brought to the Carceri Nuove, where he is waiting to be interrogated. I have been told that he was caught in the act. Given that you're available, I fear that this task will fall to you, because the other avogadori haven't arrived yet.'

Short and skinny, Tiralli, who came from a bourgeois family and, like Pisani himself, had studied law at the University of Padua, was a valuable collaborator. Entirely devoted to his office and completely lacking anything resembling a sense of humour, he would often talk as if reading from an official document and was rarely seen to smile.

'Well then, Tiralli, let's see what it's all about,' Pisani sighed. Straightforward cases held little interest for him. 'It seems to be an open and shut case, probably a robbery that ended badly. Tell me what you know as we walk over to the prisons.'

Among their other tasks, the three avogadori di Comùn were responsible for preparing trials and prosecuting charges. Marco didn't mind this aspect of his position, since it brought him into contact with people, and often he didn't stop at summoning witnesses but instead preferred to visit them in person, taking the place of the guards, and the judges and soldiers from the criminal court. But as he didn't get involved in political issues, and never used his prerogative to overturn decisions taken by the other high magistracies in the event that he believed them to be unlawful, no one had ever complained.

As they crossed the bridge joining the ducal palace to the prisons – a massive stone building that had been erected a century earlier because there were not sufficient cells inside the palace itself – Tiralli updated Pisani on the facts. 'They speak for themselves,' he ended. 'This young Tommaso Grassino was found holding the body.'

Tiralli was precise and honest, but he sometimes jumped to conclusions. When the prison guard opened the cell on the ground floor, Marco almost burst out laughing. The prisoner stood pressed against the wall, shaking like a leaf, as if he wished the stones would swallow him whole, and looked at him beseechingly with reddened eyes.

'So, this is the dangerous murderer Tommaso Grassino?' asked Marco.

'Yes, Your Excellency, no . . . I mean, no, sir,' stammered Maso. 'My name's Grassino but I'm not a criminal.'

'Well, what were you doing holding the body of Marino Barbaro this morning?'

Maso told the story and explained that he went that way every day on his way to the workshop, adding that his acquaintances could testify that he was an honest man with a job and a future. He added that His Excellency could ask his mistress, the owner of the manufactory where he worked.

'You mean the master's wife?' clarified the secretary.

'No, sir, I mean my mistress, or rather Signorina Chiara Renier; she's unmarried and she owns the workshop. She inherited the business from her father and she's very talented. You know,' Maso added with a note of pride in his voice, wiping away his tears, 'we make the most beautiful brocades and gold cloth in all Venice and we export them throughout Europe. Signorina Renier knows me well. What motive would I have had to kill that poor man?'

Pisani was quite ready to believe him. It was clear that the young man had merely had the misfortune to find the body and then to run into a foolish guard who thought he'd caught the murderer. Apparently Barbaro really was penniless, so it was difficult to imagine anyone wanting to rob him. Who knew why he had been killed?

'For the moment,' Marco said, 'you've been arrested and charged, and you'll have to stay here for a few days, as prescribed by law. Your relatives can come and visit you and bring you food, you'll be treated well, but until such time as we find something that exonerates you, I'm afraid you cannot be released.'

Pisani also thought to himself that the excuse of building the case would allow him to protect this young man from being interrogated by the soldiers from the criminal court. They were quite capable of making a naïve youngster like him confess to anything they liked.

Back in the guardroom, Marco Pisani stopped to look at the dagger, which still had slight traces of blood on it, and to question the guards who had arrested Maso and carried the body home. The oldest, Luigi Biasio, seemed a bit more on the ball than the others. 'What more did you learn?' Marco asked.

'Barbaro lived in a run-down place in Dorsoduro, near Campo San Barnaba,' the man explained. 'He was looked after by an elderly maid, who started crying when she saw him in that state. We laid him down on the bed, alongside the rope he'd been strangled with. The maid is sure that he would have been going back to his mistress, Lucrezia Scalfi, with whom he often stayed until dawn; she said she knew nothing about his situation. But in any case, we've got the murderer.'

'Yet if the dead man was still clasping that bloody dagger,' Pisani objected, 'the killer must be wounded, and young Tommaso Grassino isn't. So why is he in prison?'

'Er . . . well . . . he was on the spot. And everyone said he'd done it . . .'

Once again Pisani found himself thinking that it was just as well that he only trusted his own judgement. Aloud, he said, 'Now that he's here, I'd prefer to keep him in prison, but there'll be trouble if you mistreat him. And get Lucrezia Scalfi to come and see me in my office this afternoon.'

When he returned to the Procuratie Vecchie to put his gown and wig back in the cupboard, Marco stopped for a moment to look at himself again. The mirror reflected a good-looking man in his prime. At thirty-five he still had the slim, muscular figure of a youth, thick chestnut hair tied at the nape, a high forehead and an aristocratic, slightly aquiline nose. Under his dark cloak he wore a knee-length jacket and waistcoat, both well cut but lacking any sort of adornment. It was the perfect outfit for passing unnoticed. Marco had no intention of renouncing his chosen anonymity, even if many regarded him as a bit of an eccentric.

He glanced quickly out of the mezzanine window, which lay below the level of the portico, and admired the sight of the piazza bathed in the pale wintery sun. To the left was Saint Mark's Basilica, an oriental fairy-tale of a building whose domes rose above the Gothic pinnacles surmounting the arches. Behind it was the miracle of the ducal palace, a lace-like fortress that looked as light as a cloud, and beyond again was the glittering sea. In front of him stood the line of the Procuratie Nuove, the pulsing heart of the state.

The huge square, paved in trachyte, hosted the usual mixed crowds: women in wide skirts, their faces covered by brightly coloured shawls or veils, were admiring the fabrics laid out by street vendors on the stalls protected by awnings; gentlemen dressed in yellow or pale blue satin with silk stockings were chatting in small groups, while merchants bustled past on business. Amongst the crowds, he could also make out a couple of Dominican monks, a few women selling fritters from wooden trays hung around their necks and the odd beggar.

Pisani had no wish to join the gossiping patricians who thronged the coffee houses around the square at this time of day, so he headed to the Mercerie and to Caffè Menegazzo, which was reputed to attract scholars and writers. He chose a corner table, ordered a few snacks – baby squid, salt cod and polenta, and sardines in sauce – and immersed himself in the newspapers provided by the coffee house for its intellectual clientele.

He was interrupted by the arrival of his friend, Daniele Zen. Daniele came from a well-off bourgeois family, and he and Marco had studied law together at the University of Padua. The meeting was extremely timely because, just as he had on previous occasions, Marco had decided to involve the lawyer in his inquiries. He appreciated his friend's discretion and sharp mind, and he was extremely fond of him.

'Being boorish as usual?' laughed Daniele, pulling up a chair to face Marco. He was very handsome, with blonde hair, blue eyes and an athletic physique. He was an habitué of the social scene, where he enjoyed considerable success with both marriageable girls and courtesans. 'You, my friend, are too serious. I bet you've been working all morning.'

'And I need to be back in the palace this afternoon,' Marco admitted. 'But on that note, I'm dealing with a case that might interest you. It involves a young apprentice who had the misfortune to literally stumble across the corpse of a barnabotto behind the church of San Silvestro; a group of idiotic guards then decided he was the murderer and they've brought him to prison. I don't believe there's any proof against him, although the death of this Marino Barbaro is a bit odd, but if I don't find the right trail soon, he'll need a good defence lawyer.'

'At your orders, Your Excellency,' joked Zen. 'But the murder of a barnabotto could be motivated by any number of causes: a gambling quarrel, fraud, debts, or who knows what else? Their sort will resort to anything. I've never really understood what they do for a living.'

'That's why you're going to give me a hand.' Pisani smiled, sipping his coffee.

Daniele was right about the barnabotti, Marco thought as he made his way back to his office. They were the scourge of the century and living proof of the decadence of the Serenissima. They belonged to those noble families who, when the profitable commerce of Venice with the Orient came to an end, had not managed to reinvest their assets in the burgeoning investments to be made by purchasing land on the mainland. What was more, finding themselves suddenly without any business interests, many of them had squandered the rest of their fortunes at the gambling table.

The ones who found themselves in the direst straits were, above all, the young men who had turned down a career in the army or a job in the magistracy on the grounds that, without money, they would have had to make do with lower-ranking positions. The more intelligent and enterprising took up posts as tutors or librarians in large households, where they were little more than servants, but the majority lived by their wits. The Serenissima granted the most impoverished nobles the possibility of using small lodgings close to the church of San Barnaba, in the Dorsoduro, hence the name barnabotti. But what was really absurd was they kept all the privileges of the aristocracy, including the right to vote in the Great Council.

Marco was sitting at his bench in the hall of the Avogaria when Lucrezia Scalfi was shown into the room. The woman bore all the hallmarks of wilted beauty: darkly ringed eyes, excessive make-up, flashy costume jewellery and clothes that had been remade once too often. A courtesan, Marco thought. She might even have been high up the list in her prime, but having failed to make provision for middle age, she was still obliged to ply her trade.

'Signora Scalfi,' Pisani began, looking straight at the woman, who bobbed a curtsey to him. 'It has been brought to our attention that you were on good terms with Marino Barbaro.'

'Yes, he was my friend. What a horrible end. But you can't possibly think that I'm involved, can you?' The defensive tone in the woman's voice was immediately noticeable.

'Don't concern yourself with my views, signora. Did he visit you yesterday evening?'

'Yes, he did,' she admitted reluctantly. 'He used to come two or three times a week and would stay for dinner. A few friends would usually join us, and . . .'

'You played cards. You are aware, I'm sure, that it is illegal to gamble in a private house.'

The woman shook her head vivaciously. 'No, of course we weren't gambling! We played music and chatted, and occasionally we would go out as a group to some tavern or other. Innocent pleasures.'

'But you make a living from such innocent pleasures.' It was a barbed remark. 'How much money did Barbaro have? Where did he get it from?'

'He had little, as you can well imagine. Sometimes he worked at the Casin dei Nobili, the gambling house close to where he lived; he kept a counter, a legitimate activity which, I hardly need to remind you, is only open to patricians. Sometimes, he was involved in deals—'

'And sometimes he sold his votes on the Great Council. Yes, I'm well aware of these things.'

The woman was silent.

'Did he give you money?' Pisani continued.

'Not much,' admitted Lucrezia. 'But I'd known him for many years . . . And occasionally he would bring a more affluent friend, so I could invite him—'

'Into your bed.'

'Well, yes, since you put it like that, into my bed.' The women smiled brazenly and adjusted a ringlet that fell across her forehead. She still had a full head of reddish-blonde hair.

'What I need to know from you,' Pisani went on, seeking to catch her eye, 'is whether Barbaro had any enemies, someone who wanted to see him dead?'

Lucrezia looked down. 'No, not that I know of. He'd done a few deals that weren't exactly above board, but nothing that merited murder . . . In my view he was killed by some drunk, probably by mistake.'

'But then why was he walking home last night? Didn't he have a gondola?'

Lucrezia burst into bitter laughter. 'A gondola? Marino? He didn't have a penny. He was always on foot. It must be at least four years since he was forced to sack his gondolier. He only kept on an old maid. Even his apartment belonged to the state.'

'And who were these friends, the ones he occasionally brought to your home?' insisted the avogadore.

Visibly shaken, the woman wound her false pearls around a finger, looking everywhere but at him. 'Well . . . I don't know. He never told me their surnames. Different men came, never the same ones. I don't know them.'

She was clearly lying and did not want to compromise her clients. But there was still time. If it proved necessary, sooner or later he would make her talk. There was no question of torture, of course – it had been banned in Venice now for many years. With a woman like this, though, he would only have to make a few veiled threats.

'When he visited, did Barbaro always go home at the same time?' he went on. 'Do you know which way he went?'

'I live close to Santa Maria Formosa, in Salizàda San Lio,' replied Lucrezia, happy to change the subject. 'He always left after two in the morning and went to Rialto, and then on down Ruga San Giovanni and Ruga del Ravano, which took him behind Palazzo Pisani and then home.'

Whoever had killed him had hidden in one of the passageways behind San Silvestro, certain that he would come that way, Marco mused. Some years ago, lighting had been installed along the route that Barbaro had taken and this must have helped his attacker to recognise him.

Of course, it's possible that he was the chance victim of a bag-snatcher, but then why kill him? It was unusual for a thief to commit murder, because it was pointless and dangerous. On realising that the victim had a dagger to hand, any robber with a modicum of good sense would have legged it.

It was more likely that Barbaro was the designated victim. Perhaps Daniele had been right: gambling debts, a swindle of some sort; who knew what else this impoverished man might have done to anger someone? But a murder? It must have been something big. There was no doubt in his mind that Lucrezia Scalfi, who was stealing glances at him, wondering if she had got away with it, knew much more than she was letting on, but he would let her go for the time being, he decided. Because now it was time to embark on a course of action that his fellow avogadori would not approve of.

Dismissing Lucrezia, he sent for Daniele Zen and also sent word to Nani, who was courting a bar girl in a tavern near San Moisè, and once they were all in the gondola, the three of them headed to Marino Barbaro's house.

CHAPTER 3

Along Riva del Vin, at the foot of the Rialto Bridge, the boatmen were hurrying to unload the last barrels of the day from the mainland. Tavern-keepers and hoteliers scrambled to load them on to their carts and push them through the crowds of commoner women laden with bags, water-sellers touting their wares and urchins getting under everyone's feet. A woman hanging from a window was shouting loudly for her son. The smoke from countless chimneys drifted into the darkening sky.

Marco and Daniele stepped out of the gondola, holding a lantern each. 'You can go home,' Pisani told Nani. 'But tell Rosetta that Avvocato Zen will be coming for supper later. Make sure that she puts out some good Burgundy! We're going for a stroll.'

What Marco actually wanted to do was examine the scene of the crime. The two friends made their way through the crowds, skirting the church of San Silvestro to get to Ruga del Ravano. They only needed to ask a few questions in the shops in order to identify the spot where Barbaro had been found.

'Look,' said Marco, lighting the passageway with his lantern. 'The murderer, the real one, could easily have waited for Barbaro out of sight, here.'

'He would have been safe: no one comes this way in the middle of the night,' agreed Zen, looking around. 'The courtyard where the body was found isn't even lit by the light from the shrine, and it was too early for people to be leaving their houses on their way to work.'

'Whoever it was meant to kill him. This was no attempted robbery,' concluded Marco. 'The rope went around his neck and he was dragged in here before he could even defend himself properly. But there was a struggle: we know that because of the traces of blood on his dagger. The murderer must have been wounded, even if only slightly. Now, let's go and have a look at the body.'

Barbaro's house was not far, on Fondamenta Rezzonico, facing Campo San Barnaba. It was a strange building, topped by a large dormer window. On the ground floor, the façade contained a second-hand clothes shop and four doorways that led to the upper storeys; a further two doorways on the side also led upstairs. In short, the building was designed so that each of the tiny apartments on the first floor had its own entrance. It was the best the Serenissima could do to preserve the dignity of the ruined nobles who lived there.

One of the doors was half open, and through another came the monotonous sound of a woman lamenting. Marco and Daniele climbed up the dimly lit staircase, trying not to breathe in the stench of damp mixed with unpleasant smells from the kitchen. From the landing they walked into a room where the peeling walls reflected the dancing flames from a fireplace flanked by two rickety benches. A table, which was still half set for a meal, and a few chairs were the only other furnishings.

Beyond an archway, beside a cold stove, a dishevelled old woman huddled on a mattress. Seeing the new arrivals, she stood up and dried her eyes with her apron. She was bent over with age and her face was thickly lined. 'It's a tragedy!' she moaned, moving towards them. 'And now where am I supposed to go? Were you gentlemen friends of my master? Can you do anything for an old woman like me?'

Marco felt instinctive distaste for anyone who felt sorry for themselves and he was about to lose patience, when Zen spoke. 'We are magistrates of the Republic here to see the body.'

'It's an honour!' The old woman curtseyed awkwardly. 'My master was poor, but he must truly have been important if such distinguished persons have gone out of their way on his behalf.' Marco rolled his eyes. 'Come, follow me.'

They walked into the bedroom, where the shutters were tightly shut. On the bed, Marino Barbaro, his hands crossed on his chest, lay on a stained cover, lit by a single candle. His face had stiffened in a terrified grimace. He was young, not yet thirty, and very thin, almost consumptive; even in death, there was something repellent about him and this was compounded by his shoddy clothing. Immediately visible around his neck was the purple line of the rope that had throttled him.

'Where's the rope?' Pisani asked.

The woman threw a questioning look at him, adjusting a lock of grey hair.

'The rope he was killed with,' explained Zen. 'The guards said that they brought it here with the body.'

'Ah, that rope,' the woman said, remembering. 'It must be here somewhere.' She started to fumble through the clothing that covered the only chair. 'Here it is,' she cried, opening a box.

'How strange,' reflected Pisani. 'It's rough and frayed. Perhaps it holds some clues.' He folded it into his jacket pocket.

'Curses on the man who did this to him!' The maid swore and managed to shed a couple of tears. 'They say that the murderer has been arrested already,' she went on in a plaintive tone. 'But where will I end up? Who'll take me into service at my age? My master hardly ever paid me, but at least I had a roof over my head and something to eat. Now, the only place for me is the hospice . . .'

Ignoring her, Pisani left the room, and waited for the others to follow. Then he shut the door and turned to the old woman. 'Now, let's talk.'

Daniele Zen found himself thinking that his friend would have made a magnificent Messer Grando, or head of police. That is, if he'd not been born a Pisani. One thing was certain: he was the only avo-gadore who didn't think twice about going into the filthiest hovels to question witnesses.

'What's your name?' asked Marco, while Zen took notes in a pocketbook.

'Lucia Piumazzo, at your service, Your Excellency, and I wasn't always as you see me now.' A hint of pride crept into her voice as she stood up to light an oil lamp with an old flint lighter. 'When I was young, I was in service in well-to-do households. I even worked as maid to the Mocenigo family. But you know what servants are like; the others were jealous and started to spread a rumour that I drank on the quiet, then they planted the odd piece of silver cutlery in my room, and eventually the major-domo fired me.'

'I can well imagine . . .' Pisani replied with a touch of sarcasm. He had already formed an opinion of this old woman. 'And how did you end up with Barbaro?'

'It must have been five years ago. I was sleeping on the streets, and one day I was waiting in line for a bowl of soup from the parish of San Polo when a gentleman stopped beside me. He asked me who I was and why I was begging for food . . . he must have understood that I wasn't like the other beggars. When he heard that I'd been a maid and that I'd had the misfortune of being sacked on account of the malice of my fellow servants, he started to laugh. "Well, you'll find nothing to steal from me," he said, "and nothing to drink either. I need a servant and you'll have a straw mattress in the kitchen and regular meals." So I went with him. But now where will I go?'

'We'll talk about that later. Who was Marino Barbaro? Does he have any surviving relatives?'

'No, he was completely alone. He'd been unlucky in life, just like me.' She started to cry again. 'Every now and again, he'd tell me that his grandparents owned land and a villa somewhere near Padua, but they lived in Venice and their factor lined his own pockets with their money.

His parents died while he was still a minor, and he was brought up by the Accademia dei Nobili on the Giudecca, at the state's expense. When he was eighteen, he left their care and they gave him this apartment.'

A story like many others he'd heard, thought Pisani. 'Where did his money come from?' he enquired.

'I swear before Our Lord' – Lucia put her hands up to touch the wooden crucifix hanging around her neck – 'that I never really knew. I think he dealt in antiques on the side: with his name, he could get himself invited into important households.'

'And he pocketed the silver.'

'No, I don't know about that. What happened, I think, was that when some young friend of his wanted to sell something, a painting maybe, or a piece of china, he was the one who took it to an antiquarian. And he often worked at the Casin dei Nobili close by . . . You know the sort of thing, he was responsible for keeping the table busy.'

'Was he a gambler?' insisted Marco.

'He enjoyed playing, yes, also for himself; every now and then he'd come back with a few ducats in his purse, but more often he'd be in despair, without a penny. He used to worry about having to dress well, otherwise he'd not have been allowed into the meetings of the Great Council.'

Marco forced back a smile as he thought of the patched garments lying around in the adjacent room. 'Did he have any women?'

'Only Signora Lucrezia, who was fond of him, I think. I never heard of anyone else.'

The old woman answered readily, and it was clear that she wanted to cooperate and gain the support of these influential visitors.

'Who were his friends?'

'I never saw any of them, and he certainly never brought them here.'

'They were high-ranking people, then?' Zen interjected.

'Well, I don't know. He never told me about things like that.'

Marco caught Daniele's eye. Old Lucia, just like Lucrezia, clammed up like an oyster when asked about Barbaro's friends. There was no point going on for the moment. Pisani already had an idea about how he could get the information he needed.

'Did you ever overhear an argument, perhaps down in the street, or hear gossip? Did you see anyone skulking around here? If someone killed him, they must have had a good reason.' Pisani was trying a different tack.

'Yes, once, but it was a long time ago.' The woman screwed up her eyes in an effort to remember. 'A man came here and asked for him. He looked like a peasant . . . he mentioned his daughter and then started shouting in the middle of the street. I shut myself in the house and he went away.'

'And more recently?'

The woman seemed to rifle through her memories, scrunching up her apron in her hands as she did so. 'The only thing that comes to mind . . . but it's really nothing at all,' she said, 'is that in the past couple of weeks I've noticed a large man, a Turk wearing a turban, going along Fondamenta two or three times. I only noticed him because the Fondaco dei Turchi is a long way from here, and you don't see many of his kind around here. I even mentioned it to my master, but he didn't seem to care.'

'And now, Daniele, you know what we need to do,' sighed Marco, getting up and pulling on his gloves.

His friend did the same. The woman looked at them with surprise, her eyes narrowed and her chin poking forward.

The two men went back into the dead man's room. They opened the window on to the icy evening and started to search through his personal belongings with evident disgust. A few coins in the pockets, used handkerchiefs, grubby underclothes. The unpleasant odour now mingled with the undoubted stench emanating from the corpse. On an old table that must have served as a desk, Daniele found some papers in a box that piqued his interest.

'Look, Marco. What do these notes remind you of?'

Marco read them aloud. '*Dogaressa*, 12 April–24 September; *Airone*, 15 May–28 October; *Sirenella*, 28 March–15 October . . . And there are others. They seem to be the arrival and departure dates of sailing ships. Why did these matter to Barbaro? And how did he get hold of them?'

At the bottom of the box, another sheaf of papers attracted their attention. One showed the cross-section of a galley, another a grappling iron or small anchor; others were sketches of different types of sail and the outline of what might have been the carriage for a cannon. There was also a sketch that was titled *Old Furnaces*. The last drawing seemed to have been copied in haste by an inexpert hand. It depicted a strange vessel, made up of two parallel hulls held together by a cylinder which ended in two cogs. Four rotating arms protruded from the cylinder, with drag buckets attached to the ends, while a small raft between the two hulls was clearly designed to collect whatever fell out of the buckets. The two men looked at each other.

'I've never seen anything like it,' remarked Marco. 'For certain, it must be some sort of dredger, but it's different from the usual ones.' Dredgers in Venice were used to clear waste out of the canals and to remove the sludge from the shipping channels in the port.

'This is clearly espionage,' commented Zen in a whisper. 'The wretch . . .' He turned quickly to glance at the body. 'The wretch was about to sell these documents from the Arsenale to some foreign power.'

'That's certainly what it looks like. Barbaro was obviously involved in something suspicious. Perhaps we should warn the inquisitors.'

'Wait,' advised Daniele. 'First, let's find out how valuable this information is. We could ask at the Arsenale.'

With the documents safely under his arm, Marco said goodbye to the old woman.

'And what will become of me, Your Excellency?' She started to cry. 'You're high up. You could find me a place, perhaps in a convent. At my age, who's going to give me any work?'

'We'll think about it,' Pisani reassured her. 'Now close the door, and don't let anyone in. Have you got some money for food?' And without waiting for a reply, he placed a few coins in the woman's hand.

'May God bless you.' Lucia curtseyed. And she tried to kiss the hand that Marco hurriedly shoved in a pocket.

Her laments followed them down the stairs, but finally Marco and Daniele found themselves back in the clean air on the street by the canal.

They walked for a while in silence, holding their lanterns. 'I didn't think of it,' said Daniele suddenly, 'but I could have taken my gondola.'

'A little exercise doesn't do any harm,' replied Marco. 'What did you make of her?'

'Well, she's not exactly a pleasant sort, but she certainly doesn't know anything. The only thing that worries her is her own future.'

'Disagreeable, yes,' Pisani agreed. 'But she, too, is entitled to a living. I'll have a word with my mother, who's involved in all sorts of charitable works, and she'll be able to fix her up in a convent.' They stopped on a small bridge and looked down at the dark water. 'To be frank with you,' he went on, 'I find this case disturbing. The abject poverty, the dirt . . . even rats wouldn't live there. How can a city that was once a world leader in terms of civilisation and wealth allow its citizens to be reduced to such conditions?' He held his hand up before Daniele could reply. 'I know what you're going to say: there are beggars everywhere, that the dregs are marginalised in every society. But two centuries ago we didn't have any, at least not of aristocratic birth. This is Venice, the Serenissima. Why have so many of our noble families been ruined? Why do so many old women end up in Lucia's position? It's like a cancer eating away at us, at the walls of the palaces, the banks of the canals. Aren't you afraid our world is coming to an end?'

Daniele shook his head. 'I'd be afraid,' he reflected, 'if our world was the best of all possible worlds. But it's not, Marco, it's not. We are too attached to the past, to traditions, to passions. We get too carried away by our feelings. You see, I believe that humankind is driven by the force of reason, which alone can point us to new paths, bringing the progress that will improve our way of life, and the economic principles that will bring well-being to all . . .'

'You're a man of the Enlightenment, Daniele,' smiled Marco. 'Yes, I've read the English and French philosophers, too. They have interesting ideas, but I do wonder whether, if the French were to come here one day to spread their ideas and put them into practice, the world would be a better place, one where people wouldn't be poor any more, where there'd be no more injustice, and where reason – French reason – would triumph? I doubt it.'

CHAPTER 4

Rosetta had once been a maid in the Pisani household, and she adored the avogadore because she'd raised him since he was a baby. Now she ran his house and kitchen with a firm hand and was a force to be reckoned with. However, she had no influence whatsoever over her master's way of life, or his work, for that matter, even if she always did what she could to interfere. She also had a soft spot for his friend the lawyer Daniele Zen, and so she had personally prepared something delicious for their evening meal.

The dining room next to the central hall on the first floor was lit by a chandelier of Murano glass and the table sparkled with crystal and silver carefully laid out on a pure white cover of Flemish cloth.

'Let's go and freshen up,' said the host, guiding his friend to the upper floor, where the bedrooms were. Marco's bathroom was beside his bedroom and was the source of much speculation in Venice, mainly prompted by the servants' gossip, because the avogadore never showed it to anyone.

Gone were the days when amber and musk were used to mask the unpleasant odour of unwashed bodies. In Venice, and across Europe, a portable tub and handbasin, together with a small table and stool for shaving, were now commonplace in many households. But even by these new and improved standards, Pisani's bathroom was rumoured to be unusually luxurious.

Before accepting the office of avogadore, Pisani had travelled to England and France, where he had come to appreciate the latest fashionable bathroom fixtures, and he had imported them to Venice for his own use without a second thought.

The walls of his bathroom were clad with dark walnut skirting, above which were huge mirrors. The very latest sanitaryware came from Paris, including a ceramic handbasin painted with blue flowers and a copper bathtub with taps to provide running water, which was heated by a boiler in a nearby room. Aromatic soaps, also from France, rested on the surrounding shelves and gave off a delicate scent of violets. But the most unusual object was housed in an adjacent closet: it was a toilet, complete with a flush, which drained into a cesspit that was regularly emptied.

'You really are quite a character.' Daniele smiled as he washed his hands and face in the basin. 'You dress like a bourgeois, only wear a wig when you absolutely have to, never give a reception, and then go and spend a fortune on a bathroom.'

'I was blessed by fate and being born the second son – I can do what I like!' his friend reminded him.

Daniele knew that Marco did not envy his older brother, Giovanni, who lived in the family palace on the Grand Canal with its freezing salons, gilded stuccowork, and ancestors' portraits on every wall. In short, magnificent but horribly uncomfortable. The bedrooms had draughts from every corner, and at dinner the dishes always arrived cold because the kitchens were so far away. Marco's parents had retired to one wing of the palace, and his brother was now responsible for the estates, the accounts and for managing a household of some forty servants. A thankless task. Giovanni pretended to be horrified by his younger brother's simple lifestyle, but at times he would have given a lot to be in his position.

'In any case,' Marco went on, 'I'm certainly not a disgrace to the family name. My position as avogadore is one of the highest in the Republic, and at least I take my duties seriously.'

'Too seriously,' laughed his friend as they went back down to the first floor. 'Whoever heard of an avogadore going in person to search a victim's apartment, or to question witnesses at home instead of summoning them to the palace?'

'Well, you see,' objected Marco, sitting down at the table and unfolding his napkin, 'I enjoy my work. In fact, I still believe that law and justice can overlap, at least here in Venice, where we don't have the absurd discriminations I came across while travelling. If you want to get to the truth in a case, you need to assess the context in which the characters in a particular drama performed. When I call witnesses to the ducal palace, they either clam up or are overcome by bravado. They're quite prepared to lie, and, even if it's only about minor things, they too can be essential. Instead, in their own surroundings, it's more likely they'll tell the truth. And I don't mind moving around and going to see how people live rather than staying holed up in my office, as my colleagues do.'

The administration of justice was one of the most complicated aspects of Venetian life. Over the centuries the Serenissima had established nearly one hundred and thirty courts and more often than not their jurisdictions overlapped. As well as the Quarantie, as the civil and criminal courts were known, there were six lesser courts that oversaw questions of inheritance, rents and the lease of ships. Then there were the courts of the Piovègo, which dealt with the waters and canals, and the six Signori di Notte, who judged nocturnal offences, both civil and criminal, and were responsible for patrolling the streets. The Giustizia Vecchia presided over work-related cases and those involving women and children, and the Giustizia Nova dealt with offences regarding foodstuffs, taverns and the wine trade. Lastly, the two powerful colleges of the Savi acted as the courts of last resort. It was a system that also helped the prudent Republic to carry out cross-checks on the activities of its own magistrates.

The dinner was delicious. It was served by Giuseppe, who had worked at Palazzo Pisani before following Marco to his own house. Polished and chubby, he was forty, but looked younger. He served a meat broth first, followed by meatballs in sauce and a roast chicken. And finally, they were served with wafer-thin biscuits accompanied by sweet wine. When they had finished their meal, the two friends settled by the fire in Marco's study to enjoy some ratafia. Plato had followed them and was curled up on the hearth, having calculated to a tee the distance between his fur and the flames, guaranteeing maximum warmth and no risk of singeing.

Above the fireplace was a splendid portrait of a dark young woman wearing a black lace dress.

'If she was still alive . . .' – Marco wistfully looked up at the portrait – 'perhaps things would be different and I'd not be so obsessed by my work. But then Virginia always encouraged me to work hard, and in her own home, in Padua, they lived simply, even though the family was well off.'

'Poor Virginia,' sighed Daniele.

Marco had tears in his eyes. The thought of his young wife, who had died giving birth to their son, still upset him deeply, even after twelve years. It would have been a betrayal, he thought, to love another woman. Sweet Virginia; she had already been sufficiently betrayed by fate, who had carried her away, and also the baby for whom they had both cherished such hopes.

There was silence in the room for a while.

'Are the Foscarinis still after you for their daughter?' asked Daniele, hoping to lighten the mood.

'Constantly. And they're not the only ones.' Marco shook himself. 'If I were to go to all the parties, concerts, balls and dinners to which I'm invited, I wouldn't be able to work. They think of me as the golden widower.'

'And now you've got a reputation for playing hard to get.'

'Look who's talking! You're the same age as me and you're still living at home, while young Maddalena Santelli flutters her eyelashes at you every time she sees you – and she's got a handsome dowry.'

'Sooner or later I'll make up my mind,' sighed Daniele with a frown. 'I'll have to marry just to keep my elderly parents happy. The Santelli girl is kind and I'm quite fond of her . . . it's just that she doesn't make my heart race.'

'And you're the one who wants to do away with passions?' Marco teased. 'But you're right about love . . . love is everything! They say that it's gone out of fashion, but that's rubbish: love is worth any form of madness. I know, because I've experienced it, and I'll never be in love again.'

'You two never stop chatting; and then you complain about us women!' Rosetta had come into the room with the usual bedtime chocolate. Venetian through and through, she was a chatterbox who did not know the meaning of servility, but where her master was concerned, nothing was too good. She set the tray with the steaming jug and cups on a lacquered table.

'Don't sit up late because there'll be plenty to do in the morning,' she warned. 'And you, Plato,' she said, turning to the cat, 'if I catch you sleeping in his bed, you'll be in real trouble.'

The cat opened his eyes a fraction and then made himself more comfortable.

'You see,' said Marco. 'She still treats me like a child.'

Plato stretched and jumped on to his shoulder, purring.

'And how do you plan to proceed with the inquiries?' asked Zen, savouring the chocolate.

Marco stroked the cat, who purred even louder. 'In theory, I should start proceedings against the accused, but first we need to find him; it's certainly not that wretch Tommaso Grassino. However, it's not exactly clear cut. We've got a body and no witnesses so I can only make inquiries about the victim. And what have we discovered so far?'

'That he was a poor wretch who lived off his wits.' Zen started to list the known facts. 'He kept suspicious documents that might link him to the world of espionage, he was strangled with a strange rope and a Turk might be involved.'

'If there are any grounds to suspect spying, I should immediately inform the three inquisitors who are responsible for state security. But you're right: better wait. I can't explain it, but it seems too soon to pass this case on to them. I'd like to make more progress with the facts, but without sticking my neck out too far. I'll follow your suggestion and go to the Arsenale.'

Daniele looked thoughtful as he toyed with the lace on his cuff. 'There's another strange coincidence,' he reflected. 'Both Barbaro's own maid and – according to what you've told me – his lover, Lucrezia, were both very reticent when it came to naming the victim's friends. They may be high-ranking, even though I can't imagine why young patricians would get involved with anyone like him.'

'So, let's hunt around for their names. I've already got a plan: tomorrow it will be Nani's turn.'

'Ah, your gondolier . . .'

'He's intelligent, he enjoys a bit of adventure and he's a good-looking chap. I can't ask the guards or soldiers from the Avogaria because no one would speak openly to them. Besides, when it comes to getting the whole story out of people, especially women, there's no one better. No matter what I ask him to find out, he always manages to come back with invaluable information. The Lord alone knows how he does it. I'll call him up now and give him his instructions, then he can take you home in the gondola.'

'No, it's too late now. Let him sleep and I'll walk home. I've still got the lantern,' replied Daniele, who lived not far away, in Campo Santa Margherita.

Marco accompanied him down to the door on to the calle, and the two friends said goodnight.

'Come on, Plato, we're off to bed,' said Marco to the cat, who'd followed them into the garden. And Plato, satisfied from the previous night's adventures, obediently followed his master indoors.

CHAPTER 5

The triumphal Porta dei Leoni and the two watchtowers above the canal stood out in all their proud magnificence against the pale blue sky when Marco, followed by Nani, walked towards the Arsenale on Friday morning, having left their gondola moored to a post.

Marco stopped for a moment to look at the marble lions standing guard by the gate and remembered with a tinge of sadness that they had come originally from Greece, in the days when the Serenissima was at the height of its power and its ships ruled the seas.

It was from the Arsenale that all the galleys and cargo ships had sailed to defend Venice from its enemies and, more importantly, to trade with the East and bring wealth to Venice. In 1571, on the eve of the Battle of Lepanto, when Christian Europe had been saved from the Turkish invasion thanks to Venetian ships, the boatyards, warehouses, offices and docks in the Arsenale covered over a sixth of the city and employed three thousand specialised workers, as well as countless labourers. In preparation for the likelihood of battle, one hundred galleys had been built in two months that year, complete with sails, stays, cannons, anchors and all the supplies for the crews.

Yet the discovery of America had shifted the barycentre of trade towards the Atlantic, benefiting the westward-facing seafaring nations and sending a shiver of foreboding through Venice. Now, more than two centuries later, the peace of 1718 had meant the loss of the Morea to the Ottomans, while in the Adriatic Venice's leadership was contested by Austria, the emerging power, which competed with Venetian trade from its port in Trieste.

As a result, new ships were very rarely built now, but the Arsenale, which was responsible for the upkeep of the merchant and military fleet and its provisioning, was still at the heart of the Republic and employed fourteen hundred workers, so access to the docks was strictly surveilled.

Indeed, an arsenal guard was now walking towards the visitors but, when he recognised Avogadore Pisani, he hastened to open the gate.

'Nani, you know what to do; ask the guards how to get to the ropeworks. As for me' – Marco turned to the guard – 'I need to talk to the Patrono.' The Master of the Arsenale was always a patrician and he, together with the Procurators and the Admiral, formed the Collegio dell'Arsenale, the high council that controlled the shipyard and the navy.

Nani turned left and disappeared around the flank of the sails warehouse. In the meantime, Marco stopped to admire the Darsena Vecchia, the old dock that was flanked by a row of covered shipyards, where a number of vessels were currently undergoing repair. At the end of the dock was a drawbridge which led into the much larger Darsena delle Galeazze, where the warships were moored.

Marco knew the way and he turned to enter the building where the council sat. No one dared to stop him as he crossed the arms room on the ground floor and he then went straight upstairs to the offices without being challenged. There in front of him was his friend's office.

'Well, this is a pleasant surprise!' Patrono Cappello stood up and walked round his large desk to welcome Marco with an embrace. Of middling height and a little overweight, he had a penetrating gaze and an ironic smile. 'We've not seen each other for a while. What fair wind blows you in our direction to visit us humble workers of the sea?'

'You'll have heard of the murder of poor Marino Barbaro . . .' explained Marco, leaving aside the usual pleasantries.

'Indeed. Yesterday morning. Here the news travels fast: even if Barbaro wasn't a person of great worth, he was still a patrician of the Great Council. But what has the Arsenale to do with it?' Cappello asked with interest.

Marco took off his cloak and opened a case from which he took the sheaf of papers that had been found in the victim's house. 'Unfortunately, I need to consult you about a very delicate matter. Absolutely nothing of what I'm going to tell you must leave this room before I finish my inquiries.'

'Does it concern state security?' Cappello's voice was now deadly serious.

'It might . . . I'm going to show you something.' Marco unfolded the drawings and laid the papers on the table. 'Have a look at these. My first impression was that they're secret documents, and this would mean that Barbaro was involved in some spy ring. Yet something doesn't quite fit, and I'd like to know what it's all about before I raise the alarm with the inquisitors.'

Alvise Cappello balanced a thick pair of lenses on his long nose and bent over the table to look carefully at the drawings. First, he focused on the sheet with the dates. 'This,' he started, 'is certainly a document of no value. It seems to be a list of ships' sailing dates, their arrivals and departures; similar lists are sold to spies employed by pirates in the Adriatic. But I can't understand how it can include the return date to Venice, which is never certain. The other papers contain drawings of ships, as I'm sure you'll have realised. I've no idea why they might be useful, or to whom. It looks like they're old designs. But . . . wait a moment.' Cappello stopped short when he saw the sketch of the dredger. 'Did you find this one with the others?' he asked Marco.

'Of course. It seems to have been copied in a hurry, and it struck me as rather strange, too.'

Cappello painstakingly polished his glasses with a lace-trimmed handkerchief and put them back on his nose. Then he leaned over the sheet again. 'You'll have understood that this is a mud dredger, then. But not one of the usual ones. The dredgers we normally use have a single hull and they're modelled on an old design by Francesco di Giorgio Martini. But I happen to know that here in the Arsenale, they're now working on one of Leonardo's projects – you might remember that he was an expert on hydraulics and engineering. One of his projects is now being developed, and it would be an undoubted improvement, but it's still a secret. So, the question is, who copied this sketch? And what was it doing in the hands of that barnabotto?'

'Whoever it was, and whatever he was doing, it was clearly important enough to justify murder.'

'It wasn't robbery, then. The youngster you've arrested isn't your man.'

'Quite so. But before freeing him, I need to understand what I'm dealing with here.'

'Give me a day or two, Marco, and I'll tell you all you need to know. I could summon a meeting of the heads of all the workshops – by which I mean munition, sails and anchors, and the shipwrights – but I don't want to create too much of a stir. Instead, I'll ask a few discreet questions myself, here and there. This is a project that any number of foreign powers would find particularly interesting: all those with ports and channels that need to be kept open,' Cappello concluded, pointing at the sketch of the dredger.

'I agree,' replied Marco, getting ready to take his leave. 'And the next time, we'll go out and eat something together at the Poste Vecie at Rialto, where we can talk.'

'Perhaps about women.' Alvise grinned, giving him a wink. 'And we'll order polenta and cod. They do a magnificent dish at the Poste Vecie.'

When Marco returned to the gondola, he found that Nani had not yet returned, so he waited nearby.

The young man had not been in a rush because it wasn't every day that he was able to take a look around the heavily guarded area containing prized military secrets. Following the guards' directions, he had walked past the sails warehouse and was about to turn right, when he'd noticed a group of young women on the quay stretching out sails to dry on long ropes. 'What's the best way to the ropeworks?' he asked, hoping it would serve as an acceptable chat-up line.

Two of them looked at him with interest; he clearly didn't work in the Arsenale, and if he was an outsider, then he must be someone important to be allowed to stroll around like this.

'From the other side,' one of them answered. 'It's at the end of the calle. You need to turn left between the metal and the tarring workshops, then you'll find the ropeworks in front of you.'

'Perhaps you could take me . . .' Nani brashly asked the blonde who had spoken. She had fine ankles and was generously proportioned.

'I'm busy now.'

'What about this evening, then? I'll wait for you at the gate,' replied Nani, with one of his irresistible smiles. 'We'll have a drink together. A glass of wine to thank you for the information. Then I'll give you a lift home in the gondola.'

'That would be nice,' sighed the blonde, 'but you'd find my husband and two children waiting for me there too.'

Nani shrugged philosophically and followed the woman's directions, finding the ropeworks without trouble. He stopped in the doorway, taking in the enormous space under the trussed roof, which was supported by a double row of large columns. There was a bustle of workers everywhere: men and, above all, women were twisting the fibres into strands on pedal-powered turning machines. Other workers laid and twisted the yarns along the full length of the rope-walks, before tarring them, or plaited two or four strands together around a central core to form ropes of differing thicknesses. The hemp workers wound the ropes around tall cylinders or piled them in coils near the door. There were coils of fine lines, thicker ropes for sheets, and anchor hawsers, all waiting to be stored in the adjacent warehouses. The atmosphere was redolent with hemp, which made his head spin, and the suffocating dust seemed to hang in the air.

The foreman, Micheli, came forward and Nani introduced himself and showed him the rope that had been found around Barbaro's neck. 'My master, Avogadore Pisani,' he explained, 'would like to know where this rope comes from, because he thinks it's an unusual make.'

Micheli turned the rope in his hands, smelled it, tested its strength and unspliced one of the ends. 'Well, it's not one of ours . . . Where was it found?'

'I'm not allowed to say,' apologised Nani, who was well aware of the rules of judicial investigations.

'Of course. Well, at first sight, I think the rope must be North African, and it seems to be made of those tough grasses that grow in some areas of Libya, close to the sea. The coarse twist reminds me of the shipyards in the Levant where the Turks use Greek slaves, who are some of the least skilled at building and fitting out ships. See how it unravels? It's also quite a thick rope, and not as easy to handle as the ones we make here.'

He took a length of rope out of his pocket and compared the two. 'Hold on while I consult someone who's a real expert. Gigio!' he shouted at a passing apprentice. 'Get me the Levantino.'

The apprentice trotted off and a quarter of an hour later came back with a huge man in sailor's garb and well-worn leather gloves.

'Listen, Menico,' said Micheli, turning to the newcomer. 'You've spent time in the Levant, and you've also worked for the Turks. What do you make of this rope? Is it one of theirs?'

The man held it between finger and thumb to examine it more closely. He had a deeply furrowed and sunburnt face and his eyes were almost invisible under his heavy eyelids. 'It might be,' he said at last, 'but I'm not sure.'

'Pay no attention to his appearance,' explained Micheli, turning to Nani. 'He's dressed as a sailor but now works on land here with us.'

'Well,' continued Menico, unperturbed, 'it's certainly made from North African material, but the rope itself could be Turkish or even Portuguese. Portugal gets its raw materials from Libya, too, and they don't have the same ropemaking skills we do. Sorry I can't tell you more.'

Thanking Micheli and the burly sailor, Nani took the murder weapon and retraced his steps to find an impatient Pisani.

'I've not learned much, paròn,' Nani began. 'The foreman seemed certain that it was a Turkish rope, but then another man joined us. He's called the Levantino because he's sailed in those parts, and he was more doubtful. He thinks it could well be a Portuguese rope.' Nani proceeded to give his master a detailed account.

'So,' Marco said, as the gondola headed for Piazza San Marco, 'the rope might be Turkish or Portuguese. Well . . . at least we know that it's not Venetian.'

Once back at the Procuratie Vecchie and dressed again in his robes, Marco headed towards the ducal palace and his office, where a guard saluted him and said, 'There's a person waiting for you. She's been there for a while.'

Marco threw open the door then stopped in his tracks at the sight of a woman standing in profile, looking out at the sky through the glass of the large window. She wore a voluminous cloak made of a warm, apricot-coloured brocade and her thick blonde hair was tied back, apart from a few rebellious curls. The early-afternoon light seemed to give her a shining halo. As she turned, he noted that her smile shone even brighter than her hair, and her eyes were the colour of cornflowers.

'Pardon me, Your Excellency, if I'm disturbing you,' she began with a small curtsey. 'My name's Chiara Renier, and I employ the young man you've arrested, Tommaso Grassino, who I'm certain is innocent.' A shadow of worry crossed her face. 'I would like to know what will happen to him and what I can do to help. I know him well and he's my best apprentice; there must have been a misunderstanding. His parents are in such a state . . .'

Utterly bemused, Marco did not move, worried he might trip over his gown if he took too hasty a step forward. He felt ridiculous in his wig compared to this graceful figure. At last, he pulled himself together and gave a slight smile.

'Please, signora.' He pointed to a wide stool facing his desk, while retreating behind it himself and trying to look as relaxed as possible. 'So . . . Grassino. I agree that he is not guilty, but until I can exonerate him completely, it's better that he stays where he is.' Then he stopped in embarrassment, afraid that he might start stuttering.

Chiara watched Pisani's change of expression with some apprehension. She felt a familiar tingling run through her and was surprised to realise it felt like a good sign. He was young for such a prestigious office and he looked sensitive, with that slightly lopsided smile that lit up his gentle, intelligent eyes. Luminous motes of dust danced in front of her eyes and she shivered. She needed to take control of herself: this was not the moment to give way to her intuitions as a clairvoyant. She closed her eyes briefly, and when she opened them the lights had faded.

'Your Excellency is right,' she replied, lowering her gaze, which made Marco feel as if the sky had clouded over. 'I have complete faith in your benevolence and won't disturb you further. I will also reassure his parents.' She stood up in a single fluid motion that revealed a brocade shoe and a dainty ankle.

'Come back whenever you want to,' Marco hastened to assure her. What on earth had happened, he wondered, to his famous nonchalance where women were concerned? 'If I have any news, where can I find you, or rather, how can I contact you?'

'In Calle Venier, close to the Jesuits.' Chiara Renier shot him an impish look and smiled. Her mouth was vibrant and generous and her smile could brighten the stormiest day. 'I own the Renier weaving manufactory. Do you see this cloak?' she added with a tinge of pride. 'We make this fabric ourselves, using the latest looms but with traditional designs, and we sell it all over Europe.'

'A cloak worthy of a queen . . .' ventured Marco.

'Yes, we supply the court of France and the court of Turin.'

A highly capable woman, and one with angelic looks. Marco wracked his brains but at that instant he could think of nothing to detain her.

'Until we meet again, signora,' he said reluctantly, and watched as she walked through the adjacent room with a light step.

He sighed. What on earth was happening to him? Perhaps she was married. But no, Maso had said that she wasn't. Perhaps she lived on her own because . . . well, who knew why? He'd have liked to know more about her. But what excuse could he use? Perhaps he could invite her to a concert or to a reception, for example, one of the ones his parents gave at the family palace. There would surely be one to mark the start of the Carnival. He'd have to think up a plan. And the next time he saw her, he would make sure that he was not wearing his wig and gown.

CHAPTER 6

Hidden in the shadows of the covered passage that opened on the huge Campo San Barnaba, Nani had been sitting for a while watching the comings and goings from the victim's house on the other side of the canal. It was only lived in by barnabotti like Marino Barbaro, each more impoverished than the last.

He had seen an old man emerge from the entrance wearing expensive silk stockings, despite the fact that his cloak was tattered. A young maidservant had popped out of another door, but only to talk to a boy who was waiting, and they had vanished around the corner to flirt. An old woman was now returning, dressed in elbow-length lace gloves and an outmoded gown, and she disappeared inside through a half-open door that was carefully closed behind her.

Now, as the sun was setting, Nani hurried across the Ponte dei Pugni and made his way into a shop.

'At your service, young man,' the girl said cheekily as she sidled towards him.

Nani pretended to browse the goods on display. He picked up a jacket that was resting on a pile of other garments, rummaged around in a box of lace-trimmed chemises of somewhat doubtful colour and made an attempt to try on a *bautta* mask, usually worn with a black cloak and often seen during Carnival.

'Are you looking for something for a party?' The girl stepped closer. Tall and well built, she had a round, peasant-like face that was not unattractive, and her generous bosom half spilled out of her tight bodice. 'Zanetta at your service,' she introduced herself. 'With your build, you could easily wear a white wig and tricorn, and everyone would take you for a gentleman. Look, try this one.'

Nani looked with disgust at the white curls draped over a wig stand in a corner. He calculated the likelihood of an infestation of fleas and stepped back a little: like master, like servant, Nani had picked up Pisani's obsession with cleanliness.

'Let me think about it . . .' he prevaricated. 'What I need now is a drink to warm me up. This winter has been fine, but it's cold. Why don't you come with me to the tavern over there? My name's Nani.' She wasn't the type of girl to be seen with in an elegant coffee house.

Zanetta didn't need to be asked twice. As well as being attractive, with his sea-blue eyes and wide shoulders, the young man seemed to be well off. 'Hold on while I close up the shop and I'll come.' She threw a lace shawl over her head, bolted the door and set off with Nani. The day had been quiet in terms of business so far, but now the end looked promising.

The drinking house was not as rough as Nani had feared, given the area. A good fire burned in the fireplace and the flames helped to light the room. The glasses on the serving counter seemed clean, and the bar lady was wearing a spotless apron. They chose a corner table and ordered two glasses of frizzantino white wine.

'Here's to health.' Nani smiled, lifting his glass. 'You'll be tired after the day's work.'

'There's not much work in San Barnaba,' said the girl. 'Those wretches who live in the palace don't have a penny to spend, even on second-hand clothes. Especially elegant, high-class clothes like the ones I sell. I get some of them from the maids in patricians' households, although the mistresses make sure that the pearls and gold trimmings are removed before they leave the house.'

'But the gambling house is nearby.'

'Oh, the Casin dei Nobili. Yes, some of those have money, but as soon as they get there they only think about gaming, and anyway, wealthy people don't buy used clothes. I'd say that many of them are scoundrels too.'

It was time to bring up the subject. 'I've heard that there was a murder here yesterday, someone who lived in the palace . . .' Nani said, almost under his breath, rather absent-mindedly.

'You're right, it was Barbaro. They strangled him, poor man.'

'Did you know him? I'm sure he'd have flirted with a pretty girl like you,' Nani continued.

Zanetta preened. 'How did you know? Every now and then he would follow me around. Sometimes he would come into the shop and wait for half an hour or more, but he never actually bought anything. He'd just hang around and make a grab for me whenever I got too close. But I'm not that sort of girl and I chased him off.' She pursed her lips with a virtuous look.

'Who killed him? I wonder. Was he usually alone, or did he have friends?'

'He had friends all right, far worse than him.'

'And did they flirt with you too?'

'No, they were gentlemen, or at least two of them were; the third was a servant.'

'Sounds like an odd trio,' Nani said, before he changed the subject; he didn't want to make her suspicious. 'Where are you from, Zanetta? You don't speak like a Venetian.'

'No, I'm from Polesine. My father is a peasant, but I managed to become an apprentice and three years ago I bought this second-hand clothes shop. Selling used garments is not too difficult, and the guild even lets people in from outside the city.'

'So, you're well off. Are you sure that Barbaro didn't want to marry you?'

'Him? Even though he was poor, he still had all the pride of the nobility, and he behaved as if he were as rich as his friends. Even that servant thought he was better than me, but as far as I could tell he was nothing more than a rogue. Sometimes, when the weather was cold, they'd wait for Barbaro in my shop – they never went into his house – and I used to hear them talk about certain things, when they thought I wasn't around . . .'

'And what did you hear?'

'Enough to know that I had to be careful.' The matter seemed closed. People in Venice loved chatting, but only if the gossip was inconsequential and harmless. As soon as someone suspected that their words could be reported to the police, they closed up like a clam. Fear of the inquisitors' court and its spies was still tangible, even if over a century had passed since its trials had been surrounded by an air of terrifying mystery.

'Did they try to hurt you? A decent girl like you!' Nani's indignation seemed genuine. But it was an effort to make her talk. How did his master manage to question people for a profession?

Zanetta seemed flattered by Nani's concern. 'Not me, but I know another girl who had a terrible time.'

'What happened? Did they . . . rape her?' ventured Nani.

Zanetta blushed. 'It was a few years ago, and I'd only just arrived. At that time, all four of them used to stand in the corner, whispering to each other. It seemed serious. So one day, when they came in for one of their secret conferences, I hid behind a pile of clothes, and I heard every word they said.'

Nani imagined the scene: the girl crouching silently, her eyes half shut but her ears straining to catch every syllable.

'There was one . . .'

'Who? What was his name?'

'A certain Labia, Paolo Labia, who said, "It's nothing to do with me. You were the ones who went whoring, so you need to sort it out yourselves." And Barbaro replied, "But we all enjoyed it. You did, too, even if you just watched."'

'What about the others?' insisted Nani.

The girl finished off her wine and Nani signalled to the bar lady, who came to refill it.

'The other two were the worst,' continued Zanetta, who had now overcome her embarrassment. She pushed her shawl back on her shoulders with a coquettish glance. 'The patrician said that it had been wonderful, that a virgin was hard to come by, and his servant insisted that, after all, they were noblemen and had done her a great honour. "But now she's pregnant!" Barbaro said. "When her father finds out, he'll kill us all. You know what peasants are like."'

'And what happened then?' Nani couldn't disguise the urgency in his voice.

'After a few weeks, they seemed more relaxed. I heard the young aristocrat grumbling, "It cost me a fortune." And Barbaro replied, "You can thank me for not letting the news spread further than your family. You had to pay because she was your maid, and as a thank-you now you can buy me one of these cloaks." And the man chose a cloak that was almost new and paid for it without a second thought.'

'But who was this man? You've mentioned a Labia, but who were the other two?'

'Why do you want to know?' The girl had finally grown suspicious.

Nani paused, unsure how to answer. Pisani had told him to find out the names of the men Barbaro hung around with, but how could he get her to tell him without her finding out he was working for an avogadore?

Suddenly he had a flash of inspiration. 'I want to know so I can protect you. You see, Zanetta, you're a beautiful girl, and I like being with you. I'm not a noble, but I have a successful food shop at Murano.' Given that he was telling a pack of lies, it was wiser to say that he lived some way off. 'I'm thinking of settling down and I'd like to get to know you better. I don't want anything to happen to you.'

Zanetta smiled with even greater pleasure. This was almost a proposal. Nani felt a twinge of remorse. 'Oh, Nani, what a dear man you are! But what can you do? They're all rich and powerful men. And anyway, they've made themselves scarce for the past year or more.'

'Even so, tell me who they are, and I'll make sure they don't trouble you any more.'

The girl made up her mind. 'The patrician's name is Piero Corner, the one with a palace on the Grand Canal, and the other one is his personal gondolier. Biagio is his name, I think.'

'I'll make sure they never bother you again. I've got plenty of friends who are policemen. And the next time I see you, I'll take you out for a meal in a trattoria where they cook the best fish in the whole of Venice.'

'Oh, and there's something else,' Zanetta interrupted, now anxious to tell him everything. 'Corner disappeared completely. He was no longer part of the group and I've hardly seen the others either, for a year or more, as I said.'

Nani, hiding his triumph at the successful completion of his mission, took her hand between his, as if to thank her, and then changed the subject. They continued chatting and drinking for a while, until Nani, deeming he'd spent enough time with her to allay her suspicions, finally said, 'It's late. Will you let me take you back to the shop?'

'When will you be back?' asked Zanetta boldly, once they'd arrived.
'Very soon,' lied Nani, backing away.

As he rowed back to the palace, he couldn't help feeling guilty for dup-
ing the poor girl; he'd have to keep well clear of Campo San Barnaba
for the time being.

Pisani was waiting for him in his study, but rather than feeling
impatient, he had spent the time thinking of Chiara. Even so, he met
Nani with a severe reprimand. 'You took your time.'

'But it was worth it,' countered Nani, not in the least abashed as he
proceeded to recount the evening's events, word for word.

When he came to the suggestion of marriage, Marco started to
laugh. 'Aren't you ashamed of yourself, Nani? Will nothing stop you?'

'It's all for the love of justice, paròn, and for the reward that I've
earned.'

When he was alone again, Marco went over the details in his mind:
so Barbaro had been part of a group of rather disreputable friends, and
they included Paolo Labia and Piero Corner, two important names, two
powerful families. Were they somehow involved in his death? What was
this story about the pregnant maid? Might Barbaro's death have been
an honour crime, perpetrated a few years later? Or had Barbaro been
killed because of his involvement in espionage? Marco realised that he
was unlikely to get any answers until his friend Cappello came back
with more details about the documents that had been found in the
dead man's apartment.

As for the two young patricians, he knew them by sight, and also
knew that they brought no honour to their family name: Corner was
a degenerate who spent his time whoring, gambling and brawling. But
then after marrying a year ago, it was rumoured that his lifestyle had

changed. Labia, on the other hand, was more of a puzzle: he had never been implicated in scandals, but there were rumours that he was a usurer and a pederast. Might these two men also be assassins? And what part did the gondolier Biagio play in all this?

He needed to talk to a professional informer, one of those shadowy figures whose services were so readily used by the secret services and by the Inquisition. It was a distasteful thought, but Marco knew it was the only way to find out what the group were up to now.

CHAPTER 7

The news about Piero Corner arrived unwarranted and unexpected, ricocheting around Venice like cannon fire.

Early on Monday morning – 11 December, to be precise – Marco found his secretary, Tiralli, visibly shaken as he waited outside the door on the mezzanine floor of the Procuratie Vecchie.

'Your Excellency!' The young man was out of breath, as if he had run fast. 'It's an awful tragedy! All Venice will soon hear of it! Something dreadful has happened . . .'

'Instead of panicking, just tell me,' grumbled Marco.

'About an hour ago, the lamplighter on his dawn rounds found a patrician's body under a portico. It was Piero Corner of the Corner family at Ca' Grande. He seems to have been strangled with a rope, just like Marino Barbaro. He was on his way back from the Ridotto. His gondolier was found nearby in the gondola, bound and gagged.'

'Where's the corpse?' exclaimed Marco. 'What else do you know?'

'The body is still lying where it was found; the guards wanted a magistrate to see it straight away, and as you're always the first on the scene . . .'

'. . . you lost no time in coming to tell me,' Pisani finished. 'Well done. But where is it?'

'Not far from here, under the portico of the Fonteghetto della Farina, where the Accademia di Pittura is. It struck me that if he was killed in the same way as Barbaro, the two crimes might be linked.'

'A good assumption. Let's go.'

It had been an anxious weekend for Pisani. Conjectures about Barbaro's mysterious murder had swirled around his mind, overlaid with the image of Chiara Renier, which came back to him more often than he would have expected. What the devil was the matter with him? He wasn't some youngster to lose his head over a woman, and as for his love life, he was content with the services of Annetta, the beautiful embroideress in the apartment near San Rocco where he had been a regular visitor for a few years now; he found her pleasant company and not too taxing.

Chiara, however, intrigued him. He'd never met such a lovely, spirited woman. He had to find a way to see her again, but he didn't know how.

On Saturday night, his sleep had been disturbed and he'd dreamed about Virginia. She was waving as she walked away from him, towards fields of light. He had called out to her, but she had not turned back and he'd woken bathed in sweat.

All Sunday, he had dawdled between his study and the salon, reading in snatches and thinking. He had tried to work on some official papers but couldn't keep his mind on them; instead the memory of Chiara kept coming back to him, and to his surprise, every time he thought of her he found himself smiling. Rosetta had looked at him quizzically when she saw him but had not said anything.

That evening he had gone to dinner with his parents in the handsome Gothic-style family palace on the Grand Canal. He had raced up the imposing staircase with the major-domo struggling to keep up, and strode across the sumptuous hall that overlooked the canal to find the family sitting together in their favourite salon, the one with the ceiling painted by Tiepolo with a fresco of Venus and Mars.

'Here's Uncle!' shouted his two nephews in unison, rushing to meet him as he entered.

'What have you brought us?' asked Stefano, a six-year-old blonde cherub.

Marco handed the boys a pack of Rosetta's sweet biscuits, a renowned delicacy.

'First me, because I'm the littlest!' cried Carlo, who was constantly on the go and headstrong to match.

Once the boys had been pacified, the adults moved into the adjacent red room for dinner, where a famous collection of porcelain and old glass was displayed on either side of the fireplace.

Marco sat opposite his father and noticed how his hand trembled a little as he held his fork. *He's getting older*, he thought sadly. Teodoro Pisani was nudging eighty and still an imposing figure, but he had lost much of the drive that had made him one of the most brilliant senators of the Republic and ambassador to England and Spain, and at times his gaze seemed clouded.

Marco's mother, Elena, much younger and elegantly dressed in a blue gown embellished with lace and a luminous pearl necklace, was talking vivaciously. 'It's the children who keep me cheerful,' she remarked at one point. 'But sometimes I think about you, Marco. I know you'll never forget your wife, but don't you ever think of making a new life?'

Chiara Renier's face came into his mind again. 'It'll have to be the right woman, Mamma. It's not that simple,' he parried.

'You make things too complicated,' replied his sister-in-law, a beautiful Venetian woman with a rose-like complexion and auburn hair. She was expecting her third child. 'Take Giovanni, for instance. He certainly keeps going.' She smiled as she pointed to her large belly.

Hearing his name, Giovanni protested. 'What's that, Rossana? You know well that it's the Lord who grants us children . . .'

'With a great deal of help from you,' his wife replied, amidst the general hilarity.

'I almost forgot,' Marco's mother said as soon as the laughter had died down. 'We'll be having our traditional reception on St Stephen's Day and it would give me great pleasure if you were not there alone.'

'Of course, Mamma. I'll bring Daniele Zen with me,' joked Marco.

'You know quite well what I mean. It'll be a wonderful evening. Just think, the famous choir from the music school at the Mendicanti have agreed to sing for us. And I've invited some artists, too, like Tiepolo, who's back from Bavaria. Perhaps Rosalba Carriera will be there, even if she rarely goes out any more. What a shame that such a great artist has been robbed of the gift of sight! Then we'll have the pleasure of the usual family friends, including Carlo Goldoni.'

As he was walking to the place where the corpse had been found, Marco thought about the previous evening with a touch of sadness: his ageing father, his nephews, his brother's happiness. He felt as if he'd lost his way.

Contrary to usual, the quay in front of the imposing buildings of the Mint and the Terranova Granaries was deserted: the food stalls against the wall were bare and the chicken coops lay abandoned in a corner. Even the gondolas moored to the wooden jetties looked forlorn. A small but colourful crowd of onlookers had gathered at the end of the quay, close to the Fonteghetto, and as he drew nearer, Marco saw that a number of police officers were holding them back. As he arrived, the guards cleared the way for him and, having crossed a small bridge, Pisani suddenly found himself in front of the body.

Corner lay on his back under the portico, his bloodshot eyes staring at the sky, his hands still clasping at the rope that had been tightened around his neck. His expensive white wig had slipped off, leaving his shaved head bare. He was in evening dress, and the face mask, which was compulsory in the Ridotto, had been cast into a corner.

The avogadore knelt, tenderly closed his eyes and removed the rope. He immediately noticed that it was the same kind as the one that had killed Barbaro. He put it in his pocket before it could go missing. Marco felt a lump in his throat: the death of a young man always seemed a terrible injustice. But the corpse in front of him also meant that an assassin was on the loose in Venice and it was his duty to stop him.

There was no need for a doctor to certify the cause of death, so, turning to the guards, Marco gave the order to cover the body. 'Get a stretcher ready,' he continued, 'and carry the corpse to Palazzo Corner. You can go on foot, it's not far, but use the cloak to guard against prying.' He took the rope from his pocket and gave it to them with the instruction to leave it in his office.

He turned to look at his secretary thoughtfully. Tiralli was dressed in black and he had a naturally official look, which made him the ideal candidate for even the most unpleasant tasks.

'You, Jacopo, go with them,' he said. 'You'll have to go ahead in order to give the family the news.'

Tiralli would have given anything not to go, but he did not dare refuse.

The crowd was thinning, and many headed towards Saint Mark's or to Rialto to look for acquaintances they could share the news with. It was then that Marco caught sight of a gondolier wearing the Corner family colours. He was sitting on the ground sobbing. Marco went up to him. 'Tell me what happened,' he said.

'Oh, Your Excellency, I could easily be dead too.' He could barely get the words out. He told the avogadore how, on the previous night, his master had gone to the nearby Ridotto, as he often did on a Sunday, ordering his gondolier to wait by the boat. But when the usual time came for his master to return, a man had sprung out of the shadows and attacked him, giving him a mighty blow on the head with a club. When he regained his senses, he was lying gagged on the bottom of the gondola, trussed like a chicken. He could remember nothing else. 'My poor master,' he sobbed, 'they really wanted to kill him!'

It was true. One of the policemen showed Marco a pouch full of ducats that had been found on Corner's body. This was certainly not robbery.

The Ridotto, where so many Venetian fortunes had been squandered, was deserted at this time of day, with only a couple of valets who were finishing the cleaning. Pisani was not a regular because gambling had never attracted him, so he looked around with a certain degree of curiosity. The place was luxurious. The large central salon – which would have been crowded yesterday, as usual – had painted ceiling beams and its doors opened on to smaller rooms used for the different games. The walls were embellished with precious damasks and adorned with paintings and mirrors, and the interiors were lit by numerous six-branched chandeliers made from gilded wood.

Pisani stood by the cashier's table as he waited for the manager. He was almost certain that he wouldn't learn anything useful, but it was best to follow up this lead, too, while it was still fresh.

The manager had dressed in a hurry and the hem of his lace-frilled chemise poked out of his breeches. 'So sorry, Your Excellency.' He bowed and awkwardly finished tucking in the stray undershirt. He had already heard the news. 'It's dreadful! I can't believe it, and just close by, while his gondolier was waiting for him outside!' As he spoke, he glanced furtively at his reflection in a large mirror to check that his wig was straight. He must have been about sixty, but he strived to look younger.

'Think back to last night, Signor Baldi,' Pisani encouraged him. 'Did anything happen? An argument maybe, or some players who traded insults? Anything involving a woman?'

'Absolutely nothing.' Baldi frowned, and his powdered complexion immediately revealed a criss-crossing web of deep wrinkles. 'I remember clearly that poor Corner joined the basset table as soon as he arrived, then he moved on to play at faro. He was enjoying himself, and there were no arguments. At around midnight, if I'm not mistaken, he went to eat something in the refreshments room. I noticed because he had taken his mask off while he sipped his chocolate. Then he went back to the table. Women? No, certainly not for Piero Corner. In the past, maybe. Until last year he would occasionally bring a courtesan here. But since he married, not once. It seems that he was deeply in love with his wife. Even more so since the birth of his little girl . . .'

'A daughter?'

'Yes, born just a few months ago. He adored her and told everyone about her.' Baldi's eyes were now tear-filled, and even Marco felt saddened at the idea that the child would never know her father. Marco wondered at his own reaction. Why was he being so sentimental?

On leaving the Ridotto, he didn't feel like going straight back to the ducal palace, so he stopped in Piazza San Marco. A few gentlemen, wrapped in brightly coloured cloaks, were sunning themselves in the winter sunlight and talking about the news. Many of them craned their necks to watch him pass, and some greeted him in the hope that he might stop to give them further details. A group of commoner women were chatting enthusiastically, ignoring the protests of the children whose hands they held. A few small dogs were barking as they gave chase across the square. Behind the Piazzetta the masts of vessels stood out, lazily rocking in the waters of Saint Mark's Basin.

Pisani handed a few coins to a youngster and asked him to find Nani. Inside Florian's, he thought it likely that he would find Daniele Zen enjoying coffee, and indeed there was his friend seated at a table at the back of the coffee house.

'Marco, what's happened?' the lawyer said, greeting him.

Pisani gave him a detailed account of events before describing his own inquiries; Nani's exploits in Zanetta's shop were met with hilarity.

'But this second murder complicates matters because it's clear that the two deaths are linked,' Marco concluded.

'Well, at least you can set that young man free from prison now.'

'True. There's no good reason for keeping him there. I do believe he's an upright citizen. On Friday . . .' – and here Marco hesitated for a second – '. . . the woman who employs him came to see me and made a statement in his favour.'

'And what's she like?' Zen asked, having noted the minute pause. He knew Marco well.

'Well, fairly ordinary. She's got a silk-weaving workshop, and she runs it on her own . . .'

'Young or old? Beautiful or ugly?' Daniele pressed, not taking his blue eyes off Marco for a moment.

Marco had blushed. 'Young, and yes . . . not ugly. But what's that to you?'

'I know you, Marco. You're hiding something.'

'Well, to tell you the truth,' Pisani gave in, 'I liked her a lot, but I've only seen her once.'

'That's marvellous. Try to see her again.' Daniele knew well how to pay court to a woman.

'The trouble is, I don't know how to. She's not a courtesan, and she's not a noblewoman, which, for me, would at least have been familiar territory. I know nothing about her, and I'm concerned that she'll think I'm being forward.' Unlike his friend, Marco was shy when it came to these things.

'Seems like you've lost your head to her,' Daniele remarked. 'You know what? Discharge that young man – Maso, wasn't it? Then put him in your gondola and take him to the workshop.'

Soon afterwards, the prison guards stood open-mouthed as they watched Avogadore Pisani invite a former inmate on to his gondola and then instruct his gondolier to row to an unknown destination.

CHAPTER 8

Chiara had felt restless from the moment she awoke, and from experience she knew that this meant something was about to happen.

Walking past her dressing-table, in her mind she had caught sight of the blurred but unmistakable reflection of the handsome avogadore in the mirror. For an instant she felt as if she were being drawn into a whirling cloud and she recognised this as the sign of one of her premonitions. The scent of blossom hung in the air as an unprecedented joy filled her heart and made her want to sing. She felt her cheek where she had sensed the light touch of a hand.

What on earth was she thinking? This wasn't one of the occasional visions brought about by her powers as a clairvoyant. These were just a spinster's daydreams.

Then she had tested the patience of the young maid who was dressing her hair, because the curls refused to stay in the right place. That stain on her green dress had not been removed and so she had to make do with a purple skirt and a generously décolleté bodice. She couldn't find her coral necklace and had emptied her jewel case in search of it, and when she finally sat down late at table, she complained that the coffee was cold.

'What's the matter with you this morning, mistress?' the young maid grumbled in exasperation. 'Did you not sleep well?'

'I'm sorry, I've had a lot on my mind,' Chiara replied, feeling guilty for taking her bad mood out on the maid. She went to sit in the fashionably decorated salon. Sunshine filled the room, picking out the cream lacquered furniture and blue hangings. A handsome glass-fronted cabinet showed off her most precious belongings, and on one wall there was a view of Saint Mark's Basin by Canaletto.

Chiara loved beautiful things and she often thanked her father for having given her a good education, first with the Ursuline nuns and then later at home, as if she were the daughter of an upper-class family, with tutors in music and literature. However, at the same time, he had also taught her the secrets of bookkeeping, double-entry accounts and exchange rates.

But today she just couldn't concentrate, so she threw down the ledger which she had been trying to read and instead went down to the weaving workshop.

All the looms were busy. They were wonderful machines, some from as far away as England, and their wooden crosspieces rose up to the ceiling, allowing the complicated web of threads, expertly threaded, to be transformed into bolts of cloth. About twenty young men were working the looms, and the rhythmic clatter of the treadles always had a calming effect on their mistress.

Chiara walked around the large room, greeting the workers, who smiled back at her in acknowledgement: they worked well with this young woman because she knew the trade and had a good eye for new designs that resulted in a stream of new orders; moreover, she was not stingy. It was just a pity that she was single and appeared to have no intention of finding a husband, even if there was no shortage of suitors among those in the business.

Chiara checked a few of the latest silk samples and offered some suggestions. She glanced at Maso's loom, which was silent, the work left unfinished, and sighed before going to sit at the desk in the small office next to the workshop. She picked up a bundle of letters from customers but couldn't concentrate. Every now and then her eyes would stray to the door.

Nani tied the gondola to a post in the canal that crossed Calle Venier and Marco emerged from the cabin and jumped on to the street, followed by Maso.

'Go and look for Baldo Vannucci,' he ordered. 'If you take a turn around the taverns in Rialto, you're sure to find him.'

'But, paròn, Baldo Vannucci is—'

'I know quite well who he is. Tell him that I'll wait for him at one tomorrow at the Osteria della Pergola at the Zattere, and that I want to know everything he can tell me about Marino Barbaro, Piero Corner and Paolo Labia. Don't say a word about this to anyone and come back and collect me in a couple of hours.'

From his reply, Nani was clearly not convinced. 'Tell me, paròn,' he couldn't help asking, torn between surprise and curiosity, 'now that we've brought Maso back home, or rather back to work, what are you going to do here for two hours, given that there are only manufactories around here?'

Marco snorted. Why did all of his servants think they should keep an eye on him? 'It's my business, Nani! Just make sure you don't mention this to anyone either.'

Young Maso hurried across the bridge, his face flushed with emotion, and slowly opened the front door of the workshop. Chiara lifted her eyes from her papers and recognised the outline silhouetted against the daylight immediately. 'Maso!' she exclaimed, running towards him. 'You're back!' She embraced him with relief.

Looking beyond Maso, she suddenly froze. Was it or was it not him?

'It is you . . .' she murmured in confusion. 'Excellency, you are Avogadore Pisani. You brought him back . . . So, Maso has been released . . .' All the anxiety she had felt that morning vanished. This was what her premonition had been about.

Marco walked in and bowed slightly. 'Yes, there is no question about his innocence. I found myself passing these parts,' he said, 'and I thought . . .' He stopped, since there was no point continuing to lie. *What an extraordinary woman*, he thought. *She runs the workshop on her own, but she has the class of a great lady.*

Chiara watched him carefully. Without his robes and wig he was a very handsome man, and he was looking at her, smiling, almost shyly, a suggestion of that half-smile which made his dark eyes shine. But why had he come?

'You're most welcome.' She pulled herself together. 'How can Maso and I thank you? Indeed, on that subject,' she remembered, 'would you allow Maso to run home and reassure his parents?'

The young man was already surrounded by a group of colleagues who were congratulating him with hugs and slaps on his shoulder. He didn't wait to be told twice before he ran out of the door, heading straight home. Chiara and Marco were left watching him in the penumbra of the workshop.

'Well, I should be getting back . . .' Faced with those smiling blue eyes, Marco again found himself not knowing what to say.

Chiara saved him. 'Allow me, Your Excellency, to offer you some refreshment. Indeed, given the time, perhaps you would care to stay for lunch.'

Pisani did not even pretend to hesitate, and he followed her upstairs to the first-floor apartment. While Chiara Renier was giving orders, he looked around: it was a pleasant house, full of books, with a spinet finely painted with pastoral scenes under one window, and even a painting by Canaletto. The mistress of the house was clearly well educated and a woman of taste.

'Are you looking at the painting?' He was distracted by her return. 'I love beautiful things, and my father was able to pass on much of what he knew before he died. My mother . . .' Chiara stopped for a moment and sighed. 'She died while I was still a child. But I was born in October, under the sign of Libra, and people like me can only find peace in harmonious surroundings.'

'Do you believe in astrology?'

'In some aspects of the supernatural, yes, even though it is a sphere still shrouded in mystery.' She sat down beside Marco on a divan. 'For example, to see the influence of the stars on a person's character, one need only think of nature: the flowers and fruits of autumn are different from those of other seasons. But astrology apart, I do think that our lives have more than one dimension.'

The conversation was taking an unexpected turn. 'Do you have a deep faith?' ventured Marco.

'I believe in a God of love and mercy, but that's not what I meant,' replied Chiara. She concentrated, looking down at her folded hands. 'I believe there is an invisible, spiritual life which runs parallel to our physical world. Artists are the only ones who can perceive and give form to this supernatural harmony. Take that painting by Canaletto, for example. He's not particularly valued by Venetians and his works sell more abroad. Here, he is often regarded as an illustrator. Yet I see something magical in his works, in the way he recreates reality, as if it were an enchantment.'

Marco looked thoughtful. Her words opened strange horizons. He glanced over at the spinet and changed the subject. 'Can you play, too?'

'I studied music for quite a few years. Music is solace for the soul. Would you like to hear something?'

Chiara played sweetly but with undoubted authority. The notes of Monteverdi sounded clear and melodious. Marco sat back as he studied this surprising woman and the unfathomable facets of her personality. A delicate profile with a slightly upturned nose, a willowy figure. He was overwhelmed by a desire to be close to her. What was happening to him?

At lunch Marco enjoyed the delicately cooked fish, fresh from the market, followed by a delectable zabaione. The conversation flowed effortlessly, and they spoke of books and music. Then Marco broached the subject of Piero Corner's murder and how the presence of an unusual length of rope linked the crime to the earlier death.

As they talked, the avogadore wondered how he could ask to see her again without seeming indiscreet. There were strict rules of etiquette in Venice regarding unmarried women, and Chiara had no parents to protect her from malicious gossip.

In the end he made up his mind. 'I would enjoy it if we could continue our conversation, Chiara. Would you give me permission to address you informally like this? And you could leave aside my title, too. My name is Marco. Would you do me the honour . . . or rather, would you care to come to the Leon Bianco with me tomorrow evening?' This was the city's most refined locanda, frequented by noblewomen and even by visiting royalty.

Chiara hesitated. She was not accustomed to accepting invitations, but this man was an avogadore, one of the highest magistrates, an esteemed figure. What was more, for the first time in her life, this was a man whose presence touched her.

'Thank you,' she said at last. 'But, Your Excellency . . . I mean Marco, you must do something: bring me that piece of rope you were talking about.' And in response to Marco's look of surprise, she added, 'I know something about fibres and yarns, and I'd be interested to see it.'

Humming the notes of Monteverdi, Marco walked back to the gondola and pretended not to notice Nani's questioning glances as he was rowed to Zen's office, close to the church of San Moisè. He walked through the room full of clerks, then entered the study without knocking and sat down in front of his friend, who was reading a bundle of papers. Marco was euphoric and it showed.

'Well, well!' Daniele grinned, pushing the papers to one side.

Marco was like a bottle of spumante whose cork was about to pop, and he wasted no time in telling his friend all about the meeting.

'You've fallen in love,' Zen pronounced when Marco had finished. 'And about time too!'

'I don't know what's come over me. There's something different about this woman . . . when I'm with her, I feel marvellous. Then I think about Virginia and I'm ashamed.'

'Your wife hasn't been with us for a long time, Marco. She would have understood, you know. But there is a problem. However beautiful, wealthy and educated this woman is, she is a commoner, and as you well know it's very difficult for a patrician to marry a commoner.'

'Yes, you need the permission of an avogadore . . .' The two friends burst out laughing. 'But before we even get that far, we need to get to know each other better,' Marco went on. 'For now, I'll be happy just to see her.'

'Lucky devil, you don't have to worry about courtship,' Marco remarked that evening, looking down at Plato, who was curled up in his armchair in the study. The room was dark, lit only by the dancing flames of the fireplace. The cat's green eyes shone like lanterns.

What luck, he thought, that the four guards had arrested Maso by mistake, otherwise he'd never have met Chiara. It was not just that she was beautiful, intelligent and a woman of refined taste, she had something else that had struck him from the first moment he'd seen her. It was hard to describe, but she shone with an inner light.

Marco looked up at his wife's portrait above the fireplace. She seemed to be smiling at him. 'You know,' he whispered, 'how much I loved you, and how desperately I mourn you and our son. You'll always be in my heart, but now I must move forward.'

He jumped as Rosetta walked in with his night-time cup of chocolate.

'What are you doing, paròn, here in the dark? Is there something worrying you?' She, too, turned to look up at the portrait, and then added, 'Your wife's been gone for a long time, and it's not good for you to stay here, brooding, all on your own.'

'You're right, Rosetta,' Marco sighed. 'Light the lamps.'

He sat down at his desk. The cat followed him and stretched out on top of some papers.

'Let's see, Plato,' Marco remarked, thinking aloud, as soon as Rosetta left. 'We've got two corpses, both strangled on the street at night using a rope that might be Turkish or perhaps Portuguese. They were friends, but one of them was in trouble and had got into bad company, and even had secret papers from the Arsenale in his apartment. What I really need to know now is what Alvise Cappello has to say about those documents. Corner, on the other hand, came from an illustrious and well-off family; he'd been a bit wild in his youth, but he seems to have quietened down after marriage. Then there's that story about the young maid. This gang of friends, which also included Paolo Labia and a servant, were involved in a rape and one of them had to patch things up . . . but how, I don't know.'

Plato mewed loudly in his sleep.

'What are you dreaming of?' his master wondered. The cat opened an eye. 'See if you can follow my line of thought.' Plato yawned. 'If Barbaro was a spy, he might have been killed by the counter-espionage agents. But the secret services remove any corpses and dump them in deep water, with a stone around their neck; they never leave them in the street. Anyway, how does Corner fit into this? He certainly didn't need to stoop to earn a pittance, like Barbaro. Unless he was killed because he knew about his friend's murky dealings. And what about that unusual rope? It's like a signature of some sort. Perhaps Barbaro was cheating a Turk, and the Turk decided to take revenge. Old Lucia said that she'd seen one passing the house a few times. But that doesn't help with the puzzle of Corner's death. I need to find out more about the whole gang, and perhaps about the maid, too, even though that was a few years ago, it seems. Yet a peasant felt able to threaten Barbaro at the time. And Corner was certainly involved in that, if I'm to believe what that young woman told Nani. Do you know what, Plato?' Marco concluded, stroking the cat. 'Let's go and have a good hot bath, and then off to bed.'

At the mention of a bath the cat jumped off the desk and, with a couple of elegant leaps, settled himself on the topmost shelf of the bookcase.

CHAPTER 9

Decked in mourning, Palazzo Corner was visible from far down the Grand Canal. Drapes of black velvet trimmed with gold hung from the large Renaissance windows and were reflected in flickering black brushstrokes in the water below. The huge family coat of arms above the doorway on to the canal was also draped in black cloth.

Marco stepped out of the gondola, followed by Daniele Zen, and together they walked up the steps that led under a triple archway to the large atrium with its multicoloured marble floor, furnished with two plain coffers.

Marco had decided to visit the deceased man's family early in the morning in order to avoid the throng of visitors who would invade the palace after the funeral.

'Nani, you know what to do,' he whispered to the gondolier, who hurried off towards the servants' quarters. 'Let's go,' he added, turning to Zen as they set off up the stairs.

On the first floor Marco recognised the major-domo, who was in black livery and led them through a series of rooms. These spacious surroundings had been designed by Sansovino in the sixteenth century, and they retained the austerity of that period: high ceilings with painted beams, plain furniture, walls covered by huge tapestries. Now, even the floor-length windows were curtained in mourning, and only a few candelabras lit the way.

Piero Corner lay on a gilded catafalque in the centre of the main salon. The light of four large candles carved flickering shadows on his waxen face. On a bench to the right of the corpse a row of nuns chanted the rosary prayers, a group of visitors whispered beside one of the windows and two elderly maidservants sobbed beside a console table.

Marco and Daniele approached the bier and stood there for a moment in reflection. Corner, who now looked at rest, was a handsome young man, with regular features. He was dressed in a long blue silk jacket embroidered in silver; somebody had thoughtfully pulled up the white lace of his collar to hide the garish weal left on his neck by the murderer's rope.

Just then another young man walked across the room towards the bier. He had a slight limp. Marco recognised him as Dario Corner, the deceased man's younger brother, who strongly resembled Piero, although he was of heavier build, with an unhealthy-looking, pale, flabby face. At close quarters you could see the scars left by an attack of smallpox in his youth. His eyes were swollen, as if he had been crying for hours.

Marco and Daniele went over to him and murmured the usual condolences. They embraced him in turn.

'It's such a tragedy!' Corner interrupted them, wiping his eyes with a lace handkerchief. 'What will we do without him? He was the head of the family since our father died a few years ago and was newly married, with a two-month-old baby girl. My sister-in-law is distraught. But, Pisani' – Corner looked at Marco diffidently – 'I imagine you're here to make inquiries about the murder?'

'I'm here to pay my tributes to the family,' said Marco. 'And I'd like to present my condolences to your mother, and to his widow.'

'My mother is not able to receive anyone at present. You must excuse her, but such a blow, and so unexpected . . . Tomorrow she might feel up to seeing you, perhaps. However, my sister-in-law is in her room with the child and I know your visit would give her comfort.' He signalled to a servant to announce the guests. 'Excuse me if I don't come with you,' he added. 'I had a nasty fall and it's very painful to go upstairs.' He pointed to his bandaged knee.

In the big bedroom on the second floor, Eleonora Corner was already dressed for the funeral, her beautiful face pinched by sadness. She was standing beside the cradle, where the baby slept blissfully unaware, her rosy cheeks looking angelic against the frills. When she saw them, she burst into sobs, which she managed to stifle with the white lace handkerchief she held in her hand, its brightness forming a striking contrast with her black gown.

'Your Excellency Pisani,' she cried, her eyes brimming with tears, 'you must find whoever did this. We were so happy together, Piero and me. Why would anyone want to destroy my family?'

Marco was shaken. The young woman's pain was genuine and it stirred uncomfortable memories of his own tragedy. Like Virginia, Eleonora came from a rich family in Padua. She had been little more than a schoolgirl when Corner met and married her, and since then he had been an exemplary husband.

'Did he have any enemies, as far as you know, or anyone who had threatened him?' Marco's question was put as tactfully as possible.

'No, everyone liked him, even the servants, who mourn him as if he had been a relative . . .' Eleonora answered in a trembling voice.

'Had he broken off relations with a friend? Sacked a servant?' The question might have seemed out of place, but Marco had in mind Zanetta's story of the maid seduced by Piero and sent home a few years earlier. Barbaro's housekeeper had also recalled a peasant who had delivered threats to the barnabotto's residence. And then there was the coarse and frayed length of rope that had been used to strangle both men. But the episode with the maid had happened before Corner had married, and Eleonora could not have known about it.

She shook her head and continued to sob silently.

Daniele took over. 'Signora, was your husband involved in any business deals, like a large purchase, for example, that might have been of interest to someone? Or did he ever say that he suspected an acquaintance of passing confidential information to a foreign ambassador? Do you know whether he had dealings with Turks, for example?' Although the Serenissima did sometimes turn a blind eye to some offences, it dealt harshly with anything that involved spying.

'No! Piero told me everything and there were no grey areas in his life. He would have told me if there had been any rivals, and he didn't know any pressing secrets. He was killed because someone wanted to rob him, I'm sure of it, and you must find out who did it.'

Marco and Daniele took their leave. Neither had mentioned the fact that the purse of ducats found on the corpse ruled out any suspicion of theft.

Outside the palace, in the calle and in Campo San Moisè nearby, a crowd was already gathering which would follow the corpse to its burial place in the church of Santi Apostoli, where the family tomb was.

The Corner family had not held back. Representatives from the guilds and from the great schools were on their way with their flags; the delegations from the main monasteries had already assembled, together with the priests from the surrounding parishes. There were a few robed magistrates and Marco recognised some patricians and numerous senators. They were all waiting to take their place in the gondolas which, draped in mourning, were now converging on the palace to make up the funeral procession.

In a corner of the campo, groups of commoners, both men and women, were enjoying the spectacle, while a few beggars had taken up their posts beside the service door of the palace, where they would be handed donations by the family to commemorate the deceased.

Marco's gondolier had found his way to the kitchens easily. The whole place was in uproar. In the largest fireplace, a huge boar was being roasted on the spit under the careful eye of an assistant, who basted it using a bundle of goose feathers every time he turned the handle. On the long wooden table, some maidservants were plucking partridges and capons, while a row of plucked cockerels already hung on butcher's hooks from the ceiling. Two stewards were energetically polishing some large silver plates.

In an adjacent room, where the walls were covered with copper pots and pans, the head cook was arranging biscuits on a tray to be cooked in the oven, while his assistants descaled some large fish on a marble worktop under the window.

Nani spotted his man immediately: he was a gondolier, dressed in the family livery, sitting downcast in the corner, with his head bandaged. He was short and stocky, with a round face liberally sprinkled with freckles.

'Hello.' He bowed. 'I am the servant of Avogadore Marco Pisani, who is visiting your masters. Is there anything to drink?'

'Elvira, bring some drink over here!' shouted the gondolier to a young woman, who, seeing Nani, promptly came over with a glass of wine and a large smile.

'Who is this handsome young man, Beppino?' she asked brazenly.

'Were you the one who was with poor Corner?' Nani asked, without looking at the girl. 'What happened to you?'

'What do you think?' he said, holding his head in explanation. 'It still hurts . . .' He sighed. 'I was there, as always on a Sunday. It was the only night when my master went to the Ridotto. It must have been about two in the morning. I was standing by the gondola and it was pitch-black because there's no lamplight in that particular spot.'

'And then?'

'I heard a rustle behind me and I turned. But I must have been hit on the head with a stick. It hurt like the devil . . .'

'And after that?'

'I came to in the gondola, gagged and bound, and I had to lie there until morning when the guards found me. My poor master!'

'Had you worked for him for a while?'

'No, just since he got married. The previous gondolier was fired by the master's mother, and then I arrived.'

'Why was he fired?' pressed Nani.

'Who knows? I wasn't here. The person who knows everything that goes on in the palace is Matteo, that old man sitting beside the small fireplace.'

Nani glanced over at the elderly man in a steward's uniform. He had a head of well-groomed white hair and was stirring a pan over the fire. 'But you,' he continued, still addressing Beppino, 'hadn't noticed anything odd in the past few days? Someone following your master, for instance?'

Beppino was tiring of all these questions. 'Who's the avogadore? You or your master?' he said resentfully. 'Can't you leave me in peace?' He stood up and poured himself another glass of wine.

Nani promptly changed his tune. 'That's fine, Beppino. Just tell me whether you mean to go on working for the family. Because I have to say I wouldn't mind working here. I can't say that I don't get on well with my master, but I have to rush around all day long.'

'After what's happened, I'm not staying here. I can honestly say the Corner family are all good people, but given that Master Dario has his own gondolier, I'd have to look after the ladies, and that doesn't appeal much.'

'Well, I'd be happy to do that,' Nani laughed. 'Even if the ladies are in mourning, they'll still go and visit their friends, and I bet there'd be plenty of attractive maids . . . But, tell me, what was your late master like?' he insisted.

'He was a real family man,' Beppino went on. 'He always seemed happy and was ready with a joke. Although he was different just lately.'

Nani was quick to jump on that piece of information. 'Different? In what way? And since when?'

'Just lately, since last week, when his friend died, that man Barbaro. That affected him badly. I told him that it was probably a case of mistaken identity, that in Venice we don't have murderers wandering around the streets, but he was really shaken. I think he may have had some premonition . . . and of course, he was murdered in the same way.'

'Did he tell you what he was frightened of?'

'He didn't exactly confide in me. Anyway, who are you? One of the guards?'

Nani realised that he'd got as far as he could with Beppino and took his leave. A heady scent wafted towards him as he passed a table where one of the kitchen boys was grinding spices in a mortar. He approached the fireplace, where old Matteo was still bending over the fire, stirring a large pot.

'What's boiling in there?' Nani asked.

The old man turned to look at him with an acute, enquiring stare. 'Beans that'll be served out to the poor after the funeral ceremony. Who are you?'

Nani introduced himself. 'I was talking to Beppino over there,' he continued. 'He wants to move on and I'd be quite interested in working here.' It was a good pretext for the questions that Nani had in mind. 'What are the family like as employers?'

'Who knows? Everything's going to change now,' sighed the old man, pointing to a chair for Nani. 'I was the old master's personal steward, but he died six years ago. He kept things on the straight and narrow. When his father died, Piero went off the rails for a while, and his mother protected him. She's quite something, Signora Francesca . . . She dismissed me and sent me down here because I would occasionally let slip that things had been better while her husband was alive. What I was forced to witness . . . best not to say too much about that!'

'What a waste to put a distinguished person like you in the kitchens,' Nani flattered him.

'Better than sacking me and finding myself in a hospice . . . I'm not young any more. Who else would give me work?'

'What did poor Piero get up to then? Who did he see? Do you think he might have been killed by one of his acquaintances?'

'No. Ever since he married, which was more than a year ago, he'd settled down.'

'But before that?'

Matteo sat back on the bench by the fire and wiped his forehead with a large handkerchief. 'Well, before that . . . he was a drinker, a gambler, and of course there were women, too. Not just courtesans. He didn't draw the line anywhere. The wives of tavern keepers, shopkeepers, and even the maidservants here in the palace.' There was a slight hesitation. 'There were dreadful stories . . .' He shook his head. 'He'd paired up with his gondolier, a certain Biagio, who was a nasty piece of work. To her credit, the signora got rid of him as soon as Piero married. Then there were another two who were always hanging around with him.'

'Was one of them that Barbaro who was killed last Thursday in exactly the same way?'

Matteo took another hard look at Nani, this time with greater scrutiny. 'You are well informed! Why are you so interested?'

'Just making conversation, and I'm curious. Also, you must admit it's an odd coincidence that they were both strangled.'

'They didn't see each other any longer, so as far as I know, it's just that, a coincidence.'

'And the other chap, Biagio, what happened to him?' Nani insisted.

'I don't know, but his mother had a drinking house near the Fondaco dei Turchi. He might be there.'

'But wasn't there some story involving a maid a few years ago?' Nani felt that he had to be blunt in order to prise out the information that Pisani needed.

'You obviously know more about it that than I do.' Matteo scrutinised him with blatant suspicion now. Then he shrugged his shoulders and got up to stir the pot again before pouring out two cups of white wine. He offered one to Nani and drank the other himself in a single swig. 'It's hot work beside the fire. You asked about the maid. I shouldn't tell you because the mistress swore us all to secrecy at the time, but seeing how she's treated me . . . Yes, there was a story. Her name was Lucietta Segati, and she came from Dolo; it must have been about three years ago. Just before Christmas. She would come down to the kitchens to cry and she told me that the master was taking advantage of her. Things like that happen all the time. But then, one day she just disappeared. She must have gone home.'

'So, the master's death might have been an honour killing.'

The old man shook his head. 'Three years later? Anyway, Lucietta was a peasant's daughter. It would be impossible for her family to come to Venice and do something like that, as if they were expert assassins. They're poor folk, more accustomed to being abused. They would soon have resigned themselves to what happened to Lucietta.'

The men were interrupted by Elvira, who brought over a tray. 'Here you are, chatting with everyone but me!' she said, looking at Nani with a glint in her eye. 'Can I tempt you with a sweet pastry?'

Nani popped one in his mouth. 'You know what it's like. I'm waiting for my master to finish.'

'And he's asking all sorts of questions because he says he wants to come and work here,' Matteo snapped.

'So who's going to inherit everything?' Nani continued as soon as the girl had walked away. 'Who'll be the new *padrone*?'

'Signor Dario, of course. Things have worked out nicely for him.'

'Why?'

'Because he's got the law on his side. His brother had a baby girl and in noble families women never inherit if there's a male relative. The child will have a handsome dowry when the time comes, but all the assets go to her uncle.'

'And what sort of man is he?'

'A good-for-nothing. He's already had his share of his father's inheritance, which was substantial. He likes to think he's an experienced businessman, just like the old nobility of Venice, but the truth is he's not got the head for it. Rumour has it that he's already wasted most of his inheritance on madcap schemes of one sort or other. Of course, us servants aren't aware of the details, but every now and then one of us overhears the old signora hurling insults at him.'

How interesting, thought Nani. But it was getting late and Pisani and Zen were probably waiting for him, so he took his leave from Matteo, blew a kiss towards Elvira, who was washing up some bowls, and left the palace to join his master outside.

CHAPTER 10

'Good news?' Marco asked impatiently as soon as he saw his gondolier approach wearing a broad smile and looking slightly tipsy.

'Very good, paròn. News worth several ducats.'

Zen laughed. 'But you're already on a salary, and a good one at that!'

'Of course, avvocato,' answered Nani, opening his blue eyes wide in laughter. 'But this is highly specialised work, and it comes at a cost.'

This time it was Marco who laughed as he stretched out to give his gondolier an affectionate cuff.

The three men walked towards Daniele Zen's office, which was not far away. Its windows overlooked Campo San Moisè and the murmur of the crowd that had gathered for the funeral rose up to meet them. The details of Nani's conversations were extremely interesting, and Marco made him recount them, sometimes going over them repeatedly while he took notes.

'What do you think?' Marco asked, turning to Daniele as soon as Nani had left to go and fetch the gondola.

'The more we discover, the more complicated it becomes,' commented Zen. 'The crimes are linked, there is no question of that. The two victims knew each other, and they died in identical circumstances.'

'But what is the link? What was so serious that it meant death? Espionage? Corner didn't need the money, but even then, who knows . . .? Perhaps he was blackmailed. Or the victim of an honour killing? The episode with the maid dates back at least three years, but it would certainly be worth discovering what happened to her.'

'You could set Nani on the trail; he's certainly much better than the police at questioning people and finding things out.'

'Yes, somehow or other, I must find that girl. You're right about Nani too. I don't know how I'd manage without him. He's bright, trustworthy, and he's certainly got imagination and initiative. He's also educated. He'd make a fantastic civil servant, and at times I'm sorry that he's a servant. Perhaps I should do something for him.'

'But there's also the fact that he's happy to work with you. He earns good money and enjoys himself. It was a stroke of luck that he came to you.'

Marco smiled as he remembered the circumstances. Five years earlier, one winter morning a youngster had come running to his gate and furiously rapped on the knocker, shouting loudly for someone to open up, as if he were being pursued. He was little more than a boy, just sixteen. He had heard that the avogadore was looking for a gondolier because the faithful Martino was getting too old and the master preferred to keep him at home to help the women, while his other servant, Giuseppe, although he knew everything about table service and polishing the silver, baulked at even touching an oar. Nani had pleaded with the avogadore, assuring him that he would never regret the decision. Of course, he'd been absolutely right.

Giovanni Casadio, who was known as Nani, had a story much like that of many other boys. He was an orphan who'd been abandoned at a church sacristy and had been brought up in the orphanage run by the Scolopi fathers. This was something that happened all too frequently in Venice, where not only courtesans, maids and poor peasant girls from the surrounding villages but also the daughters of noble families freed themselves in secret from their unwanted and illegitimate infants. Throughout the city, orphanages would care for the children until they were sixteen, giving them something of an education and teaching them a trade.

But Nani had proved highly intelligent, and to his dismay the Scolopi fathers had planned to place him in a seminary and turn him into a priest, even if he showed no inkling whatsoever of a vocation. So one night the boy had escaped and run as fast as he could to Pisani's house in order to seek his protection. As a result, Pisani had hired him and had compensated the Scolopi with a generous donation.

'And how's it going with Chiara?' asked Daniele, changing the subject.

'I've invited her to the Leon Bianco this evening as I can't pay court to her at home, given that she lives alone. It's the most elegant *locanda*, in my opinion, and I hope she won't be disappointed. You're good at this courting thing – so, what should I do? Should I arrive with the gondola at dinner time? Or should I write her a note first?' Marco had not spent these years as a widower in complete chastity, but the thought of Chiara made him as uncertain as an untested adolescent.

Daniele stood up. 'Put on your cloak and come with me,' he ordered.

He led his friend to the Mercerie, the most exclusive shopping street in Venice, which was filled with elegant crowds since, by now, it was almost midday. In the window of a shop called La Piàvola there was a magnificent gown, 'à l'Andrienne', in green brocade, a style that was the height of fashion in France and had a mantle that fell from the shoulder to form a short train. The two friends walked in.

'Don't even look at the gown,' warned Daniele. 'The gift of a gown is reserved for a lover. If I were you, I'd choose a fan.'

Shortly afterwards, Nani, who could hardly contain his amazement, was sent to Chiara Renier's workshop to deliver an elegant package and a note, which Marco had taken the precaution of sealing, knowing full well how inquisitive his gondolier could be.

'But, paròn,' Nani barely had time to remonstrate, 'she's a beautiful young woman. She'll think that your gift is a token of courtship . . .'

'Nani, mind your own business . . .' warned Marco. 'What else should she think? Just make sure you're polite and come to the Zattere at around three o'clock.'

'So that's why you wanted to accompany that young man you released from prison and then you spent two hours there,' Nani muttered as he left. 'I might have known there was a woman involved.'

'I really don't understand' – Marco smiled as he turned to Daniele – 'why none of my servants show me any respect. If that loudmouth goes around gossiping about this, I swear I'll wring his neck.'

The Osteria della Pergola on the Zattere, facing the Giudecca, had a large room which, even by day, was lit by oil lamps that hung from the ceiling beams among a selection of bacon and legs of ham. The tables were covered by chequered tablecloths and set with pottery bowls and plates. It was already full of customers, including numerous retail merchants fresh from the Customs House, shopkeepers, wholesalers visiting from outside the city and a handful of sailors.

Wrapped in a voluminous cloak and wearing anonymous clothing to prevent him being recognised, Marco walked in and immediately spotted Baldo Vannucci sitting at a table beside the wine counter not far from the large hearth, from which came a waft of appetising smells. The *padrona* was busy frying stuffed sardines, handed to her by an assistant who drenched them with flour. A young maidservant was stirring stew in a copper pot.

Vannucci was middle-aged, short and rather thin, wearing a baggy garment that had seen better times. He owned a small second-hand jewellery shop near Campo Santo Stefano and acted as a spy for the inquisitors. This was the man whom Pisani had arranged to meet through Nani the day before. When he caught sight of the avogadore, Vannucci stood up and ceremoniously removed his hat.

Pisani did not like using informers because he knew that, in exchange for a few ducats, some would not hesitate to give false information, even about friends and relatives. But no one knew the city's undercurrents better than Vannucci. Indebted nobles, courtesans past their prime, thieving servants, as well as travelling salesmen, workers and penniless writers would all confide in him when they tried to sell their valuables. Moreover, they were all ready to gossip about their neighbours and reveal any dark secrets they had heard from whatever social circle they moved in. Vannucci knew who he could turn to when he needed information and, among the many spies from all different walks of life, he was regarded as one of the more reliable.

They ordered some food and then Marco broached the subject. 'I don't need to remind you that the matter we are talking about is of the utmost secrecy.'

Vannucci nodded vigorously.

Marco continued, 'I know that the two young patricians who were murdered recently – I'm referring to Piero Corner and Marino Barbaro – were frequent companions until a year or so back. I want you to tell me everything you've heard about their group and what they got up to. Did they run up debts or offend anyone?'

'Yes, Your Excellency. Yesterday your servant hinted at the reason for our meeting, which does me great honour—'

'Let's get straight to the point,' Marco interrupted.

Vannucci set all ceremony aside, knowing it was wasted on Avogadore Pisani, and he stopped to gather his thoughts for a moment. Then he spoke in a low but clear voice, carefully weighing his words.

'I had heard some talk,' he admitted, 'but in the past few hours I've been able to put together a clearer picture. Before Corner married, there were four young men in the group. There was Corner, and you know about him. His pockets were well lined – too well lined – because his mother let him have a free rein and, as head of the family, she made sure that he lacked for nothing. He gambled every evening at the Ridotto and in other casinos reserved for the nobility. Moreover, he was frequently seen in courtesans' salons, and not only those of the first rank, since he would often be found in Calle delle Tette with the common prostitutes. I've even heard rumours – although I couldn't vouch for them – that he seduced a young maid in his own household and got her pregnant. He and the group would go drinking in the lowest drinking dens and the others would often have to hold him upright as he staggered home. It's a miracle that he wasn't drowned in a canal, but the others never left him alone: he held the purse strings, so they had a vested interest in looking after him.'

'Do you think it was an enemy taking revenge for something?'

'Apparently not, because one way or another, the Corner family's money always smoothed things out.'

'But then he changed.'

'After he married. His mother couldn't bear to let him continue such a dissolute way of life so chose a bride and forced him to marry her. By some miracle, as soon as the two young people met, they fell madly in love and he became a reformed man.'

The boy arrived just then with their food and for a while they fell silent.

'And what about the others?' Marco continued, savouring the polenta, which was accompanied by a stew of small birds. The jug of cold white wine was also very pleasant.

Baldo was on his best behaviour, eating small mouthfuls. He was rather in awe of his table companion, as it was not every day that he ate with an avogadore. He wanted to be as thorough as possible. He knew that Pisani would remember him if his information was accurate, and being on good terms with such a high-ranking individual would undoubtedly serve him well, especially in a profession like his.

'I believe you already know everything about Barbaro,' Baldo continued. 'A good-for-nothing who was a disgrace to his honourable family name. He made a living from petty deals, often bordering on fraud, and he amused himself at the expense of the Corner family. It was Barbaro who encouraged Corner to drink and gamble, and I've been told that Barbaro would get a kickback from the various locales. He used to flatter Corner by saying he was the cleverest, that the rules didn't apply to people like him, and so on. The third one in the group was Paolo Labia.'

The information that Zanetta had given Nani was right, Marco thought, but Vannucci was filling in the details.

'Labia,' the other man added, 'was the most innocuous of the group. No one ever saw him take the initiative in a prank, but he eagerly followed the others. He also enjoyed himself, drinking and gambling. But no women, because he seems not to like them . . . but some of the prostitutes tell me that he didn't turn down an opportunity to stay and watch. The Labia are a very rich family, too, but Paolo was kept on short rations, so the Corner purse paid for him as well.'

Marco wondered what dark corners of the city he had scoured to obtain such detailed information, and in the course of just one day. 'And the fourth member?' he prompted.

'The fourth was Biagio, Biagio Domenici, a shady sort if ever there was one. He used to come to me occasionally to sell stolen goods . . .' Vannucci stopped, frightened that he had said too much. A worried look came into his sharp eyes.

Pisani signalled to the padrona for another wine jug. 'Go on, I'm not interested in your affairs,' he encouraged Vannucci as he filled both their cups.

'Well, Domenici seems to have been Barbaro's gondolier until four years ago. Then Barbaro couldn't afford to pay him any longer and Corner took him on, in order to keep the group together.'

'And he was fired exactly a year ago, when Corner married,' concluded Pisani.

'That's right. But I've discovered something odd: Biagio's mother had a small drinking house close to the Fondaco dei Turchi, a dingy place that barely gave her enough to live off. Then last summer, six months before her son was given the sack, she bought a large, well-furnished tavern in the same neighbourhood, and no one can tell me how she paid for it.'

'And where is Biagio now?'

Vannucci drank his wine. He was relaxed now, almost smiling. 'Apparently he lives there with his mother and spends most of the time gambling. The place attracts shady types – Turks, Albanians, passing sailors – but Biagio has certainly found his niche because, given its location, the place is always full, even if it's not very clean.'

Here was the Turkish lead again, Marco thought as he sat in the gondola on his way to the Arsenale. There was still time to pay a visit to Alvise Cappello before he was due to meet Chiara; perhaps his friend might have discovered something about the papers they had found at the barnabotto's place.

As for Lucietta Segati, the maidservant who had been seduced and – if the rumours were true – had had a child, the only way to find out what had happened to her was to go and look for her on the mainland, in her home village.

CHAPTER 11

Alvise Cappello was waiting for Marco in his office at the shipyard. He stood up as the avogadore walked in and went towards him. The two friends embraced.

'You gave me a challenging set of riddles to solve, you know,' Alvise laughed. His small, piercing eyes twinkled in amusement above his long nose. Laid out on the table were the documents that Pisani had found in Barbaro's apartment.

'What's worse,' Marco affirmed, as he took off his cloak and walked over to the desk, 'is that we now have two corpses. You'll have heard about Piero Corner, who was strangled with a length of the same kind of rope found around Barbaro's neck.'

'Yes, of course I've heard about Corner, but not about the rope.'

'The other day, while we were talking here in your office, I sent my gondolier, Nani, to the ropeworks. It seems it might be a Portuguese rope, or a Turkish one.'

'Who identified it?' Alvise asked, a note of curiosity in his voice.

'A man they call the Levantino, who's worked in the East . . .'

'Of course. That's Menico. A fine man. Now that his daughter's departed, he sometimes sleeps here in the Arsenale so as not to go home to an empty house, poor man. But he's extremely reliable. Tell me,' Alvise came back to the point, 'if this really is espionage, was Corner involved in it too? Although, presumably, he didn't need the money.'

'Who knows?' sighed Marco. 'But let's see what you've found out. What are they?' he asked, pointing at the drawings.

'They're nothing of importance, mostly,' explained Alvise, putting on his glasses. 'The anchor, the sails and the cannon barrels are models well known throughout the Mediterranean, and the drawing of a galley dates from a century ago. If your Barbaro thought he could sell this stuff to a foreign state, then he would have been disappointed. Anyone with a smattering of nautical know-how would have realised that it was a fraud. I believe he obtained the papers from the Naval School, where drawings like these are used in lessons.'

'Well, well. So he thought he could outwit a foreign spy. And what about the furnaces?'

'The same thing. These are old casting furnaces which are going to be dismantled because they're out of date. However, what we have here' – he pointed to the sketch of the dredger, and his tone became much more serious – 'is quite a different matter. I made discreet enquiries and, as I thought, this is a copy of a secret project which our architects are developing, based on an ancient design by Leonardo. As you'll have noted, the vessel has twin hulls, which gives it greater stability, and a cogwheel mechanism winds the mooring line around an axle, allowing the machine to be pulled forward. What's more, the shovels at the ends of the rotating arms tip the detritus into this small barge, and that means they don't need to be cleaned all the time.'

Marco looked thoughtful. 'It's a brilliant design,' he remarked, 'one that would be very useful to many foreign states. They all need to keep their harbours clean, especially where there are rivers that tend to make the ports silt up. But how did it get into Barbaro's hands?'

'Undoubtedly through one of the offices here in the Arsenale.'

'Do you mean that Barbaro sneaked in here?'

Cappello laughed. 'Not necessarily. So many people come and go. Suppliers and their assistants, sailors staying in the dormitories, even the wives of some of the workers living here on Rio Tana. Someone must have found these drawings, put a few in their pocket and hastily copied the others. Then they thought they could make a bit of cash by selling them to some fine fool, or in this instance to Barbaro. And perhaps they didn't even realise that, among the other rubbish, there was something of value.'

'Or maybe it was Barbaro himself who came in unobserved and snatched what he could lay his hands on . . .'

Alvise nodded. 'It's quite possible. As I told you, our workers are on guard, but there are so many ways in and out, and at night, darkness makes it easier still.'

'So we'll never know how Barbaro managed to get hold of these documents, and perhaps we'll never even know if he realised how important the dredger project is . . . But I do hope to discover whether he got in touch with any foreign spies, and whether any of them had been shown these papers recently. Perhaps the assassin was spying for the Ottomans or for the Portuguese, and then, for some reason, he feared he'd been betrayed. Something of the kind might have happened if they'd disagreed on the price, for instance.'

'Your guess is as good as anyone's.' Cappello walked over to the window and looked out at the old dock flanked by its covered dry docks and, further to the east, the drawbridge that opened into the galley dock. There was not much movement and the docks were almost empty. 'I would rule out the Portuguese,' he went on. 'Now that the bulk of maritime trade is focused on the western routes and on the Atlantic, stretching up to the North Sea, Holland, Germany, England and Portugal have all produced innovations in ship design. It's only the Turks who are interested in ours.'

'I keep coming up against the Turks in this affair,' Marco commented.

'I know what you're thinking: it's not easy to question them. The Ottomans have no diplomatic representative in Venice, although

Matteo Vitali is the merchant who's officially appointed to look after their interests.'

Marco was only half listening, absorbed by his own thoughts. He joined Alvise at the window to look at the Arsenale basins. 'Perhaps there is a way of finding out who Barbaro was in touch with,' he murmured, not expecting an answer. 'If he was a customer at his friend Biagio's tavern, there are plenty of Turks who go there, and he might have made contact with one of them. If so, someone could have seen him . . . That's something else to ask Biagio when I pay him a visit.' There was a moment's silence. Then Marco continued, 'That list of ships' names, what's it got to do with all this?'

The pair came back to the desk and Alvise opened the document in question. 'Another example of swindling,' he began. 'As you understood, it's just a list of the sailing dates of commercial and passenger ships. But where the arrival date is noted, then it means that the voyage has been completed. I matched up the list with our records and it seems that the dates all refer to last year. It's perfectly useless, and anyone who tried to sell it would make themselves a laughing stock.'

'That means Barbaro was not only a cheat but he wasn't very clever either. From what you say, it seems he misjudged the importance of the material. What he was best at was tapping his friend Corner for money. But what's Corner got to do with spying? Why has he been killed too? It's common knowledge that the family is extremely wealthy, and the two brothers seem to have squandered money left, right and centre.'

The Patrono was silent for a moment as an idea started to form in his mind. 'Now that you mention it,' he said, 'you know that the younger brother, Dario, nearly ruined the family last year? It's a story that we patricians here at the Arsenale know well, but we kept it quiet out of respect for the family.'

Marco looked surprised and pulled up a chair to sit by the desk as he prepared to listen. Cappello poured out two glasses of Cyprian wine and did the same.

'This Dario,' he continued, sipping the wine while his eyes twinkled, 'thought he could get the same sort of return on his capital as patricians did in the past when they engaged in seaborne trade.'

'Well, he must have known something about it, so where exactly did he go wrong?'

'A little over a year ago he acquired a major shareholding in a ship leaving for Constantinople with a cargo of valuable goods – gold damasks and silks, you know the sort of thing. They go crazy for our Venetian fabrics. Only he didn't have enough ducats for the whole venture and so he decided to cut corners by relying on good weather rather than drawing up the usual insurance policies. Fortune was against him. In the middle of the Adriatic the ship ran into a storm and, since it was laden to the gunnels, it sank. The crew managed to survive thanks to the pilot boats, but the cargo ended at the bottom of the sea, and Dario Corner lost his entire investment, down to the last soldo. Since it came from his own share of the family wealth, he was practically ruined.'

'I can see why the family wanted it hushed up. They must have done everything to protect the family name and their standing,' Marco acknowledged. 'Lucky for him that he's now inherited . . . Indeed, that's interesting; he stood to inherit.'

'What do you mean?'

Marco hesitated for a moment, then he pulled himself together and drained his glass. 'No, nothing. I saw him this morning when I visited the palace to pay my respects. He seemed shattered by the news.'

As Pisani crossed Saint Mark's Basin, heading for home, the winter sun was just setting. The sky behind the basilica was streaked with pink, as it often was on clear days, and the last golden rays bathed the domes and the bell tower.

What a marvellous city, he thought. He had lowered the gondola cover so that he could admire the scene. As he looked, he was aware that the twilight also represented the city's decline, yet it remained heartachingly beautiful. Its ancient palaces with their lace-like marble carvings, the peeling plaster, the sinking foundations and flooded atriums . . . how much longer could they survive? Inside the apartments, Marco knew that many of the window hangings were literally disintegrating, the wall coverings fading, and a steady stream of masterpieces were being shipped north to England. The situation was even worse in the churches. Here, the artistic treasures were neglected, the gilded plasterwork flaking and the silverware tarnished. At night, the streets were full of scurrying sewer rats. Nothing seemed to stop them flourishing.

It seemed a thousand years ago since Venice had been a great power, but in fact only a century had passed. Now that Austria ruled the Adriatic and the new trade routes were dominated by England, Holland and the Baltic countries, the Venetian ships were forced to undertake long, dangerous voyages. Commerce was at an all-time low and industry was stagnating. Venice still retained the lead in glass and silk, but for how long?

The city still had its rich families, like the Pisanis, but they all owned land and farms on the mainland. Venice seemed to have lost its drive. How many of the young patricians were good-for-nothings like the Corner brothers? How many impoverished nobles only scraped a living, like Barbaro?

One of the many things that concerned Marco about the decline of Venice was the fashion for private gambling dens, those small casinos, often in rented apartments, where the young – and not so young – met to play cards, dance and flirt. There must be around a hundred and twenty in the city now! By using rented premises for these receptions many nobles deluded themselves that their poverty would be disguised. They dressed in lace and silks, spending the last of their wealth and hoping to fob off the creditors, turning a blind eye to disaster while they partied their lives away.

Those in power had run out of ideas for economic recovery and there were no signs of a rally in international trade. In a continuing spiral of gloomy thoughts, Pisani reflected that among the three hundred or so patricians in the Senate, barely twenty had a grasp of the issues debated at meetings. Having to sit through these sessions was often little more than torture.

All the vitality and entrepreneurship in the city now came from the tradespeople, the workers and the small retailers. They profited from the luxurious tastes of the patricians and, increasingly, from the demands of foreigners who flocked all year round to the city's festivities. What was more, there were thriving pockets of the economy in the Republic's provincial cities on the mainland, driven by shopkeepers, professionals of various kinds and the factors who managed the large agricultural estates. On this slightly more upbeat note, Marco smiled to himself as he thought of the evening ahead and of Chiara, who was waiting for him.

A private room had been reserved at the Leon Bianco for Avogadore Pisani. Its walls were covered with ivory-coloured silk and the chandelier could be seen reflected in each of the large mirrors. As she sat down, Chiara took off her cloak and smiled at him. It was rather a cheeky smile that started with her eyes. Now that he was actually with her, Marco felt embarrassed. Yet he could not help but smile back, even though it was one of his characteristic half-smiles. Chiara unfurled the magnificent blue fan that she had received that afternoon.

'Er . . . I hope it met with your approval . . .'

'I've never owned such a beautiful one.'

The waiter arrived just then to take their orders and to fill the goblets with sparkling white wine. They raised their glasses and smiled again.

Chiara was wearing a necklace of aquamarine stones that shone like her eyes, and her hair was wound into a coronet around her head that shimmered like gold. Marco's heart was beating fast and he was afraid to speak for fear of saying the wrong thing. The young woman waited for him to speak with bated breath.

'Chiara,' Marco whispered at last, 'I don't know how to start because I'm not accustomed to paying court to young women. I'm not a regular at the salons, and I don't pay my respects to society ladies; I don't even go to the theatre or to receptions much. A real old curmudgeon, that's what I am, and old-fashioned with it. All I want to say is that I hope my company doesn't bore you.'

'I don't expect the most esteemed of Venice's three avogadori to be a ladies' man who spends his time flirting.' Chiara smiled. 'What's more, I'm a working woman, a commoner, and I don't suppose those gallants would seek out my company.'

'I'm not sure about that,' commented Marco, gazing at her. She looked enchanting.

The waiter interrupted them as he returned with a dish of steaming risotto. For the moment, the spell was broken.

'How are the inquiries going?' asked Chiara as soon as the man had gone.

Marco gave her a broad overview of the investigation. He felt that he could trust her to be discreet. He had told Chiara about Corner's death the previous day, and now he described his visit to Corner's widow and mentioned the possibility of espionage, the dissolute lifestyle of the four men and Lucietta's disappearance.

'How have you discovered so much in so short a time?' she asked, genuinely curious.

'Certainly not by using the police guards. I've not yet even updated their head, Messer Grando, or the Council of Ten and the inquisitors, for that matter. But now that Corner's dead, because he belonged to such an illustrious family, I'm sure they expect an official statement. I have my own methods, you know. I visit the witnesses personally, mostly unannounced, and when it seems necessary to question the servants – who wouldn't talk freely to me, of course – I send my gondolier.'

'The handsome lad who brought us here and who didn't take his eyes off me for the entire trip?'

'Yes, that's Nani. He's as inquisitive as a magpie and isn't used to seeing me with beautiful ladies.'

The waiter returned with a splendid roast duck and proceeded to serve them as they sat in silence.

'But you aren't bound by monastic oath, are you?' resumed Chiara when they were alone once more.

'Almost.' Marco nodded. He was surprised to hear himself talking to her and describing his solitary life, his devotion to his work and his love of sobriety. He also spoke about his ideals, and the illusory hope that dedication to justice might make even the slightest contribution to universal order.

'I, too, am alone,' she said in a low voice, 'and I also love my work. I remember nothing about my mother because, like I told you, she died while I was a small child. My father was wonderful, but he's been gone for five years now.'

With a light caress, Marco placed his hand over the young woman's, and Chiara surprised him by lifting it up and turning it over. She studied the lines on his palm.

'You are a person of great sensitivity,' she said in a serious tone. 'Do you see the Mount of Venus?' She pointed to the rise at the foot of his thumb. 'You're capable of great love. And you're strong and courageous,' she continued as she looked at the swelling below the little finger. 'But . . . what's this? What happened?' She stopped suddenly and looked at him uncertainly.

Marco's sad smile and his firm gaze prompted her on.

'You were very much in love with a woman, and she's no longer here.'

Marco flinched and the pain was etched on his face. 'Continue . . .'

'She went to heaven many years ago.' She smoothed out his hand before looking at it again with even greater concentration. Her voice faded to a whisper. 'Now she's in the light . . . together with a child. They both protect you . . .' Chiara suddenly understood what she was saying and burst into tears. 'Pardon me, Marco, I had no idea.'

'She was Virginia, my wife,' he explained, his eyes glistening. 'She left me twelve years ago, together with the son who had just been born. I've never mentioned them to you . . . How did you know? Is it written on my hand? I've always believed that fortune tellers are charlatans.'

'Most of them are,' admitted Chiara as she pulled herself together. 'To read a palm, you don't just have to know the lines, you also need to have a special connection with the person.'

'How did you learn?' asked Marco, his interest piqued.

'I'll tell you. But first, did you bring the rope, as I asked?' Chiara sounded anxious, as if she had just been struck by another thought.

'The rope that was used to strangle Barbaro? It's a very odd request to come from a woman. Yes, it's in the gondola.'

'Good. Then let's go back to my house.'

CHAPTER 12

Gliding forward with each of Nani's rhythmic and powerful strokes, the gondola moved silently through the back canals of Cannaregio towards Chiara's house. As the blade cut through the water it left trails of bubbles that shone brilliantly in the moonlight.

Marco watched the procession of palaces, houses and small squares, some of them just tiny spaces between the buildings, while Chiara and Nani talked in a relaxed fashion. Marco had been caught off guard by her invitation. *A strange woman*, he thought. *Why is she taking me back to her house? I treated her with immense respect, and now she's behaving like a . . . No, it can't be possible. I couldn't have been so mistaken? Chiara is what she seems. She'll have a good reason.*

They walked into the empty house from a small door that opened from the calle and climbed up to the first-floor apartment. Chiara removed her cloak and led Marco through the salon and the dining room and into a gallery where, without a moment's hesitation, she opened the door of her bedroom, which was lit by two chandeliers. Confused, Marco looked around: he was not ready to enter this intimate space, not yet.

His embarrassment continued as Chiara took a key from her purse and opened a small door in the room, hidden by the wall coverings. She headed into the darkness and lit two oil lamps. 'Come in,' she called, without a thought for his unease. 'You need to know something about me.'

With growing surprise and a touch of apprehension, Marco stepped inside. The space was deceptively large and almost empty. The windows had been bricked over and, along the walls, a few shelves held large vases like those you would find in a pharmacy. On a table were pestles, mortars, retorts and stills, as well as a few old books.

Chiara closed the door behind them. 'Don't worry, I'm not a witch. But since it takes very little for people to start gossiping, I keep what I do inside here absolutely private.'

'And what do you do?' Marco said in a low voice, not understanding.

'Drugs. I prepare drugs. My grandmother knew all the field herbs and their medicinal properties. It's a gift that is passed from generation to generation in my family. She taught me to recognise the plants, to pick them at the right moment and to use their healing properties to treat people. When the doctors would only recommend purges and bloodletting, she would offer remedies that healed wounds, helped the pain of toothache and banished fever, and even worms. In those days, mothers would frequently go to the priest and ask them to pray for nine days to heal their sick children, but illness belongs to this world, not the next, and it is the earth itself that gives us the remedies to combat it.'

Here was a new facet to this odd young woman. Marco was amazed and curious to hear more. He looked at the vases lined up on the shelves and neatly labelled. 'What do you use those for?' he asked.

'In that vase,' Chiara answered, pointing to one, 'there are fenugreek seeds. They're used as a tonic after illness, and they also induce lactation in women who have just given birth. In that other vase I keep dried savory, which is an excellent remedy for diarrhoea and colic. With the vinegar in that bottle I clean wounds to make them close rapidly, but it's even more effective to use the oil I make from cloves. It's in that little flask up there. I keep it there because it's so expensive. So, no witchcraft, as you can see.'

Marco was keen to know more so he pointed to another shelf, further away. 'And what's in those containers?'

'That's where I keep the rye I use for decoctions to treat colds, and that other bottle contains the oil I extract from pomegranate seeds. It's an excellent vermifuge. But I've not brought you here just to show you my medicinal drugs,' Chiara ended. 'Come back to the salon, because I want to perform an experiment.'

The room was dimly lit and the glimmer of the fire burning in the fireplace threw dancing shadows on to the walls. Chiara lit the candles in a pair of candleholders on the table, and their glow illuminated the painted spinet on which she had played for Marco during his first visit. He sat on the gilded divan upholstered in white brocade, the fine quality of the fabric drawing his attention.

'Do you like it?' she asked as she took two engraved glasses and a bottle of rosolio out of the glass-fronted cabinet. 'It's made here in my manufactory. We made an equal length for the Savoy hunting palace at Stupinigi.' She handed a small glass of liqueur to Marco and then sat down in an armchair facing him. 'Do you have the rope used in the crime?'

Marco pulled it out of the pocket in his jacket and placed it on the table between them. 'What are you going to do?' he felt compelled to ask.

Chiara smiled. 'As I said, it's an experiment. And I'm not certain it'll work. If you don't mind, we'll talk about it afterwards. For now, just watch without interrupting because I have to concentrate.'

She picked up the rope and went to sit in another chair by the fire. At that moment a log rolled, causing sparks to fly up the chimney. In the silence that followed, Marco could only hear the steady tick of the pendulum clock on the shelf.

Chiara seemed to go into a trance as she watched the snaking flames, the gleaming colours reflected on her face. She looked serious but relaxed, her eyes half shut. Marco was transfixed and couldn't take his eyes off her. Was something about to happen?

After a minute or two, she sighed and started to speak.

'I see something. There's a body . . .' Her voice was flat, monotonous. 'A woman's body.' She ran a hand through her hair. 'She's wrapped in a cloak, a red cloak, made from that special cloth . . . scarlet, Venetian scarlet.' She fell silent for a few moments. 'I can see blonde hair against that red, perhaps also blood, and the blood is as red as Venetian scarlet . . .'

The flames in the fireplace sprang higher, almost marking the tempo of the woman's voice. Looking at her, Marco felt a sense of peace, as if time itself stood still.

'A man has come into view now,' continued Chiara. 'He's young, but I can't see his face. Wait!' she exclaimed, stretching a hand out as if to stay the vision. Her other hand squeezed the rope more tightly. 'I can see his clothes: he's wearing a sash around his waist, like a gondolier. Now . . . but he's gone. How strange . . . a young gondolier, a scarlet cloak, blonde curls . . .' Chiara pulled herself together. 'It's over.' She sat quietly for a moment in thought, then stood up to get her glass from the table. The rope slid to the floor.

'I don't know whether I've helped you,' she commented, taking her place again opposite Marco. She sipped the liqueur. 'What I saw . . .' She shook her head and her pale curls rippled, stealing the light from the candles. 'You told me about the deaths of Marino Barbaro and Piero Corner, both of them strangled with a rope, about their profligate lives; you also mentioned the possibility of espionage and the story of that maid, Lucietta, who's vanished. None of it ties in with my vision . . . Only the girl . . . perhaps,' she added in a low voice. 'Although if she's the blonde in the cloak, then—'

'Explain what you mean,' interrupted Marco, disconcerted.

'The cloak was stained with blood . . . but I might be wrong.'

Marco sighed. 'There's no shortage of surprises tonight.' He smiled. 'At the restaurant you read my palm and guessed I was a widower—'

'I didn't guess,' interrupted Chiara. 'It's written there, in plain sight.'

'You yourself said that what counts is the sense of harmony between the seer and the subject. So this is a supernatural event.'

'Not supernatural,' replied Chiara. 'The only facets of the world that we know are those we can perceive with our senses, but there are invisible energies all around us, criss-crossing like cobwebs. Just take the most commonplace, for example: thought. It can't be seen, but of course it exists. Surely you don't believe it would be impossible for someone to read another person's thoughts? Science has never found tangible proof of this communication, yet it exists. I'm sure you, too, have experienced times when you knew what someone was going to say even before they'd opened their mouth.'

'It's true,' reflected Marco.

'But,' she continued, 'for that to happen when you want it to, you need to have a special awareness.'

The evening had taken a strange direction. Who was this extraordinary woman who reasoned like a philosopher and moved in a parallel world filled with invisible forces?

'You frighten me . . .' Marco hadn't meant to say that aloud. 'And what about the visions?'

'Do you want to know what I feel? It feels as if I'm immersed in the flowing current of a river, a timeless river, and it's a pleasant sensation . . . like being one droplet among billions of other drops of water . . . Then I start to see scenes. They appear like flashes, and at the time I have no idea what they mean. Sometimes they're crystal clear, but most of the time they're blurred, like a mosaic that hasn't yet taken shape. On other occasions I hear voices, or just fragments, a few words. I never lose consciousness, but it's like being half asleep, that moment between being awake and being asleep. Afterwards, I can describe what I've seen; I always remember it.'

'Why did you say that this was an experiment, then?' he asked. 'When you knew very well what would happen? You can reveal people's secrets by looking at their palms and you can see things by looking into the fire.'

Chiara smiled with a tinge of sadness. 'I've frightened you,' she said. 'Now you won't want to see me again . . . It's true, I can often tell someone's character, even their destiny, from the palm of their hand, but as I said, it's only because I have a greater awareness than most. I prepare medicaments to treat people's illnesses using country herbs, and that is based on science. In fact, the ancient Egyptians used many of these drugs. My mother did, and so did my grandmother. As for the rest, these are nature's gifts that pass down from generation to genera-tion in my family. My mother and my grandmother had visions, as do I . . . I don't know why. I mentioned earlier that we are surrounded by energies of different kinds, and sometimes we can establish contact with these energies . . . but perhaps I'm wrong. It's true that, every now and then, I feel as if time has stopped. It happens suddenly, but I don't know why.'

Chiara looked so delightful as she tried to find the right words to express what she felt. She held her head between her hands, as if to focus more clearly.

'But can it happen when you're not expecting it to?' asked Marco.

'I've come to realise that it often happens when I am looking at something that's in motion, whether it's clouds sweeping across the sky, or waves, or the flames in the fireplace, like this evening. I don't fall asleep, but for a minute or two it's as if I am isolated from everything around me, and I see things, things that will happen in the future, or that have already happened. They're like flashes of insight, but without being connected in any way. Or sometimes I realise that what I'm seeing has happened or is about to happen in real life. I never talk to anyone about this. I know that they call people like me clairvoyants, but it takes very little to be suspected of witchcraft, even if there hasn't been a witch hunt for years. In my family, they call it the Gift. I was taught to use it only for the good of others, and never for money.'

'Is there a rational explanation for it?' insisted Marco, who had never come across a similar phenomenon before. Above all, he wanted to understand all that he could about this strange, fascinating woman and her mysteries.

Chiara stood up and poured herself a glass of water. She drank thirstily. 'I've tried to explain it to myself,' she continued. 'I believe that it's not just thought that's invisible. All matter is imbued with energy. We're filled with life-giving energy and I believe we're immersed in an endless flow of energies that intersect and interact with each other. Even the objects around us are immersed in this flow, so it's not that strange to think that a place or an object that witnessed or was used in a dramatic event, like a crime, receives a charge of energy that it retains, therefore preserving the memory, or even absorbing the thoughts of anyone involved in that drama.'

Marco drew closer and took Chiara's hands into his own. They were icy cold, and she looked pale and breathless.

She gathered her courage. 'But you asked why I spoke about an experiment,' she continued. 'Well, in the past my visions have usually been spontaneous, and I've only managed once or twice to go into a trance on purpose. Also, this was the first time that I've ever attempted to use my gift while actually holding a murder weapon . . . But I don't think I told you anything that actually helped with your investigations.'

'Who knows . . .?' reflected Marco. 'So you did this to help me, is that right?'

'I wanted to try.' Chiara finished the rosolio in her glass, and the alcohol brought a touch of colour to her cheeks. 'Searching for the truth is one of the permitted uses for the Gift.'

A female corpse, blonde hair, a gondolier. Nothing that might be linked to the deaths of Barbaro and Corner, or even to Ottoman spies, thought Marco. Yet Chiara's vision was certainly intriguing, and perhaps it had opened new avenues for the inquiry. Moreover, this fascinating woman attracted him more than ever.

'Might it have been Lucietta, the maidservant from the Corner household, whose body you saw?'

'I don't know, Marco. The visions never relate to a specific time.'

'Well then, please will you come with me to Dolo the day after tomorrow? That was where she lived, and I need to know whether she went home. I could send someone, but I think it would be wonderful to go together. We'll take the Burchiello up the Brenta, then get off at Dolo. Also, if we actually find Lucietta, she'll be much more willing to talk to another woman.'

'I'd love to come.' Chiara smiled. 'But Marta, my housekeeper, will come with me. She keeps an eye on me night and day.'

At that very moment, footsteps could be heard hurrying along the corridor and the door flew open without so much as a knock. As if conjured up by Chiara's words, a tiny woman stood there, trim and neatly coiffed, although it would have been hard to say how old she was. She curtseyed politely.

'Your Excellency. What an honour to have you in this house! I must thank you for having freed our Maso.'

Chiara started to laugh. 'Here is my dearest Marta!' she exclaimed. 'You didn't see her the other day because she'd gone to visit her nephews and nieces.' Then, turning to the housekeeper, she said, 'You might think of knocking next time, Marta.'

'Why should I?' said the elderly woman in an offended tone. 'Ladies never have anything to hide. I've prepared a good jug of chocolate, which is steaming and freshly whipped. I'll go and get it now. But Chiara, tell me the truth. Have you had one of your visions? You're looking pale and dishevelled, as you always do when you've been visited by spirits.'

Chiara sighed. 'Marta would like me to stop having visions, although she knows full well that it's nothing to do with me. I've also told her again and again that spirits don't come into it. But she insists that, sooner or later, something terrible will happen to me—'

'Nonsense!' interrupted Marta. 'I only say that because spirits shouldn't be trifled with.'

On the way home, Nani sung Chiara's praises with each stroke. 'She's really a beautiful woman, paròn, and so friendly. Just right for you.'

'You mention this to anyone, Nani, and there'll be trouble.'

'Oh, paròn, you know me! I'll be as silent as the grave. But you didn't stay long. I thought I might have to spend the night in the gondola.'

'Impudent boy! She's not that sort of woman, so watch your tongue and talk about her respectfully. In fact, come to think of it, don't talk about her at all.'

Nani hid his smile. *So this is serious*, he thought. *And high time too. The paròn deserves a good woman!*

As Marco walked through the gate leading into the garden, still feeling exhilarated from his fascinating evening, he nearly tripped over Plato, who was stalking out, his tail held high. 'Where are you off to at this hour? Have you got an assignation?' The cat rubbed against Marco's leg, purring, and then trotted off into the dark.

Upstairs in his bedroom, Marco saw a note on his bedside table. Intrigued, he opened it.

Why haven't you been to see me for over a week? Have I done something to offend you?

Good heavens! He had completely forgotten, and now his conscience was pricking him. It was Annetta, the embroideress. Something would need to be done, but in the morning.

CHAPTER 13

'She's the most beautiful woman in Venice, I swear! I've never seen anyone like her. What's more, she's elegant, a real lady!'

'A lady, eh? Have you ever heard of a lady living near the church of the Gesuiti and managing a weaving manufactory?'

'It's not just birth that counts! Signorina Chiara Renier is more of a lady than most of the gentlewomen I've met!'

It was early morning and Nani was squabbling with Rosetta in the kitchen on the mezzanine floor of Marco's house. It was a well-lit and scrupulously clean room, and the sunshine beamed off the pewter plates hanging on the walls. A stew was already bubbling on the stove, giving off an inviting smell, while a basket of shellfish was suspended above the copper sink to catch the drips. The two servants, old Martino and Giuseppe, had gone out and Nani was enjoying an early-morning bite in the company of Rosetta and Gertrude, the cook. Plato was licking up a saucer of milk and looking a little the worse for wear after a night of adventure.

The conversation had turned to their master's exploits the previous evening. Nani was not one to keep quiet and his description of Chiara was not short on detail.

'She wore a fur-lined cloak and a velvet gown. Absolutely breath-taking. As for her hair, it's like a cascade of golden curls. Her eyes . . . well, all I can say is that it's like looking at the sky on a cloudless day!

She talked to me for quite a long time, you know.' Feeling pleased with this description, Nani craned his neck to look into the garden, checking that his master hadn't yet come down.

'I certainly wouldn't call her a lady! She's far too forward,' intervened Gertrude, frowning as she plucked a partridge. Short and plump, she looked much older than twenty-nine because of her flat nose and receding chin.

'Oh, Gertrude, we all know you've got a soft spot for the master,' teased Rosetta, 'but you're really not his type.'

Gertrude blushed a deep red. 'I never had the honour of meeting Signora Virginia, but she was a great lady – God preserve her in his mercy! Her portrait says it all.'

'But he can't spend the rest of his life looking at a painting. He's entitled to make a new family, and he shouldn't only think about work!' Nani burst out.

'I agree,' chimed Rosetta. 'The poor man has done nothing but work for the past twelve years. He's been faithful to her memory – may she rest in peace – and now it's time for him to start afresh. But this woman is an artisan; she may well be the owner of the workshop, but couldn't he choose a noblewoman?'

'Signorina Renier is better' – Nani's defence was heated and he struggled to find an apt comparison – 'better than those spoilt darlings who've never been outside a palace and are only capable of giving orders and gossiping.'

'Just because she paid you some attention doesn't mean she's a real lady. She probably only did it to impress the master,' Rosetta snorted.

'Exactly,' Gertrude intervened again. 'There isn't a woman in Venice who wouldn't throw herself at the master. She'll be no different.'

Nani was about to reply when he heard the click of the garden gate. He looked out of the window.

'Hallo, is your master at home?' Daniele Zen's booming voice was unmistakable.

'Make yourself at home, avvocato, and I'll call him straight away.' While Rosetta went to summon Marco, Nani went down and led the guest into the main room.

Pisani happened to be walking downstairs, freshly shaven and perfumed and ready to go to the ducal palace. Instead of his usual boots, he wore silk stockings and kid shoes.

'You have to save me, Marco,' beseeched Daniele with a twinkle in his eye that belied the gravity of his words.

'At your service. Nani, bring us a cup of coffee.' Unusually for him, Marco was wearing a brocade waistband under his long jacket, which he had thrown back over his shoulder. He gestured towards a small table in the salon.

'The Santelli family have invited me to lunch,' Zen explained as he pulled over a chair.

'Ah, your fiancée, Maddalena . . .'

'She's not my fiancée yet. That's why I'm here. This time the excuse is that they want me to meet a cousin of hers who's the attaché at the embassy in Constantinople – they even say he's the right-hand man of the *bàilo*. But I think it's just a pretext to catch me and give an official gloss to a relationship that honestly doesn't exist. I can't think of a way out without offending them. But if you come too, then it won't look so compromising, and you can help steer the conversation on to general topics. Anyway, they'd be so happy to have an avogadore with them they'd forget about their schemes. You're my only hope!'

'Sounds like you're not in love with the lady . . . I'll do what I can. But first I've got a meeting with the three inquisitors' – he swept his hand in front of himself derisively – 'which is why I'm dressed up like this.'

Pisani had decided to ask the three powerful magistrates for a meeting because they, not the criminal court, would be the ones who would hear the case against the murderer – if one was ever found – given that Piero Corner had been a patrician. It was a good moment to provide them with a fuller picture of the investigations, not to mention a prudent move. Above all, there was still the lurking suspicion that the Ottomans might be involved and, if it did prove to be espionage, then the sooner he involved the inquisitors the better.

'And before meeting them, I've decided to ask our prince for some advice about how much I should tell them,' Pisani continued. 'In short, I have to go now but I'll be free for lunch.'

'I knew I could count on you.' Daniele stood up, visibly relieved. 'I'll meet you later at the palace.'

'Fine, but you can do something for me too. Later this afternoon, we're going to pay another visit to the Corners. I need to question Piero's mother and it would be better to have a lawyer present,' Marco joked.

'Yours or hers?'

'Definitely mine. Everyone tells me that she's rather tricky.'

The Sala degli Scarlatti and the Sala dello Scudo – the latter dominated by the reigning doge's family coat of arms – were crowded with a throng of nobles, complete with wigs and silk stockings, as well as with magistrates in their distinctive gowns. But as soon as the guard was informed that Avogadore Pisani wished to be received, Marco was waved through to the Sala Grimani. He entered swiftly, unaware of the murmur of disapproval behind him, and approached the slim, delicate man who was seated on a high-backed chair.

'A friendly face at last!' exclaimed the doge, rising and giving the younger man a warm embrace. 'Your visits are far too rare, even though you work practically next door. You've abandoned this old man to the company of a bunch of untrustworthy and grasping courtiers and gossips!'

Marco sketched a bow. 'I don't want to take up too much of your time, Most Serene Prince. But when I am dealing with grave matters, I know I can always rely on your experience.'

'There was I thinking that only courtiers fawned!' joked Francesco Loredan, taking Marco by the arm and guiding him towards the old-fashioned armchairs by the fireplace. 'Don't you remember when you used to call me Uncle Francesco?'

The Loredan family had always been close friends of the Pisanis, and before he became doge, Francesco had spent many years as a successful merchant, never moving far from Venice and always turning down diplomatic positions. He had been a frequent guest at Palazzo Pisani, where he and Senator Teodoro would enjoy long conversations.

He had watched Teodoro's sons grow up and had spent many a day riding in their company during summers on the Brenta. What was more, he had never missed one of Signora Elena's receptions.

'How's your mother?' he asked.

'She's as lively and full of energy as ever, especially now that she has the grandchildren to look after. You'll remember, Prince, that when my brother and I were young, she refused to hand us over to the maidservants but instead brought us up herself.'

The doge smiled and his face crinkled into a web of fine lines. 'Your mother is a great woman, Marco, and one of the most beautiful in the city, which is saying something, given that our women are the best-looking in Europe. If only I'd met a woman like her! But I chose bachelorhood, and now I feel I'm a prisoner in these four rooms . . .' He gestured around the room, with its magnificent blue and gold ceiling, before adding, 'I'm desperately lonely.' Indeed, his expression had grown quite melancholy.

Marco understood him perfectly. As the official figurehead of the Serenissima, the doge attended all the meetings of the highest state councils, but he had no power except for his own vote. He was simply the servant of the Republic. Shut in the palace, which he only rarely left, he was surrounded by the members of all the official bodies and the civil servants; the high points of his life were the ceremonies and banquets, where he appeared, carried on a chair, with all the trappings of office – the *corno*, his cloak of gold cloth and his sword – surrounded by standard bearers and heralded by eight silver cornets. For the Marriage of the Sea ceremony, he would stand in the prow of the *bucintoro*, the golden vessel that was the envy of the world, as it was rowed out to the mouth of the lagoon, followed by a fleet of gondolas and boats of every kind in a triumphal procession.

But the cost of all these solemnities came from his own pocket. He was no longer particularly rich, given the massive outlay the family had invested in his public office, nor even held in special regard, because the criticisms and grumblings that had undermined his predecessor, Pietro Grimani, the poet doge, had also affected him.

'Stay for a while, Marco,' continued Loredan. 'I'll call for a cup of chocolate for you.' He shook a bell and gave orders to the steward who had appeared.

'But the antechamber is full of people waiting . . .' prompted Marco.

'Let them wait,' replied the doge. 'Usually I have to fit in with their wishes, so for once . . .' He trailed off as the steward reappeared.

As they sipped the aromatic drink, the old doge and the young avogadore drew closer to the window overlooking the courtyard, which bustled with functionaries, secretaries, magistrates and military men.

'What's bothering you, Marco?' Loredan broke the silence. 'And what brings you to me?'

'You'll have heard,' Pisani started, 'of the death of the two patricians, Barbaro and Piero Corner . . .'

Loredan nodded. 'Yes, they were strangled. I believe you are in charge of the case and that, as usual, you've taken it on yourself to make the inquiries rather than handing them over to the police. I know, I know . . .' He waved away Pisani's explanations and continued, 'And don't think that I don't believe you're right. The police don't have your training and expertise: it's an old problem that has plagued our administration. So tell me all about it.'

Marco gave the doge a full account of how matters stood, dwelling on the mysterious presence of an unknown Turk in many of the statements given by witnesses, and on the drawings found in Barbaro's apartment, especially those of the top-secret plans for the dredger. 'Later today,' he ended, 'I'm meeting the three inquisitors, who need to be informed because Corner was not just anyone. But what I'm not sure about is whether it would be better to suggest that espionage might have been involved, even if I have no firm evidence as yet . . . Indeed, as I said, I'm also pursuing a number of completely different trails.'

The doge shook his head. 'You're right, Marco. The inquisitors see spies everywhere they look. It's pointless to alarm them, and in addition, the drawings do not appear to have left Barbaro's apartment, therefore they weren't even in foreign hands.'

'I wouldn't like to start a diplomatic scuffle with the Sublime Porte . . .'

'Exactly,' ended Loredan. 'Don't say a word about anything to do with the Arsenale and the Ottomans. Just continue your own investigations and let's see what happens. In the meantime, I'll try to gauge whether any of the officials are concerned about the presence of a foreign spy in the city.'

Dressed in full official robes and wigs, the three inquisitors were waiting for Pisani in the hall of the Supreme Court, seated in high-backed wooden chairs. Messer Grando, the head of police, was also with them, looking sombre in his long black cloak.

As on every other occasion, Marco found the dark room with its gilded leather wall-hangings oppressive. And as before, he drew inspiration from a brief admiring glance at Tintoretto's large pictorial cycle on the ceiling.

The meeting was friendly because, although Avogadore Pisani was renowned for his eccentricities, he was nonetheless well liked by the most powerful magistrates of the Republic because he never questioned their authority and, it had to be said, he brought a good number of criminals to justice.

Pisani gave a concise account of the facts: finding Barbaro's corpse the previous Thursday, namely on the morning of 7 December, then Corner's death on the night between Sunday and Monday; the grounds he had for thinking that the same murderer had committed both crimes; and the kind of rope used on both occasions. He described the poor nobleman's precarious lifestyle and hinted at the patrician's dissolute youth, but he omitted the story of the maid's seduction and he avoided any mention of the strange links between the victims and the gondolier Biagio, let alone Paolo Labia, particularly because he was not yet clear about the latter's role. Most importantly, he never referred to the documents that had been found in Barbaro's possession.

'Pisani, do you still insist on carrying out your own investigations?' asked Antonio Condulmer, smiling.

'Yes, I'm convinced that in many crimes the setting plays a key role. What's more' – here Pisani turned to Messer Grando – 'in this case, I need to move in an aristocratic world, and I need to question people who would never talk to the police.'

'Quite so,' agreed the head of police. 'But if you need help, you can rely on us.' When all was said and done, he wasn't at all displeased that Pisani had taken on such a thorny problem.

'When do you think the trial will start?' asked Pietro Fontana, who, as usual, had followed Pisani's outline somewhat distractedly up until now.

'I have to say that I've no idea,' admitted Marco. 'As I said earlier, I've not yet identified the guilty party. If these were cases of murder following robbery, I could focus my inquiries on the underworld, and even pass the matter to the police,' he explained, gesturing to Messer Grando. 'But on this occasion two patricians have been killed. They were friends and the methods used are identical, so I'm inclined to believe that there's a precise motive for their deaths. Once I've discovered the reason – perhaps revenge, or perhaps rivalry in love or business; who knows? – then I'll be able to identify the culprit.'

'It's not an easy task,' said Condulmer. 'We're all in your hands, Pisani. But we think that this is not yet the moment to bring the matter to the attention of the Council of Ten.'

CHAPTER 14

As he walked out of the ducal palace at around midday, Marco concluded that the few clues he had were still extremely sketchy. True, he had yet to question the other two members of the group – Biagio the gondolier and Paolo Labia – and some new pointers might emerge from their testimonials. Moreover, if he were to trust Chiara's vision, there was a dead girl involved in all of this, who might or might not be Lucietta Segati, the maid from the Corner household. But perhaps his visit to Dolo the following day would clear that mystery up.

Daniele Zen was waiting for him near the Procuratie. Under his cloak, Marco glimpsed a crimson brocade coat and an embroidered silk waistband. His face was framed by a wig.

'I thought I'd dressed up a bit today, but you make me look positively shabby,' said Marco, greeting him. 'It's lucky you're the one who's engaged, because I clearly don't come up to scratch,' he ended with a laugh.

'You can laugh all you like, but I think you're the one who's about to become engaged. How was the dinner?'

Marco left the question hanging in the air. The more intimate he grew with Chiara, the less willing he was to talk about her. Anyway, yesterday evening had left him confused. He was strongly attracted but he wasn't at all sure that she felt the same way about him. Moreover, he had been shaken by the discovery of her skills as a clairvoyant and, for the moment, did not want to mention these to anyone.

He pretended to watch a gaggle of people in the centre of the piazza who were gathered around a large chair on which a toothless old woman sat. A maid held out her palm and waited nervously for an answer. Groups of women and a few young men queued up behind her. 'Old Rina, the soothsayer, is back,' noted Marco, and his thoughts immediately flew again to Chiara. 'It's been a while since our fortune teller has been seen around here. What do you think . . . should I ask her who killed Corner and Barbaro?'

Daniele laughed. 'I'm not sure she'd be able to help. Come on, let's get this over with.'

The Santellis were rich grain merchants and lived in a handsome building on Campo Santa Maria Formosa. The ground floor was used as a warehouse and was stacked with grain, while the mezzanine was given over to offices.

Marco and Daniele were warmly welcomed by the family, who were gathered in the principal room. Giovanni Santelli oozed joviality from his round, pink face and generous girth, and his plump wife, Agostina, wore a glittering array of gold rings and gems. Maddalena was small and graceful, but it was clear that over time she would acquire her mother's rounded figure. Daniele blushed when he saw them and lowered his eyes to the floor.

'What a pleasure, Your Excellency,' cried Santelli, moving forward to greet the newcomers and bowing before Pisani. 'This is an unexpected honour.'

Marco accepted the introductions with good grace. He met the bàilo's famous assistant, a certain Giorgio Priuli, a slight figure with feminine looks and wise eyes. A couple called Zardo were also present – they were landowners on the mainland – and finally there was Berengo, a lawyer. All of them appeared to be long-standing family friends.

As the conversation started to flow again, he looked around. The Santelli family's prosperity was evident from the highly fashionable decorations and furnishings: lacquered divans, small tables in exotic woods surrounded by chairs with silk cushions, recent portraits of the owners.

When they were finally seated at the large table and had been served with a soup made with rice, vegetables and mutton, small talk of a wholly Venetian sort got underway. Giorgio Priuli started by lauding the beauty of Constantinople, the blue mosque, the sunsets over the Bosphorus, the wealth of its bazaars. 'As for the sultan's palace!' he exclaimed. 'It's a wonder to behold! The rooms are decorated with ornately carved stone, the floors are covered with mosaics, and the gardens . . . Ah, the gardens are filled with flowers and the cool spray of fountains.' It was obvious that he was accustomed to having an audience and liked the sound of his own voice. 'But the most extraordinary thing,' he continued, 'is the harem. The sultan has dozens of wives, each more beautiful than the last, and he never lets them be seen in public.'

'You know that here in Venice,' interrupted his cousin, 'some have more than one wife. And many wives have more than one husband!'

'Giovanni, how could you!' scolded his wife. 'What are you saying? Remember Maddalena . . .'

'You're right, dearest, excuse me. But I wasn't talking about our families. We take great care to protect our wives. I was referring to some of the aristocratic families—'

Daniele Zen interrupted him by coughing and glancing over at Marco, who was highly amused. Both of the hosts blushed hotly and went quiet. Signora Zardo came to their rescue: 'I've heard that Maddalena has made great progress with her singing. After lunch, would you sing for us, dear?'

'With pleasure,' stammered the girl. 'But I don't want to bore the avogadore.'

'I would be delighted,' declared Marco with genuine enthusiasm, which won him a scowl from Daniele.

The guests were now being served a superb dish of boiled meats and for a while there was silence. Then Avvocato Berengo addressed the company in general: 'Have you heard about the deaths of those two young men, Barbaro and Corner?'

'Oh, yes,' replied Maria Zardo, who had lit up at the mention of their names. 'Sooner or later something was bound to happen, so it was hardly unexpected . . .' she added mysteriously.

'I know, that's what I thought,' agreed Agostina Santelli. 'That Barbaro was a shady character. I didn't know him personally, of course, but my maid tells me that he left debts everywhere he went and was often drunk. His sort drags down the honour of our aristocracy,' she concluded, giving Pisani a knowing smile.

'Oh, I wasn't thinking of him,' continued Signora Zardo, eager to draw the attention back to herself. 'There's something very wrong in the Corner family of Ca' Grande, which is, after all, the principal branch of that illustrious family.'

Marco was suddenly alert. He had no intention of revealing that he was in charge of the investigations, but information of any kind might prove valuable. 'Yes, my gondolier has told me something similar,' he said, inventing a lie to cover himself. 'Yet they are such a rich family.'

'Undoubtedly, Your Excellency, but they quarrelled.'

Daniele immediately understood Marco's tactics and joined in. 'Who quarrelled?' he asked.

'Well, the two brothers, of course. It's not widely known, but I was told about a terrible argument that happened some time ago. This is what I heard.' Signora Zardo looked around her, pleased to have everyone's eyes upon her. 'I use the same dressmaker as Signora Francesca, their mother. She charges extortionate prices, but she's the best in Venice. I was due to visit the dressmaker, probably about a year ago, when poor Piero was still unmarried, and I found her in a terrible state.

She didn't want to tell me about it at first, but then she told me how she had visited Signora Corner a couple of hours earlier to show her some new fabrics, heard shouting outside the door, and the two brothers, Piero and Dario, burst into the salon. They were arguing furiously and practically coming to blows.' Maria Zardo sipped her wine, while her audience waited with bated breath.

'What were they arguing about?' prompted Agostina, eager to hear more.

'Dario completely lost his temper,' continued Signora Zardo. 'Apparently his brother had refused to lend him the money he needed to pay for the insurance on a cargo of silk to be transported to the East. Piero insisted that his mother should remind Dario that none of his ventures had ever succeeded and he'd already thrown his inheritance to the winds. "Look who's talking!" Dario railed. "What with your whores and your gambling! And we all know how that scoundrel Biagio managed to buy a tavern for his witch of a mother. But you refuse to give your brother even a penny!"'

'What did their mother say?'

Signora Zardo took another sip before she replied. 'My dressmaker said that she was struck dumb, as if paralysed, and as white as a marble statue.'

'And what did Piero say to defend himself?' asked Marco, who was also engrossed by the story.

'It seems that Piero shouted that he was head of the family now, so it was up to him how the family money was spent. He admitted that he had enjoyed life over the past years, but he had done nothing to ruin the family and, if he had given money to Biagio, it was in exchange for a favour. Dario grabbed his brother by his shirt and shook him violently enough to tear off the lace – very expensive lace, according to the dressmaker. "I'll get you for this! Sooner or later, you'll pay!" Anyway, they carried on fighting, and at one point, Dario even got his hands around his brother's throat.'

'Dario Corner's got a hot temper and he might look soft, but he's as strong as an ox,' observed Avvocato Berengo. 'Once I saw him pick a fight with some chap in a tavern because he was sitting at the table that Dario usually used. At one point, he picked up the solid wooden table – which must have weighed as much as a man – and turned it upside down as if it were made of paper.'

'And that's not all,' Signora Zardo resumed, dragging everyone's attention back to her. 'At one point, so my dressmaker told me, Biagio came into the salon. He was Piero's gondolier and perhaps he thought he should defend his master. Dario let his brother go and turned on him instead, shouting at him to get out and calling him an opportunist and saying that he and Barbaro were bloodsuckers. Apparently he said something like, "You've done nothing except drain my family's wealth. And my brother's given you a free rein. The day will come when I'll put an end to it!" Then he hit him with a powerful left-hander that knocked him to the floor.'

'And all this time, didn't his mother do anything?' asked Zen.

'It seems that, after the initial shock, she pulled herself together and tried to keep the brothers apart. It was at that moment that she realised the dressmaker was still in the room and she sent her out with a warning her to keep her mouth shut.'

'The irony of it all is that Dario was right to ask for the insurance money,' intervened Giovanni Santelli, who'd been quiet until then. 'I heard that the ship transporting the goods sank in a storm, and because Dario was uninsured, he lost everything.'

Exactly what my friend Cappello told me, thought Marco as he was served a magnificent custard tart for his dessert.

'So Dario Corner will now inherit everything . . . he's had a stroke of good fortune,' continued Santelli. 'Lucky for him, too, that Piero's child is a girl, so the patrimony stays in the family, otherwise he'd have been penniless. Poor Piero is dead so there'll be no more male heirs unless Dario provides them.'

'It's sad to think that Piero had completely reformed his ways after he married,' ended Berengo. 'Apparently he'd started to show a real interest in his estates, and was becoming quite an expert on agronomy and livestock, and knew the best markets for his produce. Who knows whether Dario will be able to start afresh and live up to the family name . . . ?'

The conversation turned to other matters, and once the lunch had concluded, the group listened politely while a nervous Maddalena sang a repertoire of songs. Unfortunately for all concerned, the progress with her singing that Signora Zardo had credited her with was sadly not in evidence.

CHAPTER 15

'I think I might be on completely the wrong track,' reflected Marco, almost to himself. 'I stay at home far too much and don't socialise. Everyone knows everything about everyone here in Venice. I'm the only one who doesn't, it seems. Even gossip is a valuable source of information.'

'It's also an art,' replied Daniele. 'To be good at it you have to be a skilled observer as well as having a good memory, and the sort of mental filing system that allows you to select the most appropriate tidbits to suit the occasion.'

The two friends burst out laughing. They were walking along Salizàda San Moisè towards Palazzo Corner, and they stopped for a moment to look at the window display of a shoemaker selling sweet little velvet slippers.

'I meant to ask,' continued Daniele, 'did Chiara like the fan?'

'I think so,' answered Marco, dodging the question again. He wasn't in the mood yet to share any of the evening's events. 'Come on, we need to face the lioness in her den.'

The avogadore had sent a message to Signora Corner earlier that morning to let her know that he would be paying her a visit, and the

major-domo led the guests through the usual series of austerely decorated rooms with sixteenth-century furnishings to Sala Cornaro, which
was more ostentatiously furnished with gilded furniture, in keeping
with the latest fashion. Heavy curtains still darkened the huge windows,
blocking out the light on this unusually sunny winter's day.

Dressed completely in black, with her spare frame held proudly
erect, Francesca Corner was waiting for them, seated at a table close
to the large white marble fireplace. A magnificent silver coffee service
glinted in the light of a candelabra.

The grand dame held out her hand to Pisani, who bent over to kiss
it. 'My sincere condolences, signora,' he murmured sympathetically.

'God's will be done,' sighed Francesca Corner, without managing to
hold back two large tears. 'But please, do sit down,' she insisted. 'Your
presence, Avogadore Pisani, is certainly due to your interest in the investigations. But before you continue, do let me offer you some coffee.'

Francesca poured the steaming liquid herself, while Marco apologised for visiting so soon after the unfortunate events. 'You're right,
signora, it is my duty to discover who might have had an interest in
your son's death, and you can help me.'

Francesca had clearly once been very beautiful: she still had the high
cheekbones, deep-set eyes and trim figure that would have made her
one of the most admired Venetian women of her time. She looked at
Marco, her expression defiant. 'What do you want to know? You can't
think that he deserved such a horrendous end? Have you seen what my
poor son looked like when he was carried home?'

This wasn't a good start. Marco thought it best to get straight to the
point. 'Who will inherit the family wealth?' he asked, even though the
entire city knew the answer.

'What are you insinuating? The house will continue under the guid-
ance of my younger son, Dario, who has already shown himself to be a
capable businessman.' Marco just managed to keep a straight face. 'The
Corner family are expecting you to avenge them, Avogadore Pisani.'

'Justice, signora, not revenge. Tell me: did your sons get on?'

Francesca stiffened visibly, her mouth contracting in what was almost a grimace. 'They were very fond of one another, and I don't understand the purpose of your question. We are a united family. Sometimes, there have been discussions, certainly, as happens in all families, but when all was said and done, they loved one another. Dario was overjoyed when Piero had a baby. Poor little girl, she's now fatherless.'

Marco didn't like provoking her at such a delicate moment, but he knew that the truth would sometimes only surface when people lowered their guard. 'I've been told that a violent fight took place last year between your sons over money,' he insisted.

'That chatterbox of a dressmaker! It's impossible for people to mind their own business. Yes, there was an argument, and then they made it up.' Signora Corner had turned purple with rage and a vein pulsed in her temple as she twisted the lace on her handkerchief into a tight knot.

'But your son Dario was ruined by that disaster with the silk trade,' continued Marco.

'It would take more than that to ruin the Corner family. It was a speculation that ended badly, nothing more. In our family, we don't break off relationships for so little.' Francesca stood up, offended, and gestured to a maidservant to clear the table.

'There is something else . . .' Marco's questioning was relentless. 'I believe your son Piero was indebted in some way to his gondolier, a certain Biagio. He purchased a tavern for him and this irritated Dario.'

'You can't believe that a Corner would be in any way indebted to a servant!' She was outraged by Marco's comments and lifted her head proudly as she spoke. 'My son was a generous man, and he was happy to give presents to those who served him well, as Biagio did. He wanted to give him a future.'

'There is also talk of a young maid, a certain Lucietta Segati.' Marco was irritated in turn by her evasive response and had no qualms in inflicting this additional blow. 'It's said that she attracted your son's attention. Some say that he seduced her about three years ago. Then the girl vanished.'

Francesca Corner sat down again and, leaning towards Pisani, she whispered, 'I am surprised, Your Excellency, that you waste your time listening to servants' gossip.' It was all Marco could do to remain silent. 'Don't you know what girls are like? When they see a young and handsome master, and especially a rich one, they're willing to do anything to secure their futures.' She stopped for a moment, her eyes filling with tears at the memory of her son. 'That Lucietta was nothing but trouble, a slut. She obviously tried to snare him, but she didn't succeed and so she packed up and left.'

'She has disappeared . . .'

'Disappeared? I think not. Girls pack up and go when they don't find what they're looking for. Today they're looking for adventure, just like men. And no one hears any more about them. For example, some time ago a young woman, a seamstress who was very pretty and well educated, used to come to the house and bring me ready-made linen and other items. She was one of the family, in a sense, and knew both my sons. I always offered her pastries and chocolate. Then, one fine day, I never saw her again . . . I heard that she walked out of her home. Who knows why? Perhaps she followed a man she loved, perhaps she was in search of adventure? She was a sailor's daughter, that might account for it. And what of Tiraboschi's wife – you know who I mean, the glassmaker?' Signora Corner broke into a bitter laugh. 'All Venice is talking about her. She just got tired of living on Murano, even though she lacked for nothing. She went off with a company of travelling players performing *commedia dell'arte*. Now she plays the part of Columbine! And have you heard about the laundress who worked for the Mocenigo family? One day she abandoned everything and set up house in a well-to-do neighbourhood at the expense of an elderly notary. Now she entertains both her elderly lover and any young men she can find! How can you have the nerve to talk to me about Lucietta?' Signora Corner shook her head. 'She'll have come to a bad end, like all the others.'

'It seems that we're back where we started,' commented Daniele later. The two friends were sitting in Caffè Florian in Saint Mark's Square, with two glasses of ratafia on the table. Under the portico, in the lamplight, the *listòn* was well underway and the two men idly watched the passers-by who emerged every evening to walk around the square, showing off their clothes and gossiping with friends. There were gentlemen wearing wigs and cloaks, a handful of religious figures, powdered ladies followed by gallants laden with packages, clerks in their dark gowns returning home from work, the usual blind or lame beggars – not all of them genuine. Every now and then a courtesan, recognisable because of her heavy cosmetics and flashy jewels, would saunter past and men would stop and stare quite openly, as they never would at a lady.

'Having listened to what his mother told us,' Marco reflected, 'I'm beginning to wonder whether the culprit might actually be Dario.'

'You could be right. The two crimes were committed at night and he could have left the palace without being seen. Moreover, he's hot-tempered and well built.'

'But . . . to kill his own brother in cold blood . . .'

'He could have paid someone else to do it.'

'True,' replied Marco. 'But then he'd risk being blackmailed for life. And if it was ever revealed, he would be executed. The Serenissima doesn't pardon murderers, even if they're patricians, and especially if they kill a relative for money.'

'Anyway, the Corner family are rich enough to cover up his business disasters. To that extent, Signora Corner was right.'

Marco looked thoughtful. 'Yet I feel we shouldn't overlook Dario's motive for killing his brother,' he said in the end. 'You know, I really don't know where to start. I saw the inquisitors today, and they're as anxious to solve the case as I am. I didn't mention anything about the possible involvement of foreign spies. And anyway, if espionage were involved, how does Corner fit into that? So maybe it is all linked to the maidservant? Hopefully, I'll find out soon. I'm off to Dolo tomorrow to look for the girl.'

'Are you? All the way to Dolo? Can't you send an agent?'

'I could, but . . . I've decided to go in person and take a trip up the Brenta on the Burchiello.'

'Ah, now I understand!' Daniele started to laugh. 'You're taking Chiara, aren't you? So matters are progressing well on that front, at least.'

'I'm not even sure what my feelings are,' confessed Marco at last, tired of avoiding the subject. 'I do like her a lot; in fact, she thrills me. But I don't know if she feels the same. She's so composed, and what's more she's always chaperoned. And what about you?' He found he was reluctant to say more. 'Are you getting engaged or not?'

'I was looking at Maddalena today while she was singing,' Zen said thoughtfully. 'She's certainly pretty, I grant you, even if she's completely tone-deaf, but I kept thinking I was seeing a young version of her mother. She'll turn plump, too, and become a gossip. And then I thought of myself, like her father, sitting on his gilded chair, with a smug smile on his face, counting his gold every evening. No, that's not for me.'

'You've got sophisticated tastes,' Marco concluded with a smile.

That evening Marco felt restless and irritable. The investigation was at a standstill, he wasn't clear where he stood with Chiara and he had been annoyed by Francesca Corner. He had no appetite for dinner and criticised the partridge and the stew.

'Women!' sighed Rosetta as she cleared his plates. 'There's not a single one who won't cause you trouble!'

This infuriated Marco even more: Nani had been talking. He'd have to teach him a lesson, and if he wasn't careful, he'd be sent packing back to the seminary to become yet another disgruntled priest! 'What's all this about, Rosetta?' he asked.

'It's time for you to settle down, but with the right woman.'

'And who might that be?'

'That's not for me to say, but it must be someone of your own rank . . . not a businesswoman.' Rosetta's words came tumbling out. 'Not a woman who does a man's job, and who knows what else.'

Marco's fist slammed on to the table and the glasses shook. 'Rosetta, I am a patient man, but I do not intend to listen to anyone preaching about my private life, even you who brought me up. And don't talk about people you don't know.'

He climbed the stairs to his study and stood looking at the portrait of his wife above the fireplace. When he was here, in this room, he sometimes fancied he could hear the rustle of her gown, as if she were still close by. All it took was the memory of a gesture and he could see her in his mind's eye: how she used to offer him a coffee cup balanced like a gift on her palm or brush her hand over his papers as she tidied them. From the portrait, Virginia seemed to be smiling at him now.

He shook his head to chase the memories away before sitting down at his desk to look through his folder of notes on the case, but he couldn't concentrate. The names danced in front of his eyes, the witness statements seemed insignificant.

He went back downstairs and picked up an old cloak, then, taking a lantern, he headed for Calle dei Preti, behind the Scuola of San Rocco, where Annetta lived.

The night was clear and cold, the city deserted. Somewhere in the distance a tenor voice was singing a boating song accompanied by a violin. The melody was pleasant, at times tender and sentimental, and it took him back to the years he had spent in Padua as a youth, when he, too, sang, under Virginia's windows.

He walked past the church of San Barnaba and threw a few coins towards a beggar hunched by the wall. As he passed the building where Marino Barbaro had lived, he turned to look up at it, then remembered that he had left the rope at Chiara's. That young woman was a real puzzle: she seemed the sweetest of women, yet she argued a point of philosophy like a professor. She was serene and smiling, yet she practised mysteries in defiance of the Church's laws. Was she really a clairvoyant, though? She had seen that he was a widower when she read his palm, and promptly grasped the dramatic events of his past. Or was the whole thing a sham based on her previous knowledge of the events?

And what about the strange scene he had witnessed as she held the rope? It's true that he had felt a mysterious force. But what did her description of the blonde-haired girl, the gondolier and that scarlet cloak have to do with the death of first Barbaro, then Corner?

Passing a narrow calle, the air filled with a stomach-curdling stench and the sound of rough voices: a few barrel men were emptying the sewer of a palace. Marco walked past a tavern, peered through the windows of the crowded room and decided to go in. He pushed his way between the card tables, where some of the players seemed drunk already. At the counter he ordered a glass of wine and downed it in one before going back out into the street, his mind still full of memories of his evening with Chiara, and this time he smiled. He knew so little about her, yet she already felt part of his soul. If she truly could see things, then that was a bonus, and he shouldn't worry about it. Chiara had nothing in common with witches and other charlatans; she made no money from her gift and instead simply used it to do good, in the same way that she gave away her potions to make people better.

In Campo San Pantalòn, he was approached by a heavily made-up prostitute who was most certainly older than she looked. 'On your own, fine fellow? D'you fancy a bit of company? I'm the best Venice can offer.' Marco held out a coin and continued on his way, leaving her bewildered.

When he reached Calle dei Preti, he stood for a while looking up at the window, deep in thought. In the small second-floor apartment, a light was visible through the drapes in the salon. Annetta was still awake, waiting. She would be pleased to see him, he knew.

Then, with a sigh, he turned and headed back the way he had come. Poor Annetta. He was her only lover.

CHAPTER 16

The lagoon was still shrouded in darkness when Marco's gondola came alongside Fusina, the small port at the start of the Brenta canal, and its passengers stepped on to the landing place where the Burchiello was waiting. Chiara was enveloped in fur, complete with a muff for her hands, while her elderly housekeeper, Marta, was barely visible under a grey cloak and hood. For once, the avogadore was wearing gloves.

'It's seven now, Nani,' said Marco, turning to the young gondolier, 'and I plan to be back in twelve hours' time. But you've got a job to do during the day: look for the tavern that belongs to Biagio, Corner's servant. All I know is that it's somewhere near the Fondaco dei Turchi. Then tell Avvocato Zen from me that he should make discreet enquiries in a few coffee houses to find out what sort of man this Labia is and where I could meet him without raising any suspicions. He'll be on edge now that the other two are dead. I'm sure he's got some interesting things to say.'

'Yes, master,' agreed Nani in a serious tone. He was still chastened by the telling-off Marco had given him for gossiping about Chiara with the other servants.

'Come back to collect us this evening at seven and then you can give me your report after dinner.'

'Oh!' said Nani sadly. 'I'd planned to go to Palazzo Priuli this evening. They're celebrating Caterina's birthday. She's a delightful blonde who laughs a lot.'

'You mean you're invited to the kitchens . . .'

'Well, Caterina's Signora Priuli's maid and it's still Palazzo Priuli. Would it be all right if I told you what I've found out when I come to collect you and take you home?'

What could he say? Marco had heard tales of these celebrations in the servants' quarters, which involved much eating, singing and dancing and no shortage of wine. 'All right, Nani, we'll meet here at seven, and then you can go off.'

'Hurray for the paròn,' cheered the young man. 'He's the best in the world!' And after raising his hat in Chiara's direction, he rowed away.

All three were still laughing when they boarded the canal boat. Marta indicated that she would prefer to sit in the servants' cabin, but Marco would not hear of it. Instead they all took seats in one of the small cabins, which had silk-covered walls and a glass pane that allowed them to see outside. The housekeeper was carrying a basket covered with a chequered cloth. 'It's our lunch,' she explained. 'In the country-side you never know what you might find to eat.'

'That's Marta for you,' said Chiara, smiling at the avogadore. 'She's like a mother hen.' Her fur coat was now open and in the flickering lantern light her cheeks were pink with cold, while her eyes danced and smiled.

Marco felt his heart tighten. He longed to kiss her and hold her tightly in his arms. He had no clue as to how she felt . . . *It's for the best that Marta is here*, he thought. Chiara had her reputation to maintain and Marta filled the place of Chiara's long-dead mother. He smiled back, one of his half-smiles with a bitter edge.

Chiara, too, was thinking how much she liked this man, and how she was growing used to his company. She wondered what his inten-tions were and hoped he didn't spoil things by making advances. She realised that she had been wrong to invite him into her room the other evening and couldn't imagine what he must think of her. *Thank good-ness Marta was in the house*, she thought. *He's a Pisani and an avogadore, and even if he lives very simply, he's still one of the most famous men in the city. What would he do with a tradeswoman like me?* She could tell that he was interested in her, but she knew that, as a commoner, she was far beneath him. *It's best I keep my feet on the ground*, she decided.

In the meantime, the Burchiello had filled up. A group of very talkative priests had occupied one of the other cabins, together with an elegant lady and her maid. Three students from Padua were lounging in the armchairs, still half asleep. A small troupe of jugglers were putting on their make-up and costumes in a corner and preparing to entertain the travellers.

Outside on the towpath, two large dray horses had appeared and were harnessed to the vessel. The Burchiello started to move as the sun rose.

As on every other occasion when he had travelled along the Brenta, Marco admired the huge endeavours made by his Venetian forebears to build up the embankments with thousands and thousands of wooden stakes, brought down from the forests further inland. They had successfully brought the annual flooding cycle under control and the swamps on either side were now fertile fields.

The countryside in winter had its own harsh beauty. The skeletal outlines of poplars and acacias were reflected in the water, and willows bent over to brush the canal surface while the red hawthorn berries provided a flash of colour in this sleeping world.

'Here's the Moranzani Lock,' observed Chiara, when the large wooden lock gates were pulled shut behind the vessel using thick ropes. Marta had only made this trip once before, using the night-time boat reserved for the locals and their goods, and she watched in astonishment as the water level rose quickly.

The Burchiello resumed its slow journey and soon the villas started to appear. These magnificent buildings had been built on the banks of the Brenta two hundred years earlier by the Venetian nobility, who had developed these estates for profit and pleasure.

'There's Villa Foscari, which people call La Malcontenta,' observed Marco. 'It's not large but it has beautiful proportions and some think of it as architecturally the most striking of the forty or so residences that line the river. The Pisani family has a villa, too. I'll point it out.'

'It's a shame that these residences are closed at this time of year,' replied Chiara. 'I've heard they're magnificent inside, and I imagine they must be beautiful and cool in the summer compared to Venice, so I don't blame the nobility for spending their summers here.'

Marta coughed. She was watching the jugglers, who'd each started to throw five red balls into the air and then catch them one by one. Then it was the turn of a singer, who sang an old Venetian song while accompanying herself on a guitar.

At Oriago, the boat stopped at Osteria Sabbioni, which was right on the bank, and Marco and Chiara got off to warm themselves with a glass of wine. The inn was large and dark, with wooden beams on the ceiling. A fire crackled cheerfully in the fireplace and some large cauldrons hung under the hood, giving off an inviting smell.

'I'm enjoying our trip,' Marco said, touching Chiara's hand. She did not draw back. 'But you know,' he continued, 'once we get there, I'm relying on you to make Lucietta Segati talk. I'm not going to say who I am, of course. I'll introduce myself as the head of police.'

Chiara smiled. 'You, a policeman? No one will believe that! Anyway, who am I supposed to be?'

'A friend . . . or maybe my fiancée?' He looked at her intently. Chiara blushed and Marco again felt his heart flutter. 'The important thing is that you encourage the girl to tell me what happened while she was working at Palazzo Corner. Although she might be the young woman you saw in your vision.' It was the first time Marco had mentioned the events of that evening at Chiara's.

'So, you do believe what I saw,' she said. 'And, on that note, you know that you left the murder weapon behind?'

'The rope, yes. I'll come and collect it later.'

The boat left soon afterwards and immediately after Oriago they came to the newly built Villa Mocenigo, and then the large Villa Gradenigo, with its frescoes by Benedetto Caliari, brother of the more renowned Veronese. Then Villa Widmann and Villa Valmarana, with its splendid boathouse and park, a setting for many festivities. A gaggle of four geese appeared on the towpath, waddling pompously in front of the horses.

The Burchiello stopped again in the lock at Mira to allow the water level to rise once more. Then the procession of villas started up again. 'That,' said Marco, pointing to the right, 'is Villa Contarini. In front of it is the factory where they make candles for the whole of Venice. And now we're coming to Villa Corner, close to that Carmelite monastery. The other building is Villa Fini,' he said. 'And that's Villa Velluti, which belongs to the famous soprano. A little further on, you'll see Villa Grimani.'

When they arrived at Dolo, the Burchiello moored in front of La Posta, an inn, where the horses would be changed. Chiara woke Marta, who had dozed off, and they crossed to the inn. Marco would have liked to order lunch, but the housekeeper wouldn't allow it. 'Who knows what they'll give you to eat! Just order some wine because I've brought plenty of food.' She opened up her basket and began serving up meatballs in a sauce with pine nuts, alongside slices of roast veal.

Marco tucked in willingly. 'You know, Marta, you're as good a cook as my Rosetta,' he said.

'You flatter me, Your Excellency. I'm just an elderly housekeeper and I would never dream of competing with the cook in the Pisani household.' Privately she thought how friendly and kind he was. If only his intentions were clearer. What was it that he wanted from her dear Chiara?

They crossed the village in a rented carriage, passing the watermills and the boatyard. Soon they were in the centre, beside a church with a tall bell tower. Inside the dark nave, a priest walked towards them and Marco asked for information about the Segati family.

'They're my parishioners,' the priest replied. 'But they moved to a new house a few years ago. If you follow the path between the fields behind the church, you'll come to a canal at the end. Turn right, and after five hundred paces or so, you'll come to the house.'

They followed his directions and soon arrived at a small farmhouse, surrounded by fields and flanked by a barn with a granary above it. The farmyard was quiet and an old man was bent over a row of cabbages in the kitchen garden beside the house.

Marta stayed by the carriage while Marco and Chiara crossed the yard in the pale sunshine and walked into the kitchen through the open door.

'And who are you?' asked a man sitting in front of a wine bottle. He wore a shabby fustian jacket and breeches that had seen better days, and although he was young, his nose was red and swollen like those of many drinkers. His tangled hair fell down over his eyes.

'I'm the head of police,' Marco said, introducing himself. 'I would like to see Lucietta Segati.'

'What's that stupid woman done now? She's probably in the barn. She's been there for the past hour or more, mucking out the animals. She still thinks she's a maid in that fancy palace. She's a lazy good-for-nothing, with that brat of hers clinging to her legs.'

Marco and Chiara exchanged questioning glances as they walked over to the farmyard. 'At least she's alive,' said Marco quietly.

At that moment a woman emerged from the barn. Apart from the fact that she was heavily pregnant, it was impossible to tell how old she was. In one hand she held a pitchfork, while the other dragged a reluctant little boy who must have been about two. She looked enquiringly at Marco, who introduced himself as the head of police and asked her name.

'I'm Lucietta Segati,' she said. 'The man in the kitchen is my husband.' Now that they were closer, it was clear that she was young, but her face was deeply etched with fatigue. Her black hair was gathered into an untidy bun. 'At your service, signore,' she added, bobbing a curtsey, as she had been taught in the Corner household.

Marco wondered at the desperate turn of events that had changed a maidservant in a grand house into a slovenly-looking woman who had aged before her time. Aloud, he said, 'We would like to talk to you about what happened to you in the Corner household. Is there somewhere quiet we can talk?'

'Lucietta!' It was her husband and his tone was impatient. 'The wine's finished! Don't stand there blathering, you need to prepare the hen feed.'

The woman hurried awkwardly into the kitchen to do as he asked, then she led the visitors into the kitchen garden, among the rows of vines. The old man came closer but remained silent. 'My father,' Lucietta said, introducing him. 'He was the one who insisted I should marry.' She sighed.

'When she came home, she was dishonoured, pregnant,' interjected the older man. These were words that he had clearly repeated to himself time and again. 'That was when Momo came forward. He was a farmhand and accustomed to work . . . I thought it was right.'

'Shall we start from the beginning?' suggested Marco, who was struggling to piece the story together.

'When did you come home?' interrupted Chiara, directing her question at Lucietta.

'It was nearly three years ago now, in January 1750. I was with child.' She looked down. 'We were desperate. But the Corner family gave me some money as a dowry.'

'I'd gone to Venice,' added her father. 'I wanted the wretch who'd seduced my daughter to marry her. That's how things work here in the countryside. But he refused even to see me, he was that arrogant. I even stood shouting under his companion's house, that rascal Barbaro. No one paid any attention to me there either.'

Marco smiled at the idea that the eldest son of the Corner family might have married a maidservant.

'And what about the dowry?' prompted Chiara. She wanted the two of them to feel at ease before she started to ask any more probing questions.

'It was quite a sum of money, a good pile of ducats,' continued the old man. He scratched his head and stretched out a hand to ruffle the hair of the child, who still held tight to his mother's bedraggled skirt. 'By the spring Lucietta's pregnancy was clearly visible, and the gossip started. That's when Momo came forward. He offered to marry the girl and let the boy use his name. He didn't have tuppence to call his own, but with the dowry we could rent this piece of land from the Barnabite fathers and also buy what equipment we needed for the fields and the beasts. I convinced Lucietta and the couple married.'

'And what a good marriage it's been!' commented the girl. 'As soon as the marriage deeds were signed, Momo put down his tools and has done nothing but drink. Instead it's me and my father who have to do all the work, even when I'm in this condition . . .' She held her prominent belly. 'And never a kind word, let alone a caress for the boy.'

'Luciettaaa . . .' Momo's rough voice could be heard shouting. 'Don't stand around wasting time! There's work to be done!'

Marco turned and strode back to the house and into the kitchen. 'Listen to me,' he said, seizing the man by his jacket and lifting him bodily on to his feet. 'You are wilfully obstructing justice and for that I could have you thrown into prison.' The man paled and started to shake. 'But that's not all. If I find that you're living off your wife's dowry, that you're drunk and make her work, and you treat both her and the boy badly, then in accordance with Law 348 of the Great Council I'll have you packed off to row the galleys for the rest of your life. And remember that, from now on, even if you don't realise it, someone will be keeping an eye on you!'

He'd spoken so loudly that when he came back Chiara looked at him, her unspoken question hanging in the air.

Marco took her aside and confided quietly, 'Yes, I made that law up. It doesn't exist, but it should! You watch – it'll have an effect.'

Chiara knew that they had to press on with the matter in hand, so she turned back to Lucietta. 'What exactly happened to you while you were working in Palazzo Corner?'

The girl started to cry. 'Why are you asking me all these questions now?'

Marco felt that he had to tell her about the deaths of the two patricians and about the investigations.

'You don't think it was us . . .' implored the old man, who looked terrified.

'Of course not,' Pisani assured them, although he had of course previously thought exactly that. 'But anything that emerges about Corner and Barbaro's behaviour might be useful to us. So' – he turned to Lucietta again – 'that's why we need to hear your story.'

'Dead . . .' murmured Lucietta. 'Piero Corner is dead.' And she instinctively reached out to hug the child.

Marco looked properly at the boy for the first time and recognised Francesca Corner's high cheekbones and aristocratic nose. Here was the male heir that Piero had not had from his wife, he thought.

'Young master Piero had had his eyes on me for a while,' Lucietta started, drying a tear with a corner of her apron. 'He'd grab hold of me whenever I passed, or he'd corner me in the kitchen when no one was around and try to kiss me. Things like that. I certainly never let him. I knew that some masters would take advantage of young girls and you had to be careful. In the evening I'd lock myself into my room. But one night, I think it was in mid-November, I heard loud voices laughing outside my door. I recognised the young master's voice and that of his friend, Barbaro. They seemed drunk. Then I heard a key turning in the lock. They must have found another one that worked. I hid under the blankets . . .' Lucietta broke down.

Chiara reached out to embrace her, spontaneously. 'Would you prefer it if we talked alone?'

'No, it's all right, I can do this. I was alone against the four of them because there was also another nobleman who stood and watched. Biagio was there, too, and I was always terrified of him. "You know what I want. Hasn't your mother told you what men do to little whores like you?" Corner said. I knew nothing . . . and I started to scream, but Biagio put his hand over my mouth while Barbaro undressed me.' Lucia flushed scarlet as she remembered the episode, but she continued courageously, 'Then Corner climbed on to me while Biagio and Barbaro held me down. I was crying. "And remember," he told me at the end, "if you blab about this, especially to my mother, I'll have some jewellery placed in your room and you'll be packed off to prison as a thief."'

'Was that the only time?' asked Marco.

'Sadly not,' Lucia admitted, staring at the ground. 'From then on, Corner would come to my room on his own, once every three or four nights. I was terrorised. Then when I discovered I was with child, I couldn't bear it any longer. "Who knows whose child it is?" he said. "Everyone knows that you're out with the gondoliers at night." That was the final insult. I braced myself and went to the mistress and told her everything.'

So much for Signora Corner and her claim to know nothing, thought Marco. Aloud, he said, 'What was her response?'

'She didn't seem that surprised. She gave me a dressing-down, saying that it was all my fault, and then she sent me packing with a little money on the side. That's how I came to settle here with Momo, but now he does nothing but drink.'

'I'm sure he'll change his ways from now on,' Marco assured her.

'One other thing, Lucietta . . .' It was Chiara who suddenly broke into the conversation. 'Have you ever owned a red cloak, a scarlet cloak?'

Lucia's eyes widened at the strange question. 'Me, a scarlet cloak? No, never. That would be far too expensive for me.'

When they walked back to the farmyard, they found Momo turning over the straw that he'd mucked out of the barn. 'You're tired, Lucietta,' he said to his wife. 'Why don't you sit in the kitchen while I finish the job off?'

Marco gave him a withering look. 'Just remember that I've got someone watching you. One step out of line and I'll send you to the galleys.'

CHAPTER 17

On the return journey, the Burchiello was almost empty. There were just two merchants playing cards by candlelight in a corner. The weather was still fine, but an icy wind had got up, which found its way into the minute cracks in the cabin. Chiara preferred to wrap herself tightly in her fur coat and stand on the stern, breathing in the river air. Enveloped in her cloak, Marta remained seated beside Marco.

'I love that girl as if she were my own daughter,' said the elderly woman, breaking the silence in a meditative tone, as if talking to herself. 'On his deathbed, her father asked me to take care of her. By then, I'd already brought her up and, believe me, Your Excellency, there's no one else like her.'

Marco smiled at her sincerity. But there was a question that had been troubling him. 'I agree that Chiara is an extraordinary woman. But, tell me, why has she never married?'

Marta sighed. 'You've just seen how that poor Lucietta has been reduced to misery, Your Excellency, and yet you ask that question. My Chiara is twenty-five years old, she's independent, educated and rich. She's accustomed to dealing with international clients, she's travelled, and as a workshop proprietor she's a full member of the Weavers' Guild; she manages her money as she thinks best, she designs the fabrics herself . . . in a nutshell, she's a businesswoman. You know quite well, and probably better than me, that if she married, all this would end. Money, business decisions, guild relations, everything would be claimed by her husband. There's never been any shortage of suitors . . . her colleagues, wealthy shopkeepers, even the owners of luxury shops, they are all queuing for her hand. But she doesn't need a man.' She chuckled. 'There's a particularly wealthy merchant, a widower who deals in silk, who's so enamoured of Chiara that he sends her a bunch of flowers every two or three months, and inside there's the most exquisite jewellery: a pearl necklace, bracelets, brooches, you name it.'

'And what does Chiara do?' asked Marco indignantly.

Marta held her cloak more tightly. 'She sends everything back, of course. With a polite note, thanking him courteously. She doesn't want to be indebted to anyone.'

Listening to Marta talking about Chiara's suitors, Marco experienced an unexpected jolt of jealousy. 'And has she ever been in love?'

'Never!' the housekeeper assured him. 'These merchants are beneath her; they're too preoccupied with their goods and their wealth.' Marco suddenly thought of the lunch with Maddalena Santelli's family and he couldn't help but agree that Chiara would never be at home in that sort of company. But he wasn't a merchant and he wasn't seeking monetary gain. Like Chiara, he had higher ideals. He had never thought he could feel like this again. But did she feel the same way?

Chiara was thoughtful, too, when she came back into the cabin. In a low voice, she was saying, almost to herself, 'Yet I'm sure I saw a woman's body. She was enveloped in a scarlet cloak . . . but she was certainly blonde, and Lucietta is dark. And she says she's never had a red cloak.'

'Is it your visions that you're thinking of?' asked Marco.

'It's strange. The woman I saw wasn't Lucietta Segati. Which means that there's another girl involved in this.'

'Not that I've heard about,' reflected Marco. 'Lucietta is alive, so you must have been wrong. Perhaps what you saw was the violent assault.'

'No,' replied Chiara stubbornly. 'There was a corpse, a body to be buried. I feel these things as well as see them. Anyway, are you going to come back with me to collect the rope?'

Marta interrupted. 'I know what you're thinking. You're planning to try again, to see if you can have another vision. But I won't let you. It's dangerous. Sooner or later you might come to harm.'

'Just this once, Marta,' insisted Chiara. 'There's something I might have missed, and I must find out what it is. Just once more.' And she planted a large kiss on the older woman's cheek.

Later, as Nani was rowing Marco and Chiara across the lagoon, heading back from Fusina to the parish of the Jesuits where Chiara lived, he told Marco about what he had discovered that day.

Biagio's mother, who didn't enjoy a particularly good reputation in the neighbourhood, had started out with a grubby little den where she served the worst-quality wine and, in the evening, various soups and fried fish. Then suddenly, the previous year, in June 1751, she had moved to a handsome premises on Fondamenta del Megio, near the Republic's granaries and just behind the Fondaco dei Turchi. The handful of people who knew her, and to whom Nani had talked with considerable care, could tell him nothing about where she had found the money.

The story matched the information that Vannucci, the inquisitors' spy, had given him, and also what Marco himself had learned at lunch with the Santelli family. The money almost certainly came from the Corner family, but what were these services for which Biagio had been so richly rewarded?

Nani had visited the tavern, but he had seen no one who could have been the landlady's son and he'd purposely not asked any questions.

Once back at her house, Chiara ushered Marco into the salon, which was warm and welcoming, while Marta hurried into the kitchen to prepare hot chocolate. The rope was still there, lying on the floor by the sofa, as if no one had dared to touch it.

'What do you intend to do? Aren't you fearful of summoning your visions again? We don't know what forces you might provoke,' Marco said anxiously. 'Please, Chiara, don't try. Leave it to me to find out how they died. I don't want you to run any risks.'

'Yes,' she admitted, 'perhaps I shouldn't repeat the experience so soon, but I feel as if I should have noticed something. I must cross the boundary once more . . .' She put a hand on either side of her temples, as if to concentrate better. 'There are some other details, ones that will certainly point you in the right direction,' she went on. 'You sit down and relax. Empty your mind, like you did the other evening.'

Marco sat on the sofa and Chiara blew out the candles, leaving the firelight as the only source of light in the room. This time she didn't sit. She picked up the rope and, holding it, paced to and fro in the dim light. 'You see,' she whispered to Marco, 'I'm not doing anything to invoke it. What would you call it . . . the memory of objects? I'm just here and alert: if any unknown force wants to reveal itself, then I am ready.'

This time it was a long wait, and to Marco it seemed interminable. There was a strange atmosphere in the room. He could only hear the lapping of the water in the nearby canal and Chiara's heels as they echoed on the floorboards.

Then suddenly the woman jumped then collapsed into the armchair in front of the fire. The flames rose higher, like red tongues that seemed to be crying out, shrieking.

Marco was horrified to realise that he, too, had fallen under the spell. Chiara was white-faced and she twisted the rope convulsively in her fingers. Then she put a hand to her throat as if she were suffocating and shouted out loud.

The light wavered and again he could hear the cries, although now they were fainter. Chiara's face was streaked with tears.

Marco leaned forward, rigid with anxiety, not daring to interrupt. Time seemed to stand still. Chiara's eyes were now wide open, and she stretched out her hands, as if to beg for mercy. The rope slid on to the floor and seemed to writhe there, like a snake.

At last, with a long shudder, she came back to her senses and looked around, bewildered, as the familiar objects gradually came back into focus. Then she fell forward on to the floor and burst into tears.

Marco rushed to pick her up and held her in his arms as her sobs became more agitated. Marta, too, hurried in and embraced her little girl as, with Marco's help, they carried her to her bed. 'What happened, little one? You shouldn't have done it again, not so soon.'

'I'm not sure,' stammered Chiara at last. 'It was terrible, and I thought I was the one who would die.' Marta made her sip a little water. 'Now, leave me with Marco,' Chiara begged.

Marco waited until she spoke. 'The vision was so clear, and it seemed endless. I've never seen something so clearly before. The girl was there again, Marco, but she's not Lucietta. I saw her blonde hair again. She's wearing a scarlet cloak, made from Venetian scarlet cloth. Behind her is a church, an Eastern-looking church. It looks like San Zaccaria.' She stopped to take another sip, while Marco held up her head and breathed in the scent of her hair. 'They are hurting her, hurting her terribly. She screams and groans. Then she's dead, Marco. I feel that she's dead and must be buried. All that red is also blood. Then suddenly I saw a ship and I knew that it had arrived from the East . . . and I felt that someone was praying for help . . .'

'Well, you sleep now, my little one,' murmured Marta, walking back into the room. 'Let's leave her to rest for a little,' she said to Marco. 'Please follow me, Your Excellency.'

She took him back to the salon and poured out the chocolate. 'Chiara has these extraordinary gifts,' she started, 'and she wants to help people. I don't interfere when she prepares tisanes and other concoctions, but when she summons the spirits I am always afraid.'

'Are they really spirits?'

'I don't know. She says she just sees fragments of reality, and that the visions are like lightning.'

'Yes, she said something like that . . .'

'Whatever these visions are, she doesn't make them up. She really does communicate with some mysterious force, whatever it might be, and it frightens me. Usually, they happen out of the blue, but she'll be in trouble if she starts to prompt them! Even she doesn't know what forces she might be unleashing . . .'

The old woman took a long sip of chocolate and remained silent and thoughtful. 'But it's even worse,' she continued, 'when she has premonitions. My Chiara manages to reconstruct the past, but at times, and much more rarely, she can foresee the future. Sometimes she realises that something terrible is about to happen and she won't rest until she's done what she can to ward it off. She always says that everyone has a destiny, but that we can change it because God has granted us free will. It's all rather difficult to understand, isn't it, Your Excellency? Living here, in this house, I've had to learn to find my way around among these mysteries. Has she told you that this Gift, as she calls it, is passed down by the women of her family?'

'Yes, she told me,' he replied, hoping that Marta would tell him more.

He needn't have worried. She was eager to confide in someone. 'I was here with the Renier family in the days of Chiara's grandmother and mother,' she said. 'You've no idea how many cases they solved! For example, once, the baker lost her child. Chiara's grandmother told her that he was on an island in the lagoon, and indeed they found him there. He had hidden on a boat and got off when no one was looking and couldn't find his way back to the city. If they hadn't found him, he would have died from the cold. Another time, Chiara's mother had a vision and told the doctor's wife that her husband, who'd disappeared, was under a particular bridge. Unfortunately, he was there, but he was dead. Then there was the time that the merchant Bembo couldn't find his father's will. The man had died suddenly, and Chiara's mother was able to tell him exactly which brick on the floor he should look under. Heavens, I could go on and on . . . But will Chiara's vision be useful to you in your investigations?'

'I don't know yet,' admitted Marco. 'If what she told me this evening is true, I need to start all over again. But it's getting late, and I should leave you to take care of your mistress.' Marco rose and collected his cloak. He needed some time to think.

When he got home, it was very late. Only Plato was still up and waiting for him in his study, purring while he lay proprietorially on two sealed letters that someone had left on Marco's desk.

Marco lifted up the cat, who growled slightly. He opened the first, which was from Zen.

> *I've asked around for news of Paolo Labia and been to the places he usually goes to, including the barber, the pharmacist and his favourite caffès. No one seems to have seen him for quite a while.*

The second letter gave off a very heady, brash perfume. It was addressed to Avogadore Marco Pisani. It was accompanied by a note from his secretary Tiralli, stating that he'd thought it appropriate to deliver it personally.

'Well, my dear Plato,' guessed Marco as he broke the wax seal. 'Here we have a classic example of a Venetian anonymous letter.' He read it aloud: '*If you want to find a lead in the right direction, look for the person who's disappeared from Castello.* Is that all?' Pisani asked his cat. 'If what I learned from the spirits this evening was right, and if this letter is hinting at the truth, then I fear I may have to broaden my search to discover who killed Corner and Barbaro. But where should I look?'

Plato had walked over to smell the letter, which was still in Marco's hand.

'Yes, I know. It's a common perfume, isn't it? Who could have used a scent like that? A courtesan, you say? But one at the bottom end of the scale. Well, give me a helping hand, old fellow: is there a courtesan, well past her prime, involved in the case? Yes, of course there is: Barbaro's lover, Lucrezia Scalfi. What's more, I was supposed to get back in touch with her, but then events led me elsewhere. Shall we lay a wager that this is her work? It means that I really have missed something. But don't worry, Plato. Tomorrow I'll lay on a proper interrogation, and I'm willing to bet that she'll tell me everything.'

CHAPTER 18

There had been a sudden change in the weather. When Friday dawned, the city was enveloped in a fog so thick that houses, palaces and bridges appeared like shadowy phantoms rising above the streets beside the canal as Marco and Daniele were rowed through the canals that criss-crossed the Dorsoduro and Santa Croce districts, heading for the tavern belonging to Biagio Domenici.

'Go behind San Giacomo and moor at Fondamenta del Megio.' Zen leaned out from the awning to give the instructions to his gondo-lier, Bastiano.

The two friends were on Zen's boat because Nani had been given a delicate mission that morning: to take Chiara a bunch of flowers and a letter in which Pisani enquired after her health. And later that afternoon Nani would be involved in further inquiries regarding Paolo Labia's whereabouts.

'Tell me about yesterday,' the lawyer went on. 'How are things going with Chiara? And what about that maidservant who disappeared from the Corner household? Did you find her?'

Marco ignored the first question and instead told Daniele all about Lucietta and the way she had been raped during her time at the Corner palace, and also the arrogance of the man she had made the gross error of marrying. 'And the little boy is the spitting image of his grandmother, Francesca Corner. He's the son that Piero never had, and he'll never know anything about his real father. Poor boy: the descendant of one of the Corners of Ca' Grande will labour in the fields like a wretched peasant.'

'Their fate was already sealed,' agreed Zen. 'But at least they're alive.'

'And we're back at square one on this case. I feel we need to hurry if we're ever going to solve it. This gang of rogues is petering out: two are dead, and there's no trace of the third. Biagio is our last chance to find out what they were up to. And I've got a feeling that the murderer may well be on Biagio's trail, just as we are.'

The tavern owned by the Domenicis was a large place standing on Fondamenta del Megio, and it might once have been elegant. Given the time of day, only a few of the thirty or so tables were occupied by customers: strange Albanese wearing amply gathered pantaloons, tall and muscular Slavs, swarthy-looking retailers of pepper and ginger from the Middle East, and Turks who came to Venice to trade cloth from Flanders and English wool. They were all men who lived and worked in the nearby Fondaco, where they were required to do business. The wine counter served both wine for the Christian clients and fruit drinks for the Muslims. A tall, buxom girl ran backwards and forwards from the hearth to the tables, serving plates of fried fish, while a corpulent middle-aged man, whom the serving girl called Lele, washed glasses in the large stone sink.

Zen approached the latter. 'My name is Avvocato Zen, and I'd like to speak to Biagio.'

'Biagio's not here,' said the man, without so much as a glance. 'Why are you looking for him?'

'Private business. Where can we find him?'

Lele scratched his head and looked at Zen, puzzled. 'To tell the truth, we were also wondering where he is. He's not been seen around here for a week. Not that he's much missed. Usually he comes here to drink and pick quarrels with the clients, or he plays cards or chases the girls. He's never given us a hand serving when it's busy! But you could ask his mother – that's if she knows anything more than we do.' Then, as an afterthought, he asked, narrowing his eyes, 'Why's a lawyer looking for him, though? Is there another inheritance around? It seems good luck always comes to those who least deserve it.'

'Where's his mother?' asked Daniele patiently.

'Signora Maria? She'll still be in bed at this time of day. I'll get someone to take you. Pina!' He shouted in the direction of a back room and a young girl, not much more than a child, popped out, wearing a stained apron and with a kerchief around her hair. 'Pina, take these gentlemen to the mistress, but check that she's awake first. If she's still asleep, you'll certainly hear about it afterwards . . .'

'If she's asleep, we'll make sure she wakes up,' grumbled Marco, who had had enough of waiting.

They left Bastiano, the gondolier, to have a glass of wine and followed the girl up a steep staircase which led to the apartment on the upper floor.

Pina knocked timidly on a door and in response came a torrent of abuse. 'What the devil is that noise at this hour of day?' It was a woman's voice, hoarse and rough. 'Is that you, Pina? Curse you. I hope you fall down the stairs and smash your face one of these mornings!' The torrent was only ended by a fit of coughing.

Marco threw open the door without further ado and walked into the dark room. He regretted it immediately because he was almost knocked over by a stench of sweat mixed with alcohol, with distinct undertones of stale urine. 'Open the window,' he ordered, and the girl hurried to obey, overawed by a voice that was more imperious than that of her mistress.

'Who are you?' shrieked the vague form under the blankets. 'How dare you walk into a lady's room? I'll call the police.'

'I'm Avogadore Pisani,' said Marco. 'And the gentleman with me is Avvocato Zen. I need to have a serious conversation with you, so make haste and don't keep me waiting.'

On hearing the avogadore's name, a nightcap emerged from the blankets, under which were a few strands of blondish hair and a pale, heavily lined face with a hooked nose, two searching eyes with deep shadows beneath them and a narrow mouth. The woman smiled, although any appeal was undermined by the sight of her rotten teeth. 'Pardon me, Your Excellency, I didn't know . . . I am far from presentable . . . Give me ten minutes and I'll be at your service.'

'I fear that Biagio has escaped,' commented Daniele as they waited on the landing.

'At least we'll hear what his mother has to say,' replied Marco. 'But what a harridan!'

Maria Domenici finally received them, dressed in a pretentious velvet gown besmirched with stains. She'd found the time to don a blonde wig, which had seen better days, and to put on some make-up, and her rouged cheeks stood out against her pale skin. She had even placed a beauty spot above her upper lip, and two gaudy rings flashed on her right hand. She was seated on a gilded chair and beside her on a table were three glasses and a bottle of red wine.

The room was large and might have been refined except for the general disorder. The sight of the unmade bed, a pile of clothing on the chair and the remains of a dinner accompanied by several empty bottles on the table under the window caused a surge of disgust in the visitors.

The woman waved to the sofa beside her. 'If the gentlemen would like to take a seat . . . Can I offer them a little of this excellent Burgundy?' When the men shook their heads, she promptly filled her own glass and raised it to her lips.

'Signora Domenici,' began Pisani, 'we are here to meet your son, Biagio.'

'Dear Biagio,' simpered the woman. 'I am sorry, but he's not here at the moment. He's away on business. There is always so much to do here, and he deals with the suppliers and entertains the clients, you know. He's the one in charge of the tavern, which, as you've seen, is a classy establishment.'

'We've noticed . . . But can you tell us where to find him?'

'I'm sorry, but I've not the slightest idea. He comes and goes, and never tells me anything. I can't help you, Your Excellency.' The woman was still mincing her words, but her eyes never left the two men for an instant.

Marco began to lose patience. 'Signora, I don't know if you've understood who I am. Do you realise that I could ask the police to search the entire city for your son and have him taken before the interrogators in the ducal palace? Also remember that I am not here to seek your help. Your son is in grave danger and I can save him.'

'My son . . . the police? But why? He's the best son in the world. He's never done anything that might involve the police. You know that he still lives here with me. I couldn't wish for a better son.' While she was talking, she reached down to take a pinch of snuff from a little box and inhaled it with pleasure.

What a way to wake up, thought Pisani in disgust. 'By remaining silent, you are shouldering a heavy burden of responsibility, signora,' he went on. 'You might live to bitterly regret it. But tell me something else, how did you come to own such a "classy" establishment?'

'Well, how do you think? Through honest hard work, of course,' said the woman, tilting her head with pride. 'As I said, my son is a good man, and people are fond of him. For many years, he was secretary to a great nobleman, and he rewarded my son by giving him this place.'

'He worked for Piero Corner as a gondolier, I think, not as his secretary.'

'Gondolier, secretary, what difference does it make? He was his trusted confidant and accompanied him wherever he went.'

'You've heard what happened to Corner? And to the other noble-man, Barbaro? Years ago, your son worked for him too.'

'They're both dead, poor things, and they came to a terrible end. But what's that got to do with my son?' The woman fished a hand-kerchief out of her pocket and pretended to wipe away a tear. But she seemed less sure of herself, and her hand trembled.

Pisani leaned forward and looked her straight in the eye. 'Your son's disappearance suggests he knows a lot about both of those men. It might even have been him who killed them.'

'Are you suggesting that my son would kill his friends?' The old woman pinched her mouth in anger and the beauty spot became unstuck and fell to the ground. 'I'll have you know we're decent folk. And anyway, he couldn't have done it.' She had regained her composure. 'On the nights when they were murdered – on both nights – Biagio was here, playing cards. Dozens of people saw him.'

'Well then, if he's innocent, he's in grave danger too. Indeed, per-haps that's why he's in hiding. If you tell us where he is, you'll do him a great favour.'

Signora Domenici looked away, and for what seemed like an age she hesitated, locked in a struggle of her own. She played absent-mindedly with the snuffbox. 'No, I don't know, truthfully,' she sighed at last, look-ing down. The moment of uncertainty had passed. 'Believe me, I would do anything if I felt it was for my son's good.'

'He's your only son, isn't he?' interrupted Daniele, changing the subject. 'And where's his father?'

It was like opening the sluice gates on a canal. 'I've only got him,' prattled the woman, in a tone that suggested this was a frequent claim. 'His father is a nobleman, a high-ranking lord from Verona. I was young and very pretty.' She highlighted the word with a coquettish gesture. 'He came to Venice frequently on business, swore that he loved me and had promised to marry me. It was to be a ceremony with no expense spared. I hadn't yet met his family, but I knew that they were preparing

great festivities. It was barely a month after I'd written to tell him that
he was going to be a father, when one morning – and I'll remember it
until the day I die – a friend of his came to visit me from Verona to tell
me that he had been suddenly struck by a fatal illness. He told me that
he died with my name on his lips. He also brought me some money.
But I was left completely alone, and with child.'

Marco and Daniele exchanged rapid glances. The woman wiped
away her tears, blew her nose, and continued.

'Everyone I knew advised me to go to one of those . . . those good-
wives who would have dealt with my problem, but I was too frightened,
and I kept my Biagio. Believe me, I was a good mother. I worked hard
to bring him up, even taking lowly jobs.'

'You had a small drinking den . . .' interrupted Daniele.

'Yes, but it barely provided enough to cover my expenses, and
Biagio was still a boy when he had to accept work from that Barbaro,
who paid him a pittance. But he was a nobleman's son, and I was happy
because I thought he would learn how to behave like a patrician. Then
he was lucky enough to find work in the Corner household, and things
were much better.' Signora Domenici took another mouthful of wine.

'Why did Corner give you this place, which must be worth quite a
lot – and it also includes this apartment, doesn't it?'

'I told you, Your Excellency. People grow fond of Biagio and his
patron wanted to reward him.'

'But he fired him . . .' insisted Pisani.

'No, who told you that? He left him to enjoy his reward in peace.'

Marco resumed his questioning, making a final attempt. 'If we take
you at your word and accept that your son is away on business, you
must at least know when he's due back.'

The old woman shook her head. 'I don't know. He only said he
had to leave.'

There was nothing more they could get from her. She had a deep-
rooted distrust of anyone in authority, as so many of the poor did, and

Marco knew she would tell him nothing more. The two men went back downstairs and headed back to the counter.

Lele came towards them, wiping his hands on his apron. 'Can I offer you a glass of white on the house?' He looked at them curiously.

'No wine, thanks,' replied Daniele. 'But there's something that the avogadore would like to ask you.' And he turned to look at Marco.

'You told us earlier,' said Pisani, 'that Biagio would usually come here to play cards and chat to the clients. Now, listen carefully and think about what you say: who did Biagio usually spend time with?'

The innkeeper frowned, pulled out a large handkerchief to wipe the sweat off his neck and then cleared his throat. 'Well, that wretch who was strangled, that barnabotto, he often came here to see him . . .'

'Marino Barbaro.'

'That's the one. They'd play cards and drink, but above all I think Barbaro came to scrounge a free meal. Whenever the mistress saw him, she would grumble and tell us not to serve him, but in the end we always obeyed her son.'

Marco fell silent for a while, before asking, 'Did they ever quarrel?'

'Now that you mention it,' admitted Lele, widening his rather small eyes, 'they did argue occasionally. Then, about a month ago, they had a real fallout . . . luckily, there was no one else here and the signora was asleep.'

'What did they say?'

Lele looked guilty. 'Of course, I wouldn't have listened to them normally, but on that occasion I was busy decanting the wine from the barrels. They were talking about money. Biagio said it was too little, that he could have asked for much more.'

'And Barbaro?'

'He was clutching a sheaf of papers in his hand and he kept slapping them on the table. "I haven't a clue what they are," he kept saying. "If I ask too much, I'll end up getting nothing!"'

Marco caught Daniele's eye with a knowing look. Were these the plans that Barbaro had filched from the Arsenale? Was Biagio involved in espionage too? And who was interested in buying them? A Turkish spy, as Cappello had surmised?

'And among the other clients,' continued Daniele, 'who did your master talk to most often?'

The innkeeper turned to look around, as if visualising the scene. 'There was a man from Albania who he played cards with, then he used to drink with a couple of Austrian merchants . . .'

'What about Turks?'

'Yes, there was one he would often spend time with, but I've not seen him around for a few months. He must have gone home.'

Daniele leaned over the counter, determined to press on with the questions. 'A Turk? What did they talk about? Was Barbaro around when they met?'

Lele shook his head. 'What they talked about, I really couldn't say. They'd sit over there in the corner whispering to each other and Barbaro was often with them. But, as I said, I've not seen that Turk around for a while. He was clearly a well-to-do sort, with fine clothes—'

'His name?' interrupted Marco.

'Why on earth would I remember that?' said Lele. 'No! Hold on a moment . . . he was called . . . Ibrahim, Ibrahim Derali. I know because a countryman once came here looking for him, and his name was written on the note.'

'Now, listen carefully,' warned Pisani in an authoritative tone. 'If this Ibrahim shows up again, you're to send someone immediately to tell me at the palace and try to keep him here. Serve him really slowly – do anything to delay him until I get here. But be careful he doesn't grow suspicious!'

The innkeeper stared at them in surprise, but Marco ignored the look and turned to leave. As they walked through the room, he felt a hand lightly touch his arm. He looked round to see the young maidservant. 'The signora . . . she does know where her son is, you know,' she whispered.

'Were you eavesdropping?'

'I . . . well, yes . . . but I didn't hear everything. There's a crack in the door and you can hear quite clearly through it.'

'Do you know where Biagio is?'

'No, I don't. But a few evenings ago, I took a man upstairs to visit the signora, and I heard them talking about the master. She said, "If that's the way things are, I'll tell you where my son is." But please, please don't tell the signora that I told you, otherwise she'll give me such a beating.'

'What sort of man was he? How did he manage to make her talk? And where did she say Biagio was?' asked Pisani excitedly.

The young girl frowned in concentration. 'He was a big, tall man, wearing an old cloak,' she remembered. 'While he was talking to her, I could hear the chink of coins which he was shaking in a bag. Then, unfortunately, I also heard steps on the stairs and had to hide in the attic. Anyway, it's not my business.'

'What shall we do now?' Daniele broke the silence once they were back on Fondamenta del Megio. 'Shall we go back and make the old woman talk, using every means possible?'

'No,' Marco replied. 'We'd get that young girl into trouble, and what's more Signora Domenici is so cunning she'd pack us off to a false address while sending a warning to her son telling him to change hideouts. Nor is there any point getting the police to search all the inns in Venice: there's over a hundred of them, without counting all the rooms you can hire. It would take the agents weeks. Anyway, who's to say that Biagio's still in Venice? I've thought of another idea.'

They headed for the ducal palace in the gondola. The sunlight was trying hard to break through the fog, but for the moment all that could be seen was a yellowish halo around the buildings. Along the Grand Canal, Bastiano had his work cut out to avoid the other vessels which loomed out of nowhere.

Daniele said abruptly, 'Well, it wasn't a complete waste of time . . .'

'These visits never are,' replied Marco. 'We now know for sure that it wasn't Biagio who killed both men. Even though he wasn't ever a real suspect. But it is odd, isn't it, that his mother provided an alibi before we had a chance to ask? A cast-iron alibi, too: she said that, on both nights, several people had seen him at the tavern. We could certainly check it. Anyway, why would Biagio want to kill Corner, the goose who laid him golden eggs?'

'Also, we've got a much clearer idea of how the group worked,' continued Daniele. 'Barbaro, the impoverished gentleman, ready to stoop to any level, even spying, in order to fund his bad habits and be part of the right social circles. Corner, the leader, accustomed to getting his own way, thanks to his mother's influence, convinced of his superiority and rich enough to do anything he liked and to surround himself with fawning helpers.'

'And then there's Biagio,' Marco said, wrapping his cloak more tightly around himself. 'He can't have had an easy life. A father who vanished as soon as he heard of his son's existence and a drunken mother with social aspirations. You heard for yourself how that woman not only believes her own ridiculous fantasies but demands that others do too. Her son must have grown up thinking that truth, honesty and integrity were very flexible principles. The ideal servant for profligate masters. Then there's the Turk the innkeeper mentioned. Could he be the same one who was seen below Barbaro's house? Was he the intended recipient for the secret papers from the Arsenale? Is he the key to the whole affair? We now know that Barbaro and Biagio argued about what price to ask.'

'Don't forget, there's still Paolo Labia. Like Biagio, no one seems to know where he's got to,' said Daniele pensively. 'They both seem terrified by the possibility of revenge. I wonder if Ibrahim is the one who's after them?'

Marco suddenly thought of Chiara's vision of the blonde girl in a bloody scarlet cloak, the groans, the gondolier who might have been Biagio. Was that the right path to follow? But for the moment he felt it was more prudent to remain silent. 'This morning, before going out,' he found himself saying instead, 'I asked Nani to find a way inside the servants' quarters in the Labia household. I'm sure he won't come back empty-handed. At this very moment, he's probably courting a pretty maid and persuading her to tell him where her master is hiding,' he ended with a laugh.

CHAPTER 19

By midday the fog had lifted and the cold was less biting, but under the porticoes of the Procuratie, usually so crowded, there were few passers-by: a handful of women coming out of the church of San Geminiano, couriers working for the public offices, beggars huddled against the atrium of Saint Mark's. Today was the first of the ten days before Christmas when it was forbidden to go out in public wearing a mask, to hold receptions or to gamble at cards, and the Ridotto was closed. It felt as though the city was holding its breath while it waited for the festivities to start.

Pisani reached his office, and there, waiting for him in the secretary's antechamber, was Maso, Chiara's apprentice. He was standing with his back to the window, rocking uncomfortably on his long legs.

'What are you doing here?' Marco quizzed him with a smile.

Maso blushed violently. 'I . . . well, er, Your Excellency . . .' He remembered to bow awkwardly, before continuing, 'I am delivering this letter from my mistress.'

A letter from Chiara! A ray of light on a dull day. 'Will you wait for a reply?'

'No, that is to say . . . it would be better if I went back to the workshop.'

Marco smiled and clapped him on the shoulder. 'Off you go. You're not at ease here, which is understandable. I'll send someone with my reply.'

Maso looked extraordinarily relieved as he hurried away, and Marco walked in. The letter was short. *Act with prudence*, it read. *I woke feeling that something serious is about to happen. I've not had any visions, but I feel troubled. I beseech you, please go carefully.*

Chiara's premonitions . . . Marco almost felt happy. Although brief and to the point, the letter revealed that she was most certainly interested in his well-being. What was more, the inquiries had been going around in circles and a turn of events would be welcome. But now there were things to be done. He called Tiralli and gave his secretary precise orders.

Having set the wheels of justice in motion, it was now time to take a fresh look at all the witness statements that had been gathered. Zen had arrived in the office and they had a couple of hours at their disposal.

Lucrezia Scalfi had been waiting for an hour before she was led into the interrogation chamber in the ducal palace. She had still been asleep when she was woken just after midday by violent knocks on the door. Her maid flew into her bedchamber in a panic. 'The police, signora! The police are here! They're looking for you!'

The woman had gone down to find the salon invaded by ten or more armed men. From his uniform, she recognised Ignazio Beltrami, the notorious clerk of the Inquisitors' Court.

'What are you doing in my house?' she had demanded, but her voice shook.

'Dress yourself and come with us.' The order abrupt and peremptory.

A boat had then brought her to the prisons. Lucrezia understood that she wasn't under arrest, but she knew that Beltrami would not have been involved unless the matter was serious.

Her heart was in her throat as she was escorted up a long flight of stairs and through several corridors, until they reached the covered bridge over the small canal flanking the palace. She was taken along a gallery and through some rooms, before being left in an antechamber, alone with her thoughts.

This had given her plenty of time to search her conscience. In general, Lucrezia was a good person. In her youth she had plied her trade honestly, cajoling her moneyed lovers to pay her large sums but never leading them to ruin. At the time, she had had a plush apartment close to Saint Mark's Square, copious food and drink and sumptuous dresses and jewellery.

She had imagined her beauty would be eternal and she had made no provision for the onset of middle age. This was why, now that she was past her prime, she couldn't afford to pick and choose the company she kept. Barbaro and his friends were scoundrels, she knew that full well, but they paid her bills and shared her amongst themselves. She was in no position to judge them, and the tacit agreement was that she would cause no trouble and allow them into her apartment at any time of night or day.

She knew she hadn't done anything wrong, so if she had been brought to the palace under a guarded escort it could only be linked to the deaths of Barbaro and Corner. She was well aware that, eight days ago, she had not been forthcoming with Avogadore Pisani. Now she had to decide whether to continue with that line or to give away their secret.

Because there was a dark secret. Those four were not just scoundrels; she was all too aware that they had committed a crime, one that had never been noticed. Indeed, she suspected that the deaths of the two men were linked to a vendetta, or a late settling of scores.

She sighed and stood up from the bench in order to look out of the window; not that it brought much comfort, because the antechamber faced the New Prisons on the far side of the small canal. She smoothed her hair because she'd not even had time to comb it before leaving.

What could she actually be accused of, after all? Would they blame her, perhaps, for not having reported the men at the time? But if she hadn't been believed, who would have protected her from them? She herself wasn't guilty – or was she? Could she be blamed for having turned a blind eye to an act that could not be put right? But now that two of them were dead, and the others seemed to have disappeared, she was in a position to talk. It was quite some time since she'd received any money from the four men, and her first consideration now was to look to the future.

But what if she was accused of being complicit? On reflection, perhaps it would be better to keep quiet. Wasn't silence always the better option before the law? In any case, she'd already done her duty as a good citizen by offering an important clue to put the investigators on the right track. But was it really the right one?

The door opened just as she was adjusting a stocking over an ankle that still looked slim. Two of the Avogadaria's soldiers led her into the interrogation chamber. It was gloomy and lined with oak; the ceiling light did little to illuminate the space and a pair of torches flamed in the corners. In the half-light she could make out the shape of the wheel used for torture. True, it hadn't been used for decades, but the sight of it was still terrifying. Ropes, too, hung from the beams, implicit in their menace.

A number of people were waiting there: sitting in the centre, in a large chair placed on a dais, Lucrezia recognised Avogadore Pisani, a handsome presence in his magistrate's robes. Could he become her protector? But one glance at his expression was enough to confirm that nothing good would be forthcoming from that quarter. To his right was his friend, the lawyer who was always in his company, and to the left

Messer Grando, dressed in a black gown. The side benches were lined with clerks, secretaries and guard officers. Such a show, she thought, might imply trial for high treason, but that was surely not the case.

Messer Grando started. 'Can you confirm that you are Lucrezia Scalfi, residing in Salizàda San Lio, parish of Santa Maria Formosa, prostitute by trade?' The clerk started to write.

Shocked by the setting, Lucrezia lost her voice and had to swallow twice. 'I confirm that I am, but I am not a prostitute; I've never been on the street, I make my own living.'

'What were your relations with the deceased Marino Barbaro and Piero Corner, and with Paolo Labia and Biagio Domenici?' Messer Grando had been informed of the latest developments.

'They were my friends,' admitted Lucrezia. She looked up, and in the dim light her wrinkled face suddenly looked aged. 'I already told Avogadore Pisani when he first questioned me.' The woman expressed herself with a certain propriety, a habit learned from years spent in drawing rooms around the city. 'They would visit me after dinner, usually to play solitaire and talk.'

Messer Grando smiled. 'But you haven't told us their names. Did they pay you?'

'Yes, they helped me, of course, but then my house was at their disposal.'

'Your bed, too?'

'I was not aware that it was a crime.'

Pisani interrupted, waving a sheet of paper. 'Is this anonymous letter from you?' A faint trace of scent wafted across the room.

Lucrezia had not expected this line of attack and cursed herself for having written the letter. She had been brought into the palace because of it; that's what happened when you tried to help the course of justice. But how did he know it had come from her?

She tried to look amazed. 'What's that? Why would I send such a thing?'

Pisani got down off the dais and walked around her, sniffing the air. 'The perfume betrayed you. It's yours. Now,' he said, returning to his chair, 'are you going to tell us what it's about? Who is this person who's disappeared from Castello?' Marco was feeling his way, as he didn't have the foggiest idea what she might, or indeed could, confess. He heard the clerk's pen scratching the paper.

Lucrezia pulled a handkerchief out of her bag and patted at the sweat that had suddenly broken out on her forehead, even though the room was freezing. She wished she could sit because she felt faint. There was no escape now, that much was clear.

'A girl has disappeared . . .' she stammered at last.

'When?' pressed Pisani.

'A year and a half ago, but . . . I beseech you, let me sit down,' she implored.

At a sign from Messer Grando, a guard carried a chair to the centre of the room. Lucrezia collapsed on to it. She asked for a drink and then drained the glass.

'Now, tell us everything,' pressed Marco again.

'It was in 1751, at the time of Ascension, after the fair of the Sensa had ended. I don't remember the exact day, but the fair goes on for two weeks.' She wiped her forehead again. 'It was the middle of the night when I heard blows on the door. When I looked down, I saw it was them, all four of them. I opened the door because the maid was away visiting her relatives that day. They came in and I immediately realised they were shaken and upset, like I'd never seen them before. They'd been drinking, but that didn't account for it. They sat for a while in silence, half stretched out on the divans. Paolo Labia was crying. Corner kept punching a cushion, and Barbaro sat staring at the floor and looking grim. I remember clearly that the first to break the silence was Biagio. "What do we do now?" he asked. Then Piero Corner stood up; he took my arm and gestured that I should go back to bed.'

All those present were fixated by her words. 'But, of course, you stayed to eavesdrop . . .' said Pisani encouragingly.

Lucrezia smiled tensely. 'In the next-door room there's a cupboard with a small opening on to the salon, although it's hidden by the wall covering. I'd made it years before so I could tell who'd arrived to see me. No one knows about it.'

'A prostitute's precaution,' added Messer Grando tartly.

'A sensible precaution for a woman who lives on her own,' was Lucrezia's retort.

'Go on. What did you see and hear?' Marco was impatient now to hear the full story at last.

'Once I'd left the room,' continued Lucrezia, 'the four men started to quarrel. "I had nothing to do with it," whimpered Labia. "It's your fault. You never know when to stop." And Corner replied, "You had as much fun as we did, and now you want to pull out!" "Enough!" Barbaro shouted. "What's done is done. Now we need to take action because we're risking our heads here. She's dead, and if we're caught, it's the gallows for us, or if we escape, it means exile. The body must vanish!"'

Lucrezia started to shake as she remembered his words.

'I was terrified,' she went on. 'It was clear that those wretches had killed some young woman, and I regretted having overheard their conversation, but I was frightened that they'd hear me now if I left the room. So I stayed. At some point after this, Labia turned on Corner. "You're incapable of controlling yourself!" he yelled. "With all the women you have, why did you have to pick on the one who turned you down?" Corner punched him with such force that Labia collapsed, rolling over as he fell. "What do you know of women?" he replied. "That girl has been flouncing past me for months. She'd come to the house to deliver her sewing, and curtsey and smile at me. She was obviously asking for it. So, when we met her and her friend at the fair, I wanted to have a little fun with them. When her friend left, I thought she'd planned it and wanted to be alone . . ." Labia had wiped away the blood streaming from his nose and hauled himself up to remonstrate, "But when Biagio caught her and clamped his hand over her mouth, she was protesting . . ." Corner replied, "You need to plead with a woman, but sometimes a little force helps."'

Those listening were silent. They had been ready for anything except this astounding revelation. The woman's words had revealed a crime that had remained unseen and unpunished for months. This was the secret that the four men had guarded so jealously. They were guilty of the rape and murder of a poor young woman, one of the gravest offences and punishable by the law with the utmost severity.

Pisani pulled himself together and continued the interrogation. 'So you heard them confess that they'd killed a girl at the time of the fair. Where did they kill her? And what happened to the body?'

Lucrezia returned to her story. From what she'd understood, the four men had in some way or other got hold of the poor girl as soon as her friend had left her. They'd dragged her into a dark alley and then Biagio had had the idea of taking her to Corner's casino, a bachelor pad not far from where they were. Here the worst had happened: the girl had probably been raped and now she was dead. That much was clear from what they'd said. They'd then pulled themselves together, to some extent, and had come to her house to decide how to dispose of the body.

While Lucrezia was talking, Marco was aware of something lurking at the back of his mind, a memory that was proving elusive. Then it came to him in a flash as he remembered Francesca Corner's words. 'Was this the girl,' he asked, 'who brought linen and other sewing to the Corner household and then disappeared?' It was the example the noblewoman had used to justify the maid's disappearance.

'Exactly,' confirmed Lucrezia, who had now decided to tell them everything she knew. 'They never mentioned a name, but I did hear them say that she lived in the Castello district. It was Biagio who took control in the end. Even though he was a servant, he seemed the most sensible. "I'll do it," he promised. "I'll get rid of the body. But I won't do it for free. You two" – he pointed at Corner and Labia – "you're so rich you wouldn't even notice it if you gave me enough to sort me out for life." They then argued for a long time, and at the end I heard that Biagio had got himself an elegant tavern and an income for himself and his mother.'

So much for having bought it with honest earnings, thought Marco. 'And what happened to the corpse?'

'That I don't know. Biagio's last words were, "We'll remove every trace and they'll all think she eloped with someone. The body's in the gondola, wrapped in a red cloak; I'll hide it so no one will ever find it and you'll have no further need to worry."'

Chiara's visions, the blonde-haired girl wrapped in a scarlet cloak, the gondolier, the screams and cries: it all fitted. He was seized by a longing to see Chiara and to look deep into her clear eyes.

The chamber was dumbstruck. Venice was a tranquil place and most of those present would never have come across stories of such an appalling murder.

'Tell me,' resumed Pisani, 'why have you remained silent for so many months and only now decided to write that letter offering this clue? You could have told me all of this when I first questioned you.'

Lucrezia sighed. 'As I've already said, Your Excellency, I was frightened they might turn on me.'

'And they provided you with a living.'

The woman pretended not to have heard. 'Strange things are now happening. There must be someone who wants to see them all dead, and I'm afraid that I'll be caught in the process.'

'It is strange,' concluded Messer Grando. 'Here we are, searching for the killers of Barbaro and Corner, and we discover that they are the ones guilty of a crime.'

Lucrezia was already on her feet, and the interrogation seemed to be over, when Zen took to the floor for the first time, having listened carefully to the entire proceedings. 'Just a moment, there's something else,' he said, turning to the benches. 'Perhaps the witness knows where Biagio Domenici is hiding.'

Of course. It was clear that Biagio had fled. Marco remembered Chiara's note, and her conviction that something was about to happen. There was a note of alarm in his voice as he turned to Lucrezia. 'Talk! Biagio is in danger – if you know where he is hiding, then we must reach him as soon as possible!'

The woman weighed up the situation and realised that, once in police hands, Biagio would no longer be a threat. 'I know that sometimes, when he was hiding from anyone who wanted to make him pay for some joke or other, Biagio would take refuge in a locanda.'

'There are over a hundred in Venice. Which one?' snarled Pisani.

'The Locanda del Principe,' confessed Lucrezia, still reluctant. 'It's on the Giudecca, behind the Redentore.'

'Quick!' Marco rapidly pulled off his wig and magistrate's gown. 'Let's go and get him.'

He was furious with himself. He'd been so shaken by Lucrezia's story that, had it not been for Daniele's question, he would have completely forgotten to ask her about Biagio's hiding place.

As the hearing adjourned, he gave orders. 'Four guards come with me, and you, too, Daniele. Tiralli, go and get two of the Avogaria's boats ready. We'll need six oarsmen, because gondolas would be too slow. We'll be down in an instant.'

Messer Grando, the clerk and other officials were at the door, while Lucrezia stood in the centre of the room.

'You're free to go,' continued Pisani, 'but don't leave Venice, because we'll need to question you again.'

Lucrezia didn't wait to be told twice. She slipped out of the room and before long stood poised, for an instant, in the palace gateway before vanishing into the alleyways behind Saint Mark's.

CHAPTER 20

The two *bissóne*, each powered by six rowers, cut through the waters of Saint Mark's Basin, heading for the island of Giudecca. It was nearing evening and the huge outline of the church of La Salute emerged like a phantom out of the misty air. The steersmen focused on avoiding the barges that were heading for the customs sheds and salt warehouses before nightfall. Marco and Daniele shivered as they sat in the uncovered prow of the leading boat.

'Do you think Biagio really is in danger? And why are you so keen to save a murderer's life?' Zen asked in puzzled tones.

'Because I need to understand.' Pisani was thoughtful. 'If the group is guilty of the crime that Scalfi woman told us about, it might be revenge that prompted someone to kill Barbaro and Corner. The next victims will be Biagio and Labia. But if we get to Biagio before this unknown person, we can arrest both of them: Biagio for having killed the girl in the scarlet cloak, and the other man for killing Barbaro and Corner.' For the time being, Marco had no intention of confessing, even to Zen, that Chiara's premonitions and her gifts as a clairvoyant had triggered his anxiety and his urgency to act.

'Shouldn't we first discover who the murdered girl was?'

'I'll know soon enough. I've already thought about that. But now we need to try and catch both murderers in a single move. Then I'll worry about Labia. By tonight I should know where he's hiding.'

Daniele preferred not to push his friend. The situation seemed extremely confused to him, but Marco seemed sure enough. But there was something that his friend was holding back from him, and Daniele knew that it was better to bide his time.

It was pitch-black by the time the two boats came alongside close to the church of the Redentore. Once ashore, Pisani, Zen and the four agents ran along a side alley for a short distance, guided by the lights and the music from an inn not that far away. It was a disreputable-looking place and Daniele left two of the men at the door before walking in with the others.

Inside it was like a cave, with a few lamps to lighten the darkness. Their flickering light showed small huddles of customers, some sitting around the tables, others leaning against the central counter. They were all staring at a pair of young and rather underdressed girls who were playing mandolins on a makeshift stage and singing a two-part song. Behind them, it was just possible to see the staircase leading to the upper floor.

An indistinct shape, crouching by the fire, turned out to be the elderly innkeeper, who was trying to fan up the flames so cooking could start. Zen spoke to him.

'Is there a certain Biagio Domenici staying here?'

The man struggled to stand, as if his knees were hurting. 'Biagio?' he said, to gain time, as if he'd never heard the name before. 'Who are you?'

'This is Avogadore Pisani,' announced Zen, 'accompanied by the Inquisition guards.'

'Ah, well, in that case . . . Biagio always told me never to let on where he was, but . . .' He patted his face dry with a corner of his apron.

'Well, where is he?' shouted Marco impatiently.

'Excellency, on the first floor, third room on the left,' hissed the inn-keeper between his teeth, and obviously with considerable reluctance.

Daniele grabbed a lamp off the table and the four men hurried up the stairs. The first room was deserted. When the door to the second was thrown open, a couple could be seen entwined in bed. Despite having her legs in the air, the woman seemed quite unperturbed at the inter-ruption, and she was clearly a whore like those in the room downstairs. This explained why the room was so crowded in the late afternoon. The third door was bolted on the inside.

'Biagio Domenici!' shouted Zen. 'You're under arrest. Open the door!'

There was silence.

At a sign from Pisani, the guards heaved against the door.

The innkeeper had appeared at the head of the stairs and started to shout. 'What are you doing? You'll wreck the place.'

The couple who'd been in bed, and were now half dressed, peered into the corridor.

The door gave way and the four men rushed into the room. They were met by a draught of cold air from the wide-open window. On the floor, a dark shape was visible at the foot of the bed.

'Lift him up and bring other lights,' shouted Marco, running to the window. It gave on to the rear of the building. A thick vine grew up the wall. At ground level a heavy man was picking himself up. He ran off, limping slightly, and was lost in the darkness of the alleys.

'You couldn't have done more. We came as soon as we knew . . .' Daniele tried to console Pisani, who was prowling around the room like a caged lion. 'But how did you know it was so imminent?'

They were alone in the room since the guards were now at the door, keeping the other customers at a distance.

Biagio's corpse, still warm, had been laid on the bed. The yellowish light of the lantern revealed a swollen face, bloodshot eyes and a rope, the usual thick, frayed length of rope, wound tightly around his neck, biting into the flesh. No doctor was needed here to verify the cause of death.

Biagio Domenici had been tall and well built. He had inherited his mother's hooked nose, which must have given him a predatory expression. His half-open lips still looked full and lecherous. He certainly hadn't been expecting the visitor, because he was informally dressed, his white chemise hanging out of his breeches.

There had clearly been a fierce struggle, as the room was a mess. A broken chair lay in a corner, the covers had been torn off the bed, and a heavy stick, with traces of blood, had been thrown across an armchair. By the door, a shattered terracotta jug lay in a pool of liquid.

Marco approached the corpse with a shiver of distaste and examined the head: there was a deep wound at the nape and the hair was matted with blood. 'That's what happened,' he remarked. 'It can't have been easy to overcome someone of Biagio's stature. The murderer knew this, and he brought a stick with him to knock him out. Then he strangled him like the others. But how did he get here before us?'

Daniele had been pacing anxiously up and down the room. 'Remember the young maid?' he suddenly said. 'Didn't she tell us that his mother had been forced to reveal her son's hiding place to someone? That was a mistake and a half! Basically, she handed her son to the killer and kept quiet when she spoke to us. How on earth did he manage to make her talk?'

'Well, she'll talk now, that's for certain. She'll confess everything, but it's too late, far too late.' Marco sighed as he stared into the darkness through the window. 'Let's go and hear what the customers have to say about this downstairs. Then we need to make arrangements for the body to be taken home.'

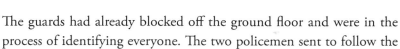

The guards had already blocked off the ground floor and were in the process of identifying everyone. The two policemen sent to follow the killer had returned empty-handed after pursuing him in vain through the dark alleyways and covered passageways.

Most of the clientele that evening belonged to a firm of builders from outside Brescia who had been asked by the parish priest to work on the restoration of the great church, the Redentore. Definitely the worse for wear after an evening's drinking, they had seen nothing and were soon sent on their way.

'What about you?' Zen asked the innkeeper. 'What can you tell us about Biagio? How long had he been here?' The girls and the few remaining customers listened in silence.

'I think he arrived last Monday. He was in hiding, that much was clear. He told me not to let anyone up to his room, and not to tell anyone he was here. His meals were served in his room. In fact, I don't think he went out all week.' The man talked without hesitation. Sitting at a table, he methodically swigged a bottle of white wine, sighing deeply between each mouthful.

'It wasn't the first time that he'd been here?'

'Of course not, but he'd never stayed so long before.'

Daniele turned to the girls, who were now dressed more modestly. 'What about you? Did you see anyone go upstairs? Didn't you hear the fight going on?'

'It was so noisy down here,' said the older girl, who'd been surprised in one of the upstairs rooms with a client. 'So that's mostly what I could hear. Although I did hear a chair falling over in the next-door room, but I didn't think anything of it—'

One of the younger girls interrupted. 'I saw someone,' she said. She had the complexion of a peach and her blue eyes still had a glimmer of innocence. 'I saw a man going upstairs.'

'Tall, short, old or young?' urged Pisani.

'Well, he was certainly tall, but he was wearing a cloak and had a hat pulled over his eyes. I noticed him because, instead of stopping to listen, as most of them do, he grabbed a wine jug off a table and rushed upstairs, looking as if he had something to do.'

'I suppose you didn't notice whether he was carrying a stick?'

'If he had one, he must have hidden it under his cloak.'

There was nothing more to be done. Pisani and Zen climbed, dead tired, back into the boats and were rowed back to the palace.

'You know what's going to happen, don't you?' Daniele said. 'Three people have been killed and, for the time being, we can't say anything about the murder of the girl from Castello, so soon rumours will be rife around the city that there's a murderer on the loose who goes around strangling people at night for no good reason.'

'Although you and I know quite well that there is a motive,' reflected Marco, 'and the killer might be Ibrahim, the Turk, who is trying to cover up his espionage dealings because, if the inquisitors got wind of them, he'd be banned from Venice for good and couldn't do business here any more. But it might also be someone linked to the girl who was killed. Although why they'd wait so long is a mystery!' By now they'd arrived, and Marco stepped ashore before concluding, 'But I'll soon know where the girl was and tomorrow I hope to have more precise details about her disappearance. I've asked Tiralli to look through the files.' Marco turned to his friend. 'Why don't you come and see me on Sunday, and we can talk about it then? I'm hoping Chiara will join us,' he said.

'In that case, I'll definitely be there. A quartan fever wouldn't keep me away. I can't wait to meet the enchantress who's bewitched you.' Zen smiled.

You're closer to the truth than you realise, thought Marco as he embraced his friend goodbye.

It was already dinner time and the ducal palace was half empty. Marco found Nani waiting for him in his office. The fire was out, so the young man was impatiently jumping up and down, trying to keep warm.

'I know everything, paròn,' he burst out. 'I know where Labia is.' Then, at a sign of encouragement from Pisani, he went on. 'This afternoon I went for a wander around his family's palace. The Labias are a suspicious lot and it's not easy to bluff your way in. But then I spotted a maidservant who was coming back with a large bundle of laundry. I offered to help her carry it and soon I was inside. She then felt obliged to offer me a glass of water, and, as always, we soon got talking . . .'

'Get to the point,' said Pisani with some impatience.

'It seems that young Paolo has a fairly disreputable lifestyle, and he left, very suddenly, a few days ago to go to the family villa on the mainland. To be precise, he left on Tuesday 12 December, just as all his peers were attending Piero Corner's funeral.'

'It's an odd time of year to go off to the villa,' said Marco. Most Venetians usually went to their country villas for the *villeggiatura* in the early summer and returned in September after the grape harvest. But right now, in December, the villas around the Brenta would be deserted.

'Well, it was obviously an excuse. He went to Villa Labia in Mira, but he wasn't alone. Apparently, he had an escort of six of the strongest male servants and gondoliers, all of them capable of wielding a sword.'

'So at least he's safe and I can go and see him whenever I want,' said Pisani – although it had to be said that he was less concerned about the safety of this wretch and more about the fact that now Labia was the only one who knew how that poor girl from Castello had met such a terrible end. 'Now,' he continued, 'you can take me to Calle Venier.' Nani struggled to repress a smile. 'But first I want you to stop off briefly at Palazzo Corner. I need you to check something with your friends there . . .'

Pisani waited patiently in the gondola while Nani went into Ca' Grande. He came back half an hour later, looking very pleased with himself.

'That was easy,' he said, laughing proudly as he sketched a bow, like a real-life harlequin. 'I hope Your Excellency will remember his humble servant at New Year.'

Marco stretched out to cuff Nani affectionately around the ears as he stepped aboard. 'Go on, tell me.'

'You were quite right. There was a young seamstress who came to the Corner household to deliver sewing ordered by Signora Francesca. Do you remember Elvira, the maid who flirted with me in the kitchen the other day? Well, she got to know her because she would occasionally stop to chat. A good girl, she says, engaged and soon to be married.'

'And who was she?'

'Her name was Marianna Biondini. She was a sailor's daughter from Castello. Apparently she lived in a calle overlooking Rio Sant'Anna.'

'What did she look like?'

'Elvira said she was quite pretty, and elegantly dressed, with blonde hair. But at some point – she thinks it was in the spring, last year – she stopped coming. Signora Corner was extremely annoyed because she'd relied on her as a seamstress. She sent one of the servants to Castello and they came back with the news that the girl had run away from home.'

After so many false trails, here at last was something concrete. 'Nani, you have my permission to ask for whatever you want,' promised Pisani as the young man started to row, guiding the boat into the side canals towards Chiara's house.

Chiara herself opened the door, looking anxious and tearful.

'Chiara . . .' he murmured, walking into the hallway. 'Chiara . . .' He looked down at her in the light from the staircase. 'Chiara . . .' He held her gently to him, stroking a curl back from her face. He had an overwhelming desire to kiss her, but he held back.

She smiled, looked up at him and brought her lips to his. At last, he felt the softness of her mouth and sensed its rose-scented sweetness.

'Chiara, I've missed you so much,' murmured Marco at last, as the strain of the last few hours dissolved. 'Will you allow me to stay here for a while?'

He was a Pisani, the city's highest magistrate, but at that moment he felt like a beggar. He had been shaken more than he cared to admit by Lucrezia's dramatic revelations that morning, the race to find Biagio at the inn and the violence of his death. But more than anything, he couldn't stop thinking about the girl and how she had died.

Chiara took his hand and led him upstairs. 'Perhaps you've not eaten yet? And neither has Nani. I'll look after you now, and Nani can go into the kitchen, where Marta will give him whatever he likes.'

She sat Marco down at the dining table and served cold meat and a delicious glass of cool white wine from the Euganean Hills. She watched him as he ate. His tired face and sad, deep eyes filled her with unexpected emotion. It was as if she had known him for ever, yet her heart was beating with the fear of losing him. She would have loved to caress his face, hold him close and make him smile.

After dinner, they sat on the divan, Marco now relaxing as he held Chiara's hand between his own. Then he told her about the tumultuous events of the day. Finally, he asked the question that had been on his mind since the morning. 'How did you know that something awful was about to happen? You didn't try to have another vision, did you?'

'No, sometimes I just have these strong premonitions, which leave me perturbed and worried. That's why I warned you to take care. I was terrified that you might be the one in danger.'

'Why?' asked Marco impetuously. 'Would you be sad if something happened to me?'

Chiara blushed and looked down. 'I don't quite know what to say. Some days ago you confided that you were terribly antisocial and wouldn't know how to court a woman, but I'm not familiar with such social finesses either.' She twisted the stray curl that hung down her neck. 'Yes, Marco, I want you to be happy, for ever.'

'Do you know what that means?' Marco spoke for them both. 'We love each other, Chiara.' He laughed. 'I love you, and you love me. We are in love!'

He held her close and buried his face in her hair. It was smooth and perfumed.

'I am so happy,' he whispered. 'Good Lord, it has been so long,' he went on, pulling back from the embrace, 'since I've felt as I do right now! Finding you is like a gift from heaven, one I dared not hope for any more.'

They looked at each other. Their reservations had been swept aside and there were no more barriers between them.

They were brought back to the present by a quiet knock. 'Excuse me, Your Excellency.' Marta's head appeared around the door. 'I've made a cup of hot chocolate.' It was the housekeeper's way of checking that her child was safe.

The couple turned towards her, smiling.

'There's no hurry, my love,' murmured Marco. 'We have all the time we want.' In response to the elderly woman, he said, 'On Sunday, dear Marta, you must accompany Chiara to lunch at my house. It's high time she sees where I live, and I want to introduce her to my friend, Daniele Zen. You, too, you'll have to summon up the courage to meet my Rosetta: she's very nosy and complains a lot, but she's the salt of the earth.'

CHAPTER 21

On Saturday morning, in the privacy of his office, Pisani looked at the papers that Tiralli had found in the archives. These were the folders relating to people who had disappeared in the spring of 1751. Given that there were only three, it did not take long for Marco to confirm the victim's identity.

The first folder was about a corn merchant who had vanished, leaving a welter of debts. Then there was the case of a young fisherman who had failed to return one morning after a storm. A week later, his boat had been found, empty, high and dry on a sandbank. These accidents were rare, but they did happen. The last folder seemed thinner than the others, but it bore the name of Marianna Biondini.

Marco read the witness statements with care, and the outcome of any searches that had been made. The disappearance of Marianna Biondini, aged eighteen, a linen seamstress resident in Calle Grimana, Castello, had been reported by her aunt, Giannina Biondini, on Monday 24 May 1751. According to the report, the girl had gone to Saint Mark's Square with her friend Angela Sporti, the previous afternoon, and had never come home.

When the friend was questioned by the guards, she had declared that she and Marianna were on the way home together after sunset, when she remembered having promised to visit her godmother. At that point she left Marianna, and she did not know what had happened to her afterwards. The captain responsible for the case, one Giandomenico Brusin, had widened the search, in line with normal procedures. From the report he had subsequently written, it appeared that the girl lived with her aunt and her father, a sailor on a cargo ship, who was away from home at the time.

A fact then emerged that, according to Brusin, might explain the girl's disappearance. Marianna was engaged to Angela's brother, Giorgio Sporti, who, because of his size, went by the name Giorgione. He was an apprentice baker who also lived in Calle Grimana, and he worked for Mastro Luca in Campo San Zanipolo. When the police went to summon him for questioning, Giorgione was also missing and, according to his parents, he had boarded a ship bound for an unknown destination.

After a month, given that no traces of the girl had been found, either living or dead, the police had concluded that she must have left home voluntarily and had probably eloped with her fiancé. Giandomenico Brusin, captain of the guards of the Serenissima, had therefore announced that the case was solved.

Pisani angrily snapped the folder shut, picked his wig off the table where he had laid it and shoved it back on his head. Then he instructed Tiralli to send for this Brusin.

'Is this the way to carry out an investigation?' he said accusingly as soon as the man was ushered into the room.

Brusin had a square face adorned with a heavy black moustache. He reeked of wine despite the early hour and his uniform jacket was buttoned wrongly, both of which led Marco to surmise that he'd been sitting around with his jacket off, drinking, even though he was on duty. 'I . . . Excellency . . . I don't understand. What investigation? What did I do?' He was visibly quaking.

'This appalling piece of work! Perhaps this will remind you!' shouted Pisani, slamming the folder down on the table, producing a cloud of dust in the process.

The captain came closer to the desk, dragging his feet, and then leafed through the papers. 'Yes, that's right . . . it was about that girl who disappeared. But it was quite a while ago . . .' He still couldn't understand what he'd done wrong, but in the avogadore's presence, he thought it safer to keep his mouth shut.

'Have you nothing else to say? Did you do everything possible?'

Brusin scratched his head. He could vaguely remember the case, but the details now eluded him. 'We carried out searches. But we didn't find anything.'

'Of course not,' snapped Pisani. By now he was pacing around like a lion circling its prey, although every now and then he snatched at his gown so as not to trip. 'Did you check the sailing dates at the Arsenale and the fiancé's destination? Did you check whether a girl of her age had boarded some other boat in the days after Marianna Biondini disappeared? Did you question the girl's friend thoroughly, as well as the neighbours and her relatives? Were you aware of any problems she had had? Had she ever left home before? Was she the subject of gossip? Where did she go when she delivered the household linen she sewed? Was there a man who was bothering her? Did the family have any debts?'

Overwhelmed by such a stream of questions, Brusin cowered, hunching his shoulders and staring at the floor.

'Enough!' ended Marco, even more irritated by the man's reaction. He pointed to the door. 'Get out of my sight, and at least go and tidy yourself up. And if I ever find you drunk on duty again, I'll throw you into a cell without a second thought.'

Bowing nervously, Brusin retreated hastily from the room.

'That's not justice,' Pisani muttered. 'People like him don't give a damn about anything. Is it surprising that those criminals got away with it?'

Marco was still trying to calm down when Tiralli brought in a note that had just arrived via one of the many couriers who walked around the city delivering the post. The handwriting was uncertain, almost childish. *Your Excellency, Pisani*, it read, *the merchant Ibrahim Derali has just come into the tavern, and I am obeying your orders by writing to advise you immediately. I will try to keep him here for as long as possible. Your reverent servant, Lele.*

Marco sat for a moment longer, thinking. Then, he turned to Tiralli and said, 'Take the *bissóna* from the Avogaria and get there as fast as you can. You need to collect an important witness, but because he is a citizen of the Ottoman Empire, I can't send the police because it might look as though he was under arrest. Is that clear?' He smiled at the young man. 'We'd find ourselves in very hot water with the Sublime Porte. You'll need to use all your charm to persuade him to come here of his own will.' He stopped, as if struck by a sudden thought. 'And before you set off, stop by at Florian's and order coffee and pastries to be brought here in an hour's time. That's diplomacy too.' Then Marco explained to his secretary exactly where to go and what to do.

Jacopo Tiralli was rushing out of the office when he bumped into Maria Domenici, Biagio's mother, who was responding to a summons from the avogadore. Holding her mistress's arm was the young girl who had told Pisani and Zen about the man who, by shaking a bag of coins, had convinced Signora Domenici to reveal her son's hideout. It was clear that the young girl was terrified and feared that her role would soon be discovered. Marco gave her a quick sign of reassurance.

'Wait outside, Pina,' ordered her mistress in a trembling voice as she walked into the office.

Pisani was sorry to have summoned the old woman, but he needed to ask her an urgent question. After her son's corpse had been brought to her the previous evening, she was still clearly distraught and seemed to have shrunk in stature, struggling even to stand. The arrogance of the previous day had vanished without trace. She wore her good gown, but the lace on the bodice now hung limp and the odd grey hair was visible under her wig.

She curtseyed with effort, her face streaming with tears, and then walked forward to kiss Marco's hand. Marco withdrew it promptly, but he helped the old woman up and led her towards a chair.

'I regret having had to disturb you at such a time,' he said, 'but there is something I need to know in order to catch your son's murderer.'

'Ask, Your Excellency. I will do everything I can to help you.' She wiped away her tears with a very damp handkerchief.

'Yesterday morning you lied to me.' Pisani looked at her severely. 'And if you hadn't, your son would still be alive.' The woman bowed her head. 'You refused to tell me where he was hiding, and in doing so you let the killer find him before we did.'

'It's not true,' she said loudly, bursting into sobs. 'How could I have known . . .? My Biagio . . . how will I manage without him?'

Pisani waited for her to calm down. 'You must now tell me the truth. You refused to tell the law about Biagio's hiding place, but you did confide in someone else. Who was it?'

Signora Domenici gave a start. 'How did you know? Who told you?' she stammered.

'We have spies everywhere!' said Marco in a mysterious tone. He certainly did not want to involve the young maid. 'Here in the palace we know about everything that's going on in the city. So, who was he?'

'Well . . .' the woman started, 'I met him, but I never really knew who he was. He came to see me a few days ago, and he said that he needed to talk to my son.'

'And despite the fact that Biagio had insisted that you shouldn't tell anyone where he was hiding, you told the first person who asked.'

Signora Domenici blew her nose energetically. 'It would be best . . . if I told you everything. This man came to see me quite late in the afternoon. He seemed to be in a terrible hurry. He told me he owed my son a large sum of money and wanted to pay him. He even showed me a bag full of coins.'

'And couldn't you have told him to come back another time?'

'Of course not! He told me he was passing through Venice and wouldn't return for another year. So I told him where Biagio was, I thought it was the right thing to do.' She buried her face in her hands. 'Was he the murderer?' she whispered.

'Perhaps,' admitted Pisani. 'But what did he look like? Did he sound like a Venetian, and how did he dress? Was he Turkish? Did he tell you anything about himself?'

'I don't know,' she stuttered. 'It was dark in the room and I couldn't see much. I can't remember how he talked. But he had a commanding tone of voice, that's true, almost menacing. He kept asking me questions, and my head started to spin . . .'

Pisani could imagine the scene; the woman's shining, greedy eyes, her lack of focus. He felt angry. 'You must have had a glass too many, as usual,' he said accusingly. 'Go now, but if you remember anything else, come and tell me.'

With a frustrated sigh, Marco flung himself into a chair and tried to gather his thoughts before the arrival of his foreign guest.

The Ottoman merchant Derali was very different to how Pisani had imagined. He spotted him as he made his way through the secretaries' chamber, just as the waiter from Caffè Florian was putting the finishing touches to the refreshments laid out on the table between the two armchairs.

Ibrahim Derali was magnificently dressed, leaving no doubt as to his important status. Short and spry, he advanced at the head of a small procession. Jacopo Tiralli was jumping around ahead of him, pushing people aside to make way, and both were followed by Matteo Vitali, the merchant who stood guarantor for the Turks in Venice. Bringing up the rear of the procession were two Moorish servants, each bent under the weight of a rolled carpet.

Having reached the avogadore, Derali made an elaborate bow. 'I came as soon as I could, to obey your orders, Your Excellency,' he said. His Italian was very good. 'And I took the liberty of asking Signor Vitali to accompany me, in case you needed to talk business. But, before we start, please do me the honour of accepting this humble gift.' He gestured to the servants, who started to unroll the carpets before Pisani.

For a moment, Marco watched in silence. Derali was dressed extremely elegantly in a short, closely fitted black velvet jacket with gold embroidery. He wore ample, dark-coloured pantaloons tucked into the finest leather boots. Over one arm was a cloak made from the finest cloth, which was as white as his turban. His dark face had regular features and an aquiline nose typical of his people, and he boasted a neatly cut black beard.

Marco reflected, with some disappointment, that he was undoubtedly shorter than he had imagined. From what the witnesses had told him, he had formed the idea of a much larger, heavily built man. To cap it all, he had himself seen the killer last night, and he could swear that he was considerably taller than Ibrahim Derali, and a good deal stouter. What was more, Derali was not limping.

'I am most grateful for your kindness,' he said at last as he invited his guest and the Venetian merchant to sit in the chairs. 'But you must know that magistrates are unable to accept any gifts. However, I am delighted by the thought and please let me accept in principle, if not in practice.' He indicated that the servants should carry the carpets away, while Jacopo Tiralli sat down in a corner to discreetly take notes. 'Moreover, my note was not an order,' he clarified diplomatically, 'but an invitation.'

Derali sat back in the chair and waited. He appeared relaxed, but his dark eyes were alert.

Pisani cleared his throat. 'I am told,' he began, 'that you are one of the most influential Ottoman merchants here in Venice.'

The Turk smiled suavely. 'Thanks be to Allah,' he declared, 'my business affairs are flourishing. As you have seen, I bring the most beautiful carpets from Anatolia to Venice. Our women weave them in the villages, using traditional designs, and I sell them all over Europe. What's more,' he added, 'I also import spices. And I return to my country with the matchless Venetian silks and the magnificent glass made in Murano.'

'Do you come from Constantinople?'

'No, I am from Smyrna, and down by the port I own the largest warehouses in the entire city.'

Matteo Vitali joined in as he served coffee. 'Signor Derali is a man of impeccable standing and is well known throughout the Ottoman Empire for the value of his business dealings.'

It was a warning to treat the guest with respect. Marco realised that the conversation would be one where much was left unsaid.

However, he pressed on. 'I imagine you have direct relations with ruling circles?'

Ibrahim leaned back and crossed his legs. 'You are asking whether the products I import from Venice are also purchased by the court? Of course they are. Our sultan, Allah protect him, and his dignitaries are highly appreciative of Venetian silks and glass.'

He's certainly sharp, thought Marco, noting how Derali had elegantly evaded the question. Marco could not now press him on his relations with the court without creating a diplomatic incident.

He decided to try another tack. 'I hear, Signor Derali, that you patronise the tavern owned by Signora Domenici on Fondamenta del Megio.'

The merchant's dark eyes flashed. 'You can't have invited me here,' he remonstrated, 'to discuss how I pass my free time? However, it's true, I do often go there because it's close to our warehouse here and I know I will find compatriots there. But I can't imagine what use this information is to you.'

Pisani was not put off. It was clear that Derali was on guard because he had something to hide and this whole set-up was intended to ward off awkward questions. 'You were often seen talking,' Pisani continued, 'with the landlady's son, Biagio Domenici, and his friend Barbaro. However, perhaps you may have heard that both were killed recently, along with their other friend, Piero Corner.'

'I don't see how this can possibly concern Signor Derali,' intervened Matteo Vitali, clearly annoyed. He then proceeded to provide his client with a cast-iron alibi. 'He only returned to Venice the day before yesterday, on the *Fulminante*, after being away for a couple of months. You can check.'

Ibrahim shrugged and smiled as he sipped his coffee. 'Yes, I've heard about the tragedy,' he admitted quietly, accepting Pisani's challenge. 'The news in Venice travels quickly. Before I left earlier this autumn, I did chat to Barbaro and Domenici occasionally,' he confessed. 'But I never saw Piero Corner. What amazes me, however, is how such a ferocious killer is still at large and unpunished in a peaceful city like Venice.'

It was clearly a provocation. Derali had understood that Pisani was trying to link him to the murders, but Vitali's alibi had let him off the hook.

'When investigating a crime,' explained the avogadore, 'every detail, however small, can prove useful. When you spoke to the two victims, what impression did they make on an acute man like yourself?'

The Turk immediately grasped Pisani's game. 'I certainly didn't admire them,' he admitted, 'but they were good company, especially Barbaro, and I enjoyed listening to their stories. They were always looking for ways to make money, and once or twice they even suggested that I might like to join them. Can you imagine! Latterly they promised me valuable information, which they would share with me on my return. I think they hoped this would make their fortune. I understood immediately that this was some shady deal, and I kept my distance.'

Was he telling the truth? Or had he encouraged them? Pisani would never know, but Derali's message to him was unequivocal: he had never touched the stolen documents from the Arsenale. Pisani knew there would be little more to be gleaned from the man, so he diplomatically turned the conversation to more general topics, before thanking him for his time and rising to show the meeting was at an end.

When they had gone and he was alone again, Marco sent a note to Cappello asking him to check the registers for a record of Ibrahim Derali's presence on the inbound ship, the *Fulminante*. It was entirely unnecessary, because it was clear that the Turk had nothing to do with the deaths: he'd not even been in Venice on the crucial days, and had never received the documents, so even if he were involved in the organisation of the spy operation, it could never be proved. Lastly, and perhaps importantly, he was skinny, and the murderer – or the man Pisani himself had seen – was well built.

The inquiries would have to focus elsewhere.

CHAPTER 22

By midday it had started to rain, a heavy rain that penetrated one's clothes and left one soaking, but Marco was not so easily discouraged. He had a quick bite of lunch at Menegazzo's and then, without stopping to read the papers, he set off on foot towards Castello.

Along Riva degli Schiavoni, icy squalls blew the rain straight at him and Marco had to wrap his cloak tighter and pull down his hat. Any passers-by he occasionally met were also walking head down and making straight for their destinations. Looking out towards the Lido, he could see how the grey sea had been whipped up by the wind into white-crested waves.

Marco was sure that he would at long last learn more about poor Marianna's disappearance when he reached the house where she had lived. He would talk to her aunt and to the neighbours, and perhaps her friend. Of course, he wouldn't let them know about the manner of her death. Lucrezia Scalfi's account still needed to be verified.

The boatyards around Saint Mark's Basin, where gondolas and small commercial vessels were built and repaired, were deserted. Marco walked past the Arsenale and the Marinarezza houses reserved for specialised workers and headed up the paved street of Rio Sant'Anna. The rain beat down on the canal, creating dark waves.

It was not difficult to find Calle Grimana, a small alley preceded by a passage that ended on Rio Tana, beside the Arsenale. He was looking for a two-storey house with a pink plaster façade. Marco lifted the brass knocker and let it fall.

'Who's there?' A window on the second floor opened a fraction and a woman's face appeared briefly. 'I'll be down right away, signore.'

Marco heard the respect in her voice. There was a sound of hurried steps on the stairs and then the door opened to reveal a good-looking and primly dressed woman, her copper-coloured hair gathered into a neat bun.

A pair of inquisitive blue eyes peered at him for a moment, registered amazement, and then the woman backed into the hall, curtseying. 'Your Excellency, to think you are here in my house, and on such a day! Please come upstairs, where the fire is lit.' She held a hand to her heart. 'Is there any news?' She was frightened now. 'Follow me, I'll lead the way.' And she headed back up the stairs.

Marco had a glimpse of two neat bedrooms on the first floor, and then he entered a large, comfortable kitchen. 'How do you know who I am?' he asked, taking off his cloak and sitting down on a bench by the fire. Feeling at home, he stretched out his legs to dry his boots.

'I doubt if there's anyone in Venice who doesn't recognise Avogadore Pisani. I've wondered so often about coming to see you after my niece's disappearance . . . But have you found her? Is that why you're here?' Her words were rushed and she looked pale.

'No news, I'm afraid, signora,' lied Marco. 'But we have started the inquiry afresh and I'm here to ask you a few questions. You must be Marianna's aunt, if I'm not mistaken.'

Momentarily the woman seemed a little calmer. 'Yes, I am Giannina Biondini, Marianna's aunt and her father's sister. What can have happened to my poor little girl?' Her eyes filled with tears. 'But what can I be thinking of? You must still be chilled, so let me make you some coffee.'

While she was busy at the stove, Pisani looked around. The room was welcoming, with two benches beside the hearth, each filled with embroidered cushions. To one side was a well-polished wooden table with a dresser behind it, and in another corner was a pair of comfortable armchairs. A couple of oil lamps added a warm glow on such a gloomy afternoon. Steaming on the stove was a large pan, which gave off a wholesome smell of broth. This was not a poor household.

They drank the coffee at the table, accompanied by some delicious biscuits.

'They were Marianna's favourites,' sighed her aunt. 'I made them this morning because my brother came home a few days ago from one of his trips. But I'm wasting your time. I am honoured that you came to question me in person. I could have come to the ducal palace in order to save you time. Please tell me how I can help.'

Marco instinctively felt a deep sense of respect for this woman, so he began, 'Signora, I've come to ask you to go over, once again, the sequence of events on the day of your niece's disappearance. Some details may come to light that might be useful to our search . . .'

'My niece,' she began, 'was a simple girl, you know, but very beautiful and kind. I brought her up because her mother – God rest her soul – had been ill for years with a bad chest. She was very delicate, and after giving birth to Marianna, she went into a decline. She died when the child was just seven.' Giannina wiped away a tear with her apron. 'I was already living with them,' she went on. 'I was there when Marianna was born, so when her mother died the child became my entire life. She was the apple of her father's eye too. My brother's a good shipwright and he is often away on the ships for months at a time. But he's well paid and we've never lacked for anything. As for Marianna, my brother was determined to bring her up like a signorina.'

'I was told that she worked,' interrupted Marco.

'Yes, that's true. Her father didn't want her to be lazy, or grow fanciful, so I introduced her to a refined trade. She was a linen seamstress in a workshop not far from here. And while she worked, she also set things aside for her own marriage coffer.'

Marco remembered that the police folder had mentioned something about a fiancé. 'Was she soon to be married?' he asked.

Giannina stood up to go and stir the fire. A stream of sparks lit up the dark interior of the fireplace. 'Yes, certainly,' she said, turning to face Pisani. The reflection from the flames served to highlight her copper hair. 'It happened just a few months before the wedding.' She turned back to the window to hide her tears. When she started to talk again, her voice sounded unsteady. 'She was supposed to marry in September, when her father was due home. Even the dress was ready . . . look, Your Excellency.'

She walked over to a cupboard and opened the door to take out an ornate silk dress, embroidered with tiny pearls. As she replaced it, her sobs were audible again.

'I've not moved it since then, just in case she comes back . . . Without her, the house feels so empty, and so quiet!'

'And what of her fiancé?'

'The best sort of young man, and they'd known each other since childhood. We all knew that they'd end up marrying each other. His name was Giorgio Sporti, and he was Angela's brother – Angela's her best friend. Everyone called him Giorgione because he was so strong and large. It was wonderful to see them together: she so blonde and delicate, and he a strapping lad.'

'Why talk about him as if he's dead too?'

Giannina sighed. 'After Marianna disappeared, he vanished as well,' she said. 'He worked as an apprentice baker for Mastro Luca in Campo San Zanipolo, but he had plans to open his own bakery soon and had started to look for a house where they could live together.' She smiled as she remembered. 'He used to work all night until dawn, but the family lives in this street opposite us, so every morning he'd stop for a moment and bring Marianna a freshly baked loaf, straight from the oven. The scent would fill the whole house. Marianna would make him coffee and they'd chat for a while, then she would go to work and he'd go off to bed.' Giannina pulled a handkerchief out of her apron pocket to dry her eyes. 'He'd already given her a ring, with a diamond. You know, one of those mementoes that are now fashionable when a couple becomes engaged. They were happy together.'

'How did he disappear?' Marco tried to hide his own emotion by pressing ahead with the questions, but the memory of Lucrezia's revelations was making him increasingly angry.

'The realisation that she wasn't coming home didn't dawn until a few days after Marianna disappeared.' Giannina hid her face in her hands before summoning the courage to continue. 'The police told us that she must have run away with a man . . . that girls always have secrets, and that we shouldn't worry because she'd come home again, sooner or later, perhaps with a child in her arms.'

Typical Brusin, thought Marco. Another telling-off was clearly in order.

'Giorgione couldn't bear it any longer. Even the stones reminded him of her,' she went on, 'so he boarded a ship whose crew needed a baker. We've not heard from him since.'

'And the police?'

'Oh, they were quite satisfied. A few weeks later, on a whim, they came back to question him, and when they heard that the ship had left, they came to the conclusion that the pair must have eloped and they could stop looking for Marianna. They said that she couldn't be dead, because they'd not found a body, so she must have gone off with her fiancé. I kept telling them there was no reason for the young couple to leave, but they refused to listen. In fact, I was on my own at the time, because her father was still away at sea.'

'Tell me about the day itself,' interrupted Pisani, standing up and walking back to the bench by the fire.

The woman sat down opposite him and gathered her thoughts for a moment. 'It was 23 May, a Sunday afternoon. The Sensa fair had just opened in Saint Mark's Square, because that year, if you remember,

Ascension was on the 28th. You know how keen girls are to go to the fair, with all the stands selling frippery, articles of clothing, glass decorations and things for the house. But Marianna had just one thing in mind: a cloak made from Venetian scarlet . . .'

Chiara's vision immediately came to mind . . . the cloak that had become a shroud.

'She'd wanted one for some time,' continued Giannina, now wholly immersed in memories. 'It was very expensive, but her father, who couldn't refuse her anything, had given her the money before he left, and so that day . . . that cursed day . . . she and her friend Angela went off in the middle of the afternoon. I never saw her again.'

Heavy steps were coming up the stairs and Giannina broke off. Silhouetted on the threshold was the powerful figure of an older man. As he walked in, Marco noted that he wore the clothes of a shipwright from the Arsenale under the ample folds of a heavy cloak. His weather-beaten face was deeply lined, but his hands were protected by woollen gloves. When he saw the avogadore, he stood still for a moment.

'Here is my brother, Your Excellency, Marianna's father.' Giannina introduced him as she helped the man take off his cloak. 'Avogadore Pisani has taken the trouble to come here because he wants to reopen the case of Marianna's disappearance. I pray to heaven that he may find her!'

Biondini sketched a bow but could not help grimacing in pain. 'Poor Marianna,' he murmured, 'she won't come back. But at least let her rest in peace.' He reached for a flask of wine from the dresser. 'Can I offer you one, Your Excellency?' When Pisani refused, he sat down at the table and poured himself a glass. 'You must excuse me,' he went on after he had drunk a mouthful of the golden liquid. 'I'm numb with cold. I'm not a refined man, Avogadore Pisani, but I am honoured by your presence in my house and your interest in my daughter's disappearance. But' – tears welled into his eyes as he went on – 'it's been a year and a half.' He hung his head. 'I have no reason to hope that I'll ever see her again. I just want to give her a Christian burial.'

'Why do you think she's dead?'

The man's voice was a monotone. 'Marianna can't have left of her own accord. She was content here, she loved Giorgione, she couldn't wait to become his wife. I wasn't here when she disappeared. I'd just left on a trip to Syria because we had cargo to deliver there. When the ship arrived in port, I found a letter from my sister which had got there before me. She wrote to tell me that Marianna was seriously ill.'

'I didn't want to tell him out of the blue, because he was so far away and couldn't do anything,' explained his sister. 'Anyway, for the first few days, I hoped that she might still come back.'

'And then a few months later, Giannina sent me another letter. By then she'd given up all hope, but to make things easier for me she told me that Marianna had died from her illness. You can imagine how I felt. As a result, all that time I knew nothing about her disappearance.'

'When did you find out?'

'Only two or three days ago, when I came back to Venice. Last autumn, when I received Giannina's second letter, I was so shaken that I couldn't face coming home and living here without my Marianna. I found myself a job in the Ottoman capital, where we Venetian shipwrights are always welcome, and I stayed there until late November, when I bought a berth on a passenger ship.'

'And what did you do when you heard she'd disappeared?'

'What could I do? I realised immediately that she hadn't eloped, and nor had she been kidnapped, as my sister hoped. Marianna was clever, and she knew how to read and write. If she'd been kidnapped, she'd have found a way of letting us know. And why would anyone kidnap her anyway?'

'What do you think happened?' pressed Pisani.

'I don't know,' sighed Biondini, hanging his head again. 'But one thing I'm sure of is that Marianna won't come back. My only hope now is to find her body . . .'

These poor people! Her aunt couldn't bear to think of it, but her father refused to countenance any illusions about her fate. Marco promised himself that he'd find the body at all costs, at least so it could be buried. It would hardly be a consolation, but it would be better than this uncertainty.

'You were telling me about the day of her disappearance,' Marco went on, turning back to Giannina.

'Everything that happened after Marianna left home I only know from what her friend, Angela Sporti, told me later. Perhaps it would be better if you spoke to her directly.' She walked over to the window. 'If you look over there, you can see where she lives: in that house at the end of the calle, overlooking Rio Tana. And she can tell you more about Giorgione.'

As he made his way to the Sportis' house, Marco felt a twinge of remorse because he'd not told them his reasons for knowing that the girl was dead. But first he needed to know what had happened to her corpse.

CHAPTER 23

The kitchen in the Sporti house was a large, dark room on the first floor of the building at the end of Calle Grimana.

Marco had knocked on the front door and after a short wait it had been opened by a pretty girl with masses of brown, curly hair that hung down over a simple pale blue dress. It was Angela. To start with, she stared with indifference at the distinguished figure standing outside the door, but then, on hearing his name, her indifference turned into plain embarrassment. She was alone in the house, and on the long table in the kitchen were rows of bowls filled with Murano glass beads which she was threading on to long strings.

As Marco explained the purpose of his visit, Angela's large black eyes widened in wonder, then concern and, finally, outright terror.

'Your Excellency,' she stuttered, 'you want to know what happened that day when Marianna went missing. But I've already told the guards.'

Marco turned his most piercing gaze on her. 'I have reason to believe that you know much more than has been reported in the minutes.'

Angela sighed as she backed towards the table. 'I answered all of their questions.'

'I'm not accusing you, Angela. But I would like to question you myself. Because you know something that you didn't tell the guards, don't you?' he pressed, remembering Lucrezia's story. 'I don't want to subject you to a formal interrogation. But you must remember that poor Marianna has disappeared, and may be dead, yet no one has paid for this crime. You want to see justice done, don't you?'

'Do I . . . yes, of course . . . but I'm afraid. It's a story that's much bigger than me.' She looked over her shoulder apprehensively. A man's jacket was draped over a chair. 'I can't talk here,' she concluded. 'My parents will be home soon. I'll come to the ducal palace tomorrow and ask to see you.'

'Time is precious, Angela.' Marco smiled. 'Let's do it this way: come to my house now and you can make your statement in secret in the presence of a lawyer. Then I'll arrange for you to be brought back here.'

'Yes, I could come, but it's late and if my parents don't find me at home they will worry.' It had stopped raining, but it was pitch-dark and the fog again hung densely over the canal. Angela took a moment to reconsider, then she announced, 'But I could leave a note for my mother, explaining that I'm out for work. That would be all right.'

As the girl hastily scribbled a short note, raked the burning embers of the fire together to keep them safe, tidied away the bowls of beads and wrapped herself in a heavy shawl, Marco noticed that the Sportis were clearly poorer than the Biondinis. Although it was clean, the kitchen seemed bare, without any trace of food, and the atmosphere was sad, as if life for its occupants had at some point come to an end. It was strange, he thought, how a crime never affects the victim alone but triggers a chain of broken lives. There were always so many people whose lives would never be the same again.

They walked down Rio Sant'Anna, turned right on the street running beside the basin and soon reached the Arsenale Bridge. Notwithstanding the bad weather, a few gondoliers were waiting for customers. Pisani instructed one of them to go to Zen's office and collect the lawyer, and then he and the girl boarded another and headed for Marco's house.

◆ ◆ ◆

Angela greedily drank the chocolate that Rosetta served in Marco's study. After the cold and the darkness, the warm, well-lit room calmed her fears.

'Did you know Marianna well?' asked Daniele Zen, setting down his cup and picking up his notebook.

The question seemed to set her further at ease and she exclaimed, 'Oh, yes! We were like sisters, practically inseparable, in our free time at least.' Then she went on, 'She was a seamstress during the day. It was a good job, one that I would have liked, too, but my family didn't have the money to pay for an apprenticeship. That's why I thread glass beads. I don't earn much, but it's better than nothing. My father's a knife grinder and he goes from house to house. But in the evening Marianna and I would meet at her house, and on Sundays we would always go out for a walk together.'

'So it was quite normal for you to be together that Sunday,' commented Marco, 'on 23 May, and go to the fair.'

'We'd been planning it for weeks and we couldn't wait to go.'

Marco nodded. The fair, known in Venice as the Sensa, was always hugely anticipated by everyone throughout the city. It started a few days before the feast of Ascension and offered the city's artisans and retailers, and even its artists, a chance to present their wares and products. People came from all over Europe to visit the stalls which filled Saint Mark's Square. One could buy chandeliers, necklaces and mirrors from Murano, leather belts and gloves embossed with gold, jewellery, wigs, the finest linen trimmed with bobbin lace, handbags embroidered in petit-point, telescopes . . . the list was endless. Renowned weavers exhibited satins, wool and silk velvets, damasks and lampas in a rainbow of colours. The leading wholesale merchants of corn, salt, spices, oil, cured meats and rare Cypriot and Malmsey wines were also there.

Every day the stalls were thronged by crowds from all social backgrounds: scholars and intellectuals were drawn to admire paintings by the leading artists and the latest books published by the city's printers.

Noblewomen and the wealthier merchants' wives sought rare perfumes and jars of scented creams, powders and beauty spots, while commoners were content to choose from the ribbons and veils or copper dishes to embellish their kitchens.

The square resounded with the cries and shouts from all sides: women selling sweet, spiced fritters, filling the air with enticing scent; water bearers; fortune tellers who told all the girls that they were about to meet the love of their life; alchemists who praised the miraculous effects of their cures.

The high point came on Ascension Day itself when, from the Piazzetta, the doge boarded the magnificently decked-out vessel known as the bucintoro, to shouts and applause from the crowds and gunfire from the canons. Preceded by flagships from the naval fleet and followed by hundreds of gondolas and bissóne, also festively decked, the procession headed for the Lido fortress, where the ceremony of the Marriage to the Sea was celebrated.

After that, the fair stayed open for a few more days to give the retailers who'd travelled from afar time to wind up their business deals.

'Marianna,' Angela continued, 'was happy because her father had finally given in and made her a present of the money to buy herself a cloak of scarlet wool. She'd been longing for one for ages. She was pleased, and I remember her singing as we walked along.'

'Was it very crowded?' asked Marco.

'It was Sunday – Sunday 23 May 1751. I'll remember the date for the rest of my life. There were crowds everywhere, so we agreed that if we lost one another, we'd wait under the campanile. But we tried to hold hands so that wouldn't happen.'

'And what did happen?'

Angela sighed, twisting her hands. 'Everything went well to start with. Marianna chose her cloak and bought it, then we joined a group of people who were watching the acrobats. I remember then we bought some fritters and stood eating them in front of the lion's cage. Then Marianna saw the fortune teller and wanted to have her palm read.'

'And then?' urged Marco. Zen wrote down every word.

'It's strange, I'd forgotten about that episode . . . We started to queue and then, when it was her turn, Marianna showed the woman her hand. She must have been middle-aged, but she was made-up and was wearing a purple silk turban. She took Marianna's palm, examined it and then her eyes widened as she looked up at Marianna's face.'

The silence that followed was broken by a thud. They all turned to look at the bookcase. Plato had been asleep on one of the shelves and had suddenly jumped off, his tail on end, as if he'd seen a ghost. Crouching low, the cat crept across the floor to the fireplace and curled up in front of it.

'Go on,' murmured Marco, turning to the girl.

'The fortune teller looked at Marianna's palm once more, then she let go as if it was red hot and shouted – I can remember it as if it were now – "Take care, child, take care! The raven's wing is around you! If you see tomorrow's dawn, you'll be safe!"'

Marco shivered. Daniele sat rigid.

'And Marianna?'

'We were both puzzled and we didn't understand what the woman meant. There were no ravens. It was a beautiful day. But I remember that Marianna forced a laugh. "She must be mad," she said, and we walked away. But the fun had gone out of the afternoon, and it was shortly afterwards that we bumped into—' Angela stopped abruptly.

'Be strong.' Marco guessed that this was the crucial moment.

'Yes.' Angela hesitated, her eyes filled with tears. 'We met a group of young men who started to bother us.'

'What do you mean?'

'They started following us, making comments about our clothes, our looks, even making insolent jokes out loud. One of them in par-ticular was fixated on Marianna. He said to her, "Isn't it about time you came along with me, you blonde beauty? I know you fancy me."' Angela put her hands up to her mouth, which was trembling. 'He even said, "Come with me and I'll help to unlace that pretty bodice. Together we'll discover what's under your skirt."'

'What did Marianna do?'

'She blushed furiously and tried to run away, but we couldn't make any headway because of the crowds. I did my best to keep up with her . . . By then it was late and the sun had set. We tried to head for the narrow streets behind Saint Mark's in order to go home. We found an open doorway and hid in the passage. It was there that I asked her, "But who are they? Do you know them?"'

'Did she tell you?' A log fell, sending sparks shooting up the chimney. Plato jumped up and shot off.

'Yes. She told me that the most insolent was Piero Corner, a member of the patrician family that lives in Ca' Grande. She occasionally went there to deliver linen for his mother, and he had been bothering her for some time. He would follow her upstairs, try and touch her and invite her into his room. The others were often with him.'

'And who were they?'

'Marianna had heard their names from a maidservant who she was friendly with, a certain Elvira. One was Marino Barbaro, the other was Corner's gondolier, Biagio, and the third man – a short, ugly man – was called Labia.'

Angela gave a long sigh as if she had freed herself from a great weight. Marco and Daniele exchanged glances.

'Then what happened?' Daniele encouraged her this time.

'What happened next was the worst . . .' Angela drank a glass of water and seemed to regain some strength. 'We left the doorway, and there was no sign of the men. There was hardly anyone around, and it was now completely dark in the calle. There was a new moon at the time. Marianna wore her scarlet cloak and wrapped it tightly, as if she were cold. We headed towards Campo San Zaccaria, where the darkness was lit by a single lamp. Here – and I'll never stop blaming myself for this – I remembered that I had to go and see my godmother, who lived close to Campo Santa Maria Formosa. I didn't want to leave Marianna, but she didn't seem worried. "Go," she said. "It's only a short distance between here and Riva degli Schiavoni, which is full of people; there's no danger any more. The four of them have tired of following us. Nothing could possibly happen to me."'

'And you left her . . .?'

'You can imagine how often I think about that moment!' Angela broke down and cried. The others were silent. 'I'd only just left her and was heading up the narrow street leading to Santa Maria Formosa,' she went on, her words interrupted by sobs, 'when I heard the shouting. They were male voices, probably men who'd been drinking. I was scared and I froze in the dark. I could hear them laughing and cracking jokes. Then I heard Marianna's voice shouting, "No! Help!" And the men laughed even more. But I just couldn't summon up the courage to run towards her. I left her alone with them. She cried out twice more before her voice became indistinct. Then I heard heavy steps again, running, and the men calling to each other, but now quietly. I realised they were coming into the side street where I was hiding . . .' Angela burst into fresh tears. 'I can't bear it any longer,' she sobbed.

It took a while before she was calm enough to talk. Marco gave her a handkerchief which he'd dipped into a bowl of water so she could wipe her face.

'Right beside me there was an alleyway and I hid there, behind a column. They passed so close to me. Two of them were holding Marianna, who was struggling, but I think she'd been gagged and I could see she was wrapped in the cloak. Then they vanished into the darkness.'

'And what did you do?' asked Zen.

'I went home. I kept hoping that she would come back. I hoped that even if they had . . . hurt her, they would let her go. Her aunt

Giannina came to ask me where she was a couple of hours later. She was worried and had hoped that Marianna was with me. I told her that we'd said goodbye in Campo San Zaccaria and that I'd not seen her since then, but the next day I knew already that she'd never come back. My conscience hasn't known a moment's peace since then.'

There were still so many loose ends, but the girl was exhausted. Marco and Daniele left her with Rosetta, who tried to revive her with risotto and a glass of wine. When they came back to the study, Angela looked less pale.

They sat down again around the desk while Plato, having enthusiastically cleaned his whiskers, curled up between them on a pile of papers.

Marco came straight to the point. He hazarded a guess and asked, 'Angela, have you told anyone else what you saw?' There was one name, another person whom the girl hadn't mentioned so far, but now she couldn't avoid it.

'I've never said anything to my father and mother, and not even to Giannina.'

'Why didn't you tell the police?'

The girl blushed. 'I was frightened. The captain called me into the interrogation room in the prison, but he only asked me where I had last seen Marianna. He seemed to be in a great hurry, and I think he might have been drinking.'

Ah, Brusin! You'll pay for this, thought Marco.

'How could I tell him about the young men who'd followed us, let alone give him their names? They were such high-sounding names too. Important people. If the guards had questioned them, they'd have said I was making it all up, and they'd have made me pay for it. I wouldn't have had the courage to show my face in the city, and Marianna was beyond my help.'

This was all true, thought Marco, glancing at Daniele.

'But then you did tell someone the truth, didn't you . . .' Daniele resumed.

Angela couldn't evade the question any longer. She drank a glass of water, hung her head and in a flat voice started to talk again. 'You'll have heard that my brother Giorgio was engaged to Marianna. When he heard that she'd disappeared, he went crazy. He walked all over Venice for two days, stopping people in the street, in the shops. At dawn he'd go and ask the fishermen landing at Rialto whether they'd found a body floating in the lagoon. Then he threatened to go to the head of police and make a scene.'

'But why didn't you come to me?' asked Pisani.

'We're simple folk,' said the girl. 'None of us ever thought about disturbing an avogadore.' Then she went on, 'My parents were worried that Giorgio would get himself into trouble, and he'd even stopped going to work. A neighbour who worked at the Arsenale found a place for him as a baker on board a ship that was leaving for the East. We had to convince him to go, almost compel him.'

'But before he left, you told him the truth.'

'He made me. He threatened not to leave unless I told him everything. Giorgio's not stupid and he'd realised that there was more to the story. So I made him swear that he'd keep my secret to himself and I explained that if anyone, even Marianna's aunt, ever knew the truth and then told others, rumours would spread and I'd be in danger. He promised and he left with our secret.'

'With the names too?'

'The names too.'

In the silence that followed only the crackle of the flames could be heard. Marco poured Vin Santo into the crystal glasses. The men drank, each deep in their own thoughts.

Zen broke the silence. 'But now he's back . . .' It was a guess.

Angela was quick to understand the insinuation. 'You don't think he's guilty of killing those three scoundrels?' Like everyone in Venice, she'd also heard about the crimes and the thought had clearly crossed her mind as well. 'My brother is not a murderer. He came back this summer, and he's no longer angry about Marianna, just very sad.'

'Where had he been all this time?'

'He hasn't said much about it. I know that he found work in Constantinople, as a port labourer, and then he found a job as a baker. He saved up quite a bit of money, and then he grew homesick and wanted to come home.'

'But he doesn't live with you,' concluded Zen aloud.

'No, he's found lodgings in the Ghetto Nuovo, where he works. He only stayed a few hours with us. He says he couldn't bear to pretend that life is still the same as it was when Marianna was alive. They grew up together, after all. They were so close.'

'Does he come to visit often?'

'No, we see very little of him.'

'Did he hear about the murders?'

'I don't know. It's been a month since I last saw him.'

While he sat thinking, Daniele played with Plato's tail, which annoyed the cat. After a while Marco said, 'But in all these months, Angela, are you sure you've never mentioned the names of those four men to anyone else?'

'Never. No one else knows.'

'That's why Marianna's family still don't know what happened to her.'

'No, and if I'd said anything, I'd only have added to their pain.'

CHAPTER 24

In the servants' dining room of Marco's house, next to the kitchen and overlooking the garden, Marta and Rosetta were seated at a table laid for Sunday lunch. From the sidelong looks, it was clear they were sizing each other up.

'I understand that Signorina Chiara is an orphan,' broke in Rosetta. 'Does she manage all right?' Marco's housekeeper was wearing a wide grey skirt and a lace shawl pinned with a cameo brooch.

Marta smiled. 'Her father – bless his soul – made sure that she was well prepared. He used to tell me, "She'll be a single woman, with a double burden; she must know how to manage a household and a business." He made sure that she learned all the techniques of weaving and how to design fabrics. This is one of hers. Isn't it beautiful?' She pointed to her gown, which was made from elegant crimson damask. 'Chiara also learned mathematics and accounting, she speaks French and English, and with her father she used to travel throughout Europe.'

'But Signor Renier didn't make any plans for the most important thing,' said Rosetta reprovingly. 'He didn't find her a husband, and it would seem that she is not that young any more.'

Marta's dainty features hardened, but she calmly picked up her fork to taste the steaming portion of rice and peas that had been served on a fine porcelain plate. Then she wiped her mouth with her napkin and sipped her wine. 'How can I put this, Signora Rosetta,' she started, in unruffled tones. 'The only girls who *need* husbands are those without any initiative, whether they're uneducated commoners or patricians who need someone to invest their dowry – if they have one, that is. You see, if she married, my Chiara would lose her independence, as her assets would be administered by her husband. She's not the sort of woman to leave others to manage her affairs while she sits around doing nothing.'

Just then Giuseppe came into the kitchen, looking even more elegant than usual in his livery and silk stockings, because on this special occasion he was serving at table. He was carrying a fragrant dish of fried fish and seafood, and hot on the butler's heels came Plato, tail held erect as a flagstaff.

Rosetta politely served her guest, and as soon as Giuseppe had left the room again, she commented, 'But His Excellency appears to be to her liking.'

Marta's patience was wearing thin. 'They're young, they're handsome and perhaps they're in love. What's wrong with that? If I'm not mistaken, both of them have experienced misfortune. If they're happy together, why do you want to interfere? Are you insinuating that Chiara's not good enough because she's not a noblewoman? I can assure you that your master would never find anyone better, even in the most emblazoned families.'

'Don't be offended.' Rosetta acknowledged that she had gone too far. 'The fact is that I've known the boy – I mean the avogadore – since he was born. I brought him up and he's like a son to me. Anyway, I must admit that no one could be more beautiful than Signorina Chiara.'

From the kitchen came the sound of energetic clapping. Nani and Gertrude the cook were having lunch around the table there, with old Martino and Zen's gondolier, Bastiano. Maso was also with them, as he had brought his mistress and her housekeeper in the firm's boat to Marco's house and had immediately been invited to stay for lunch. Nani had firmly placed himself beside him.

'What a magnificent woman your mistress is,' said Martino, turning to Maso. 'And with exquisite manners, a real lady. If you don't mind me saying, in the many years I've been working here with the family, I've seen several people of quality, but there's something special about her. I can't put my finger on it . . .'

'Yes, sir,' agreed Maso. 'She's also generous and kind-hearted. She's always told me that I'm good at my job and now she's teaching me how to weave the most complicated fabrics.'

Bastiano looked up from his plate. He had a healthy appetite and had done justice to the food until that moment. 'I hope my master, Avvocato Zen, will meet someone like her. But he doesn't seem to be trying very hard – indeed, sometimes I have to take him to one of those houses . . . you know where I mean. Of course, they're honourable women, the best in Venice, but I'm sorry all the same.'

'Young men, eh, what can you do?' sighed Martino, who all his life had dreamed of what it might be like to be in a courtesan's house. Instead he could only conjure up a rather unsatisfactory image of the temptations that he would now never experience.

'Stop making so much noise!' It was Giuseppe, bringing the plates back to the kitchen again. 'Those two can hear you next door, and I bet they can hear you in the dining room upstairs as well. You wouldn't be this loud if we were at Palazzo Pisani. The major-domo used to keep everyone under strict control there, and he still does.'

Everyone fell silent, but it was short-lived, for as soon as Giuseppe left the room Nani raised his glass to Maso in a friendly toast.

'What does your father do?' the gondolier asked him.

'My father?' repeated Maso, blushing furiously. There was really nothing to be ashamed of, but Maso couldn't help it. 'He has a fruit stall at Rialto. Mamma often helps him. I've also got two sisters, but they're young and still at school with the nuns. When Mamma heard that I'd been arrested – and what's more, arrested for murder – she fainted. The doctor came and wanted to use his leeches to bleed her. My father objected and, luckily, Signorina Chiara then arrived. She gave Mamma one of her remedies and she soon recovered. I must say, if your master hadn't done what he did . . .' He stopped, amazed at having spoken for so long.

'Yes, he's a good man,' commented Nani. 'Look at me: the Scolopi wanted to turn me into a priest. Imagine that! He took me under his protection, and here I am.'

'Remedies?' interrupted Gertrude. 'What remedies does this Chiara have?'

'Signorina Renier,' said Maso emphatically, 'was taught by her grandmother how to prepare syrups, poultices, medicines, for all sorts of illnesses. So many people come to her to be cured, and all for free, because she won't accept payment. She says that leeches and purgatives don't work, in fact they often do more harm than good.'

Gertrude was thoughtful for a moment, her low forehead deeply furrowed. 'That means she's a witch,' she burst out after a while. 'Your mistress is a witch.'

Maso turned an even deeper shade of red. 'A witch! How dare you!' he shouted. 'If anything, she's an apothecary. She knows all the herbs and their properties better than any of those high-sounding academics!'

It was old Martino who changed the subject. 'Tell me, Nani, given that you're always with him, what's the latest on the investigations into those three men who were murdered? At the market yesterday, the talk was all about this killer who's on the loose and goes around strangling people, and the authorities aren't doing a thing to stop him.'

'Just idle gossip,' said Nani loftily. 'I can't comment, you know, because of confidentiality, but I can tell you that my master's hot on the trail. I can say one thing for certain, though: the three who died were certainly not saints.'

'What, even Piero Corner?' interrupted Bastiano, who had stopped eating to listen.

'I can't say any more.' Nani made a gesture of biting his tongue. 'Yes, him too . . . Perhaps not now, but in the past . . .'

'To our good health! And to lifelong friendship!' In the airy dining room on the first floor, overlooking Rio San Vio, Daniele Zen raised his glass to Chiara, while Marco joined in the toast.

The lawyer had been bewitched by Chiara Renier from the moment he'd watched her disembark on the small jetty by Marco's house. Enveloped in her fur-lined cloak, and pink-cheeked from the cold after the boat trip, she looked like a creature from another world, with her tumbling curls and sky-blue eyes.

'You must be the famous Daniele,' she had said with a sudden smile.

'And you're the girl who has cast her spell over a magistrate,' Daniele had replied as he offered her his arm.

Then they had walked together towards the house, chatting like old friends.

'To lifelong friendship,' Marco repeated, beaming at his guests, delighted to see how well they were getting on. 'Now let's enjoy lunch, and then we'll move into my study and see where we are on the investigations.'

With Gertrude's help, Rosetta had excelled herself. The seafood antipasti were so delicate that they melted in the mouth; the rice blended perfectly with the peas, which had been brought specially from the mainland and must have cost a fortune. The huge platter of fried fish included tiny sole, tender octopus and red mullet small enough to eat in a mouthful. It was accompanied by grilled polenta with a side dish of pale pink prawns, anchovies and small flatfish called *zanchette*. Marco also noted that Rosetta had set the table with the best silverware and crystal especially for the occasion.

Daniele turned to Chiara to ask her a question. 'Tell me, how do you organise everything on your own? You create the designs for the fabrics, you train the workers, you correspond with your suppliers and customers, you keep the books, you attend the various guild meetings. Where do you find the time?'

Chiara smiled. 'My father was a wonderful teacher. He taught me how use my time wisely. My weaving shop focuses on quality, and so the volumes are not huge. The secret is to keep the accounts in good order and train the workers.'

Marco listened to them and felt happy. How long was it since he had had an ordinary moment of domestic serenity like this? This woman had the ability to put anyone at ease and to talk frankly. Perhaps not everyone, he admitted, because Rosetta still seemed to be on the defensive, but every time the austere Giuseppe came into the room bearing new dishes, Marco noted that he had a smile of approval on his lips. Nani, too, had been won over right from the first day, and here was Daniele, who seemed perfectly comfortable in her company.

'Marco tells me,' Chiara continued, looking at Daniele with a degree of curiosity, 'that you're not married, or even engaged, even though Venice is full of girls who'd be more than happy to oblige.'

Zen looked embarrassed. 'Well, yes, I've never really thought about it, although I now realise that I'm at the age when I should be thinking of having a family. Who knows what fate has in store for me . . .?'

'Would you like to know?' asked Chiara. She looked questioningly at Marco, who immediately understood.

'Watch out, Daniele,' he said. 'She can read your fortune. Do you want to, Chiara?' He smiled at her.

'Now that you've given my secret away . . .'

In the servants' dining room, Marta and Rosetta were eating dessert. They had made peace over Chiara. 'My master,' observed Rosetta, daintily sampling a sweet fritter, 'is a very rare sort of man. Do you know, Signora Marta, that he finances an orphanage entirely at his own expense? As for the amount of work he does! I often find him working late into the night over his papers. When he's dealing with a case he won't rest until he's got to the bottom of it. Of course, when his wife was alive, it was all very different!'

'Was he married?' Marta asked, curious to know more. Chiara had not told her anything.

'Oh, yes.' Rosetta poured some sweet Cypriot wine into her guest's delicate crystal glass. 'Poor Signora Virginia. May the Lord bless her and keep her! She left us twelve years ago, together with the young son to whom she had just given birth.'

Both women sighed. There was a stirring of friendship and the beginnings of a bond forming between them.

Rosetta broke the silence. 'But do you think they are really in love?'

'I've never seen Chiara smile so often,' remarked Marta, sipping her wine. 'In the evening she goes over to the window and looks at the sky, and every now and then I hear her singing.'

'My master doesn't even smile at the angels, but he's calmer and in a much better mood, that's certain. Tell me, has Signorina Chiara never been engaged?'

'No, never. She's very naïve in these matters, like a young girl. I don't want to see her hurt.'

Rosetta made a move to stand up so she could check how things were going in the kitchen and order coffee. But she sat down again quickly, with a grimace of pain. 'Oh, my back!' she exclaimed. 'When the weather's bad, these aches never go away. There doesn't seem to be anything I can do about it.'

'My dear Signora Rosetta, let me see what I can do.' When Rosetta looked at her with an enquiring glance, Marta added, 'For generations, the women of the Renier family have handed down secret recipes that can cure all sorts of illnesses. Every now and then, Chiara gets up at dawn and goes into the fields on the mainland to pick herbs, berries and bark, which she then uses to prepare the remedies her grandmother taught her. Chiara's mother died when she was very little, you know . . . I think she uses a tincture made from willow bark to treat these seasonal aches and pains. Apparently it's extremely old – Egyptian, even. It's quite miraculous. Tomorrow, I'll send Maso over with a phial for you.'

A gale of laughter came from the kitchen.

'Have you really never been with a girl?' Nani asked poor Maso, who was now even more embarrassed than ever.

'The problem is, I'm always on my own,' Maso said lamely. 'After work the other weavers all go off and I just go home. I can't exactly stop a girl in the street, can I?'

'After lunch,' promised Nani, 'I'll take you to the coffee shop behind La Salute. It's a respectable place, so there are no drunks or time-wasters there, but they're not snobby either. I'm not saying that you'll find any bourgeois daughters – they'd never be allowed to step outside the front door – but it's where the best maidservants in Venice go, and young widows, as well as some of the young market sellers. People of a certain standing. I always manage to meet someone to chat to, and on a good day, even a decent bed I can slip into.'

'Nani,' said Gertrude in scandalised tones, because she'd already set her sights on Maso. 'Aren't you ashamed of yourself? It's bad enough that you behave so indecently and brag about it, but that you want to drag a decent man like Maso along with you, that's really too much!'

'But it's not indecent,' laughed Nani. 'Love is the most beautiful thing in the world.'

'Here we are,' said Chiara pensively, holding Daniele's left hand, which he had offered somewhat timidly. 'You're a very balanced person, loyal to the end and highly intelligent, capable of analysing situations in depth. I'd say you're the ideal person to be a lawyer, and to act as a consultant to an avogadore.' She looked at Marco with a smile.

Daniele watched her, his curiosity mixed with trepidation.

'But . . .'

'Is there a "but"?' asked Daniele seriously, widening his blue eyes.

'Yes, look at these signs: your life line is long and free from illness. You have before you a career which will take you to high posts and will be very successful, but your heart line is troubled.'

'I disagree,' interrupted Marco. 'I know how many women he sees!'

'No, no,' Chiara objected. 'There's only one woman here.' Daniele went pale. 'Look, you see all the others – these little lines – but they don't count. This deep line, which is broken here, indicates a single, great love, a love that would seem to be . . . secret.'

'It's not possible!' Daniele's words came rushing out in the anguish of his embarrassment.

'Secret?' said Marco. 'Daniele has no secrets from me.' He looked at his friend's face, now a torment of confusion, and stopped talking.

Chiara immediately realised what was happening. 'Forgive me, Daniele, I've been indiscreet, as usual. I am led on by what I see in someone's hand and I don't realise that this might be uncomfortable—'

'Go on . . .' interrupted Daniele. He seemed lost and his voice was barely audible.

'If you want me to.' Chiara started again, while Marco looked on, dumbfounded. 'The woman you have always loved, and whom you will love for ever' – Chiara sighed as she spoke these words – 'she is not yours. You've always known, and this is why you have hidden the depth of your feeling from everyone.'

'And this is what's written on my palm?' asked Daniele in astonishment.

'On your palm and in your mind, which I can also read, thanks to your hand.'

'You frighten me,' exclaimed Zen. 'Who are you? A magician?'

Marco interrupted. 'Chiara isn't a magician, she's only a clairvoyant. All the women in her family have been seers. But she keeps it secret because it could lead to trouble. In fact, it was she who pointed me in the right direction in these investigations.' Marco told his friend about Chiara's visions and her powers as a healer.

'Good heavens!' Daniele exclaimed, while Chiara watched his reactions. 'Now I see why she's bewitched you. Oh, sorry, I see that's not a very appropriate word choice. But I've never told anyone about my secret love, not even Marco.' He looked down but went on talking, as if to himself. 'I know well that it's hopeless, but I can't let her go. That's why I pretend not to care when it comes to matters of the heart. She's an exquisite creature, but she was forced into an arranged marriage at a very young age. I know that she has feelings for me, too, but it's best for us both that we stay apart. It wouldn't do either of us good, and I would certainly never want a clandestine relationship.' He sighed, then smiled and said, 'Well, that's a weight off my chest. I've never spoken about it before, Marco, even to you, because I didn't want anyone's pity. Even now, I won't tell you her name, unless Chiara can read that, too, in my mind.'

'No,' Chiara reassured him. 'Names are beyond my powers. But I've not quite finished. Show me your palm again and be silent for a moment. Look at this point, Daniele,' she continued, 'here the line joins up again. It means that one day, indeed quite soon, there will be no need to maintain this secret. This isn't a hopeless love. There is a chance that you might be very happy, but you mustn't intervene, you must let events take their course. All will be well.'

Daniele gave a faint smile. 'It would be wonderful, but I don't dare hope. Her husband isn't an old man and he's still in excellent health.'

'That's strange; there is no sign of a marriage here. What I mean is this woman doesn't seem to be married . . . Are you sure? Is she not still engaged?'

'Yes, I'm sure . . . more's the pity. He's a well-known figure in Venice. She doesn't have children, but she certainly has a husband. Well,' he said in a resigned tone, 'I've now bared my soul to you. I trust you will respect my secret.'

'For us, it will be a sacred pact,' said Marco.

The three of them raised their glasses once again, this time with greater solemnity. At that instant, Giuseppe walked in carrying the coffee pot.

It was already getting dark, and in the servants' dining room Rosetta was stoking up the fire and lighting the lamps, while Marta sat on the sofa with a rug over her knees, enjoying a pastry.

'Of course, it would be bliss,' she suddenly said, as if following a train of thought, 'to have children around the house again. The older one gets, the more one longs for their laughter, their delight.'

Rosetta came to sit beside her. 'I would love to have children to care for again. The avogadore was such a delightful little boy. He would play jokes on me sometimes and then come and say sorry in such a serious little voice and give me a big hug.' She smiled at the memory. 'His mother, Signora Elena, is still a most beautiful woman, even today, but she wasn't the sort who left her children to the servants, and she was always personally involved in their education. Yet, in that little boy's heart there was room for me too.'

'Now that you've mentioned the Pisani family . . .' Marta thought that the time had come when she could dare to ask the question. 'If our two wards were to get engaged, Signora Rosetta, do you think the avogadore's parents would object to the fact that my Chiara is a commoner?'

Rosetta smiled at her new-found friend. 'Marta, you don't know the Pisani family . . . they are unique. They don't need anyone else's blue blood because they are aristocrats through and through, and that means they can choose to marry where they like.'

'Would they not be opposed to a marriage between . . .?'

'Signora Elena can't wait to see her son happily married again, after all that has happened. She'd welcome Signorina Chiara as a daughter.'

CHAPTER 25

It was mid-afternoon and in the study the lamps were already lit and the room was filled with the scent of the logs burning in the fireplace. On the marble shelf, a candelabra lit the portrait of Virginia, and its wavering flames appeared to animate the young woman's face.

Before sitting down around the desk with Marco and Daniele, Chiara stopped to look at the portrait with a slight smile. 'She was very beautiful,' she murmured, almost to herself.

Plato then strolled in, filled with delicious tidbits from lunch, and lazily stretched out on an armchair, from which he looked up at Chiara with some suspicion. The young woman walked over to stroke him, but she was met with an irritated yowl. *He's jealous*, she thought. *He'll get over it.* The cat furiously licked his fur where he had been stroked.

Marco was the first to talk. He gave an account of the previous day's meetings and told the others about a message he'd received from Alvise Cappello that morning. The Ottoman merchant, Ibrahim Derali, had been telling the truth: he had left Venice in October on the ship called *Fulminante* and had only returned a few days ago. Then Marco shared Angela Sporti's revelations. 'The last few hours have been so tumultuous that I've not had a moment to reflect on it,' he added. 'Unfortunately, we've not got much time, though, because the city's now awash with rumours about a mysterious killer who picks his victims at random and then throttles them. We know that the choice is far from random and there is someone who hated those three men, but until we can lay our hands on Labia and hear his confession we'll be unable to silence the rumours.'

'To be more precise,' interrupted Daniele, 'we mustn't forget that we are dealing with two distinct criminal acts, even if they may be linked by cause and effect. A year and a half ago there was the murder of poor Marianna Biondini, and we know the names of her killers. And then, during the past ten days or so, someone has been eliminating precisely these men. Three of them are already dead, which only leaves Labia.'

'It certainly helps to explain my visions, which seemed so out of place,' said Chiara. 'The blonde girl, the scarlet cloak, the church of San Zaccaria, where I saw the scene happening, and the gondolier, who might have been Biagio: it all now makes sense, although who knows where he hid the corpse? The only thing that hasn't yet been explained is the ship arriving from the East . . . perhaps it was the ship that brought back the "avenger", if I can call him that.'

'Careful, Chiara,' warned Marco. 'These were all murders. No one can take the law into their own hands.'

Daniele was absorbed in his own thoughts. 'Agreed, the Turk has an alibi. Although perhaps he isn't as clean as he'd like us to think: I think he may have encouraged the victims to embezzle the confidential material, and he might have been interested in the mud dredger, but he certainly never actually laid his hands on any of the documents, and he never killed anyone. But are we sure,' Daniele asked, 'that the killer is one and the same as the person avenging Marianna Biondini's death? And if so, who could it be?'

'Let's take another look at the facts,' Marco invited them. 'What exactly do we know about this shadow who kills in the darkness? First, he's a tall, well-built man. He was seen by the maid at Biagio's tavern, and I saw him when he escaped from the locanda on the Giudecca. Oh, and another thing: he's slightly lame, although I'm not sure if that's the result of a temporary injury or a permanent disability. What's more, he must still have a visible wound on his body somewhere, because the dagger which was found close to Marino Barbaro's body ten days ago had blood on it, and the killer's scar, even if slight, can't have healed properly yet.'

'Second,' Daniele went on, 'he's either a Venetian or he's been in Venice for at least ten days, and I would suggest much longer, because he's been able to study his victims' habits, their daily movements, the routes they took. And he also has money – remember the coins he showed to Signora Domenici?'

'Third,' added Chiara, 'he uses a special rope from the Orient, or perhaps from Portugal. It's like his signature. So, he's someone who has contacts abroad.'

'He's not a loner,' clarified Marco, 'because he's accustomed to talking to people; otherwise, he wouldn't have been able to make enquiries about his victims. And there's something else too: if he's someone who's taking revenge on behalf of that poor girl, he must be someone who was close to her, and we're all thinking of the same person.'

'Giorgione, her fiancé,' concluded Daniele.

'Exactly,' Marco continued. 'Giorgione knew who was to blame, and he's had enough time to prepare his attacks because he's been back in Venice for at least five months. He came from the East, so he'd have been able to procure that special kind of rope and, above all, he has a valid motive. Perhaps he brought some savings back from Constantinople, and we certainly know that he fits the build. But we know nothing about his character, or where he's hiding. Tomorrow, I'll send Nani to the Ghetto Nuovo to ask some discreet questions.'

'And will you arrest him?' asked Daniele.

Marco thought about this for a while. 'I don't know. If he's innocent, I don't want to torment him for no good reason.'

'But if he's innocent,' countered Chiara, 'then who's to blame?'

They were interrupted by Giuseppe, who came in with a tray of glasses and a carafe of Cypriot wine. The conversation resumed as soon as he had left.

Daniele thought aloud while taking notes. 'If the deaths of these three young men are linked to that of the Biondini girl, we need to look around the Castello neighbourhood, among the girl's acquaintances. But no other names have come to light yet, except for Giorgione, that is. Marianna's father has only been in Venice for three days, and before his return he had been told that his daughter died of an illness and not that she had disappeared. I can't think of any other suspects. But the four of them were certainly not saints, and they could well have offended others, or have perpetrated some other crime . . . Don't let's forget that, before Marianna, Corner raped the maidservant, Lucietta.'

'Even so,' Marco interrupted, pouring wine into the glasses. 'I asked Baldo Vannucci, who works for the inquisitors, and he didn't know of any serious crimes that the four men might have committed. But then he doesn't know anything about Marianna Biondini's death, or about Lucietta, as the group has managed to keep their crimes secret.'

'And Lucrezia Scalfi knew of nothing else apart from the possible death of an unnamed girl. Even though the four of them talked quite openly at her house and she, in her own words, certainly didn't think twice about secretly spying on them.'

Chiara was thinking as she sipped the wine. 'Let's try to think about it this way: the first motive we need to consider is revenge, but what if we were wrong and the motive was quite different? Who would stand to benefit from the death of these three men?'

Marco shot her a smile. 'Well done, Chiara,' he exclaimed. 'We've forgotten the Corner family. Biagio and Barbaro were impoverished wretches, so they can't have been killed for money. But for Piero Corner, things are different. His death makes his brother, Dario, an extremely wealthy man.'

'And Dario's a tall, well-built man,' interrupted Daniele. 'Apparently he's very strong too.'

'I've also noticed that since around the time of his brother's death he's been wearing a bandage on his knee and limping, like the shadow who jumped from the window after killing Biagio. But if it was him, it won't be easy to prove,' noted Marco. 'We need to know exactly where he's been. Daniele, do you think you could question some of the servants, informally? That old man, Matteo, for example, who bears a grudge against his masters.'

Chiara had been listening in silence up to this point, but she now spoke. 'I'm not sure. I've got the feeling that we're not yet on the right trail. I don't think Dario Corner comes into this at all.'

'Don't give in to the temptation of trying to have another vision,' warned Marco. And when Daniele turned to him with a questioning look, he added, 'The last time she tried she was taken ill. Those who dare to enter the world of unknown forces pay a heavy price. We'll continue with our investigations using the means we have. Chiara's visions have been enlightening, but that's enough.'

'Well, what will we do now?' asked Daniele, looking at the empty wine carafe.

'Tomorrow you should summon Matteo by sending one of your secretaries to the Corner palace, but do it as discreetly as possible. Then you'll question him about relations between the brothers and about Dario's movements. If you can find out what Dario was doing on the nights of the murders, so much the better. And remember to tell Matteo that he mustn't tell a soul about any of this. If I can, I'll come along, too, to listen to what he has to say. In the meantime, tomorrow morning I'll send Nani to the Ghetto to look for Giorgione. That way we'll know where to find him when we decide to question him. Nani knows how to do this sort of thing well, and he'll find him without raising any suspicion. Then, on Tuesday, we'll go under official escort to Villa Labia, in Mira, to arrest Paolo Labia. But we need him to confess everything before we bring him back to Venice, where his family might tamper with the evidence.'

'And how are you going to square this with the inquisitors?' Daniele reminded him.

'That's going to be difficult. I think I'll have to visit them tomorrow morning and tell them how things stand. There's no doubt that Labia is guilty, and they can't object to his arrest.'

But on Monday 18 December, Marco's meeting with the inquisitors had to be postponed because, on arriving at the ducal palace, he found a man waiting for him in his office. At first, he didn't recognise him. He was fat and rather elderly, shabbily dressed, and in his hands he was twisting what seemed to be a pink rag.

'Your Excellency,' he began, with an awkward bow, 'my name is Antonio Cotti, the landlord of the Locanda del Principe on the Giudecca.'

'Oh, yes, the brothel,' said Pisani.

'It's a respectable house,' replied the man, offended.

'Let's leave that to one side for now. What brings you to the palace?'

'I'm an honest citizen who wants to help the law,' the old man continued, still twisting the pink rag tightly in his hands. 'Yesterday morning, which was Sunday, I walked under the window of the room where poor Biagio was found dead. It was the first time that I'd actually walked around the house since Friday, when the awful events happened, because it has been raining so heavily.'

'And what happened?'

'While I was looking around, I found this piece of fabric caught in the vine – you know, the one the murderer climbed down. I'm sure it must belong to him. The guards didn't notice it because it was dark at the time.' With these words, Cotti handed Pisani the soaked piece of cloth.

Marco turned it over and saw immediately what it was: it was a sash like the ones that gondoliers wear around their waists. But this one was different: embroidered in a corner, and unmistakable, were gold and blue chevrons and two lions rampant inside a shield. It was the Corner family's coat of arms.

The inquisitors were waiting for him in the Sala di Tintoretto, together with the head of police, Messer Grando. Resplendent in his formal robes and wig, Pisani apologised for the delay and immediately made a start on the thorny subject that could not now be postponed any longer.

He told them about the group of four profligates, two from old noble families, plus a barnabotto and a gondolier, who until a year and a half ago had formed a gang whose only objective was their own amusement. These men, who spent their days gambling and drinking, chasing women and forcibly seducing maidservants, and who would stop at nothing, even serious crimes like theft and fraud, brought shame on the Republic. But one day, Marco continued, the four scoundrels had overstepped all limits and, having kidnapped a girl, they then found themselves with her corpse.

'Has the body been found?' asked Condulmer.

'Not yet, but I haven't lost hope,' Marco went on. 'And there is ample evidence to prove the crime, and tomorrow, with an armed escort,' he added, turning to Messer Grando, 'I shall go to arrest the only survivor of the gang, who can clarify any points that are still unclear.'

'And who is that?' asked Bragadin.

'Paolo Labia. He's fled to the family villa at Mira. As you know, Piero Corner, Marino Barbaro and the gondolier Biagio Domenici have been killed.'

'But were you not making inquiries into their mysterious deaths?' interrupted Pietro Fontana, who had not been listening, as usual.

'As I've already explained,' Pisani repeated patiently, 'we are dealing with a double case. The victims and Labia were guilty of a repugnant crime. The first three are dead, but Paolo Labia is not, and he must pay.'

The inquisitors rolled their eyes. 'A pity it has to be Labia,' sighed Condulmer. 'The family will cause trouble. But in Venice we pride ourselves on the fact that everyone is equal before the law and, if the charges are serious, he must be brought to trial.'

'This is why I'm going to Mira. To question him and bring him back to Venice in chains.'

'And who killed the other three?'

'I am not certain yet,' admitted Pisani. 'It might be someone who wanted to avenge the Biondini girl, but money might also have been a motive.'

'Could you explain more clearly?' Bragadin insisted.

'I don't want to draw any hasty conclusions, but some clues appear to give credence to the former hypothesis, while others appear to point to the Corner family . . .'

The inquisitors again sighed heavily and rolled their eyes. Marco left them to their business, but he had deliberately not told them that Marianna's fiancé was back in Venice or that a sash with the Corner coat of arms had been caught in the vine in the exact place where Biagio's murderer had been seen escaping. Nor, given that Derali had an alibi, had he mentioned that the men were also suspected of espionage.

It was almost midday when Marco came out of the ducal palace and found Nani waiting for him in front of the mezzanine office at the Procuratie Vecchie. 'Well?' he asked anxiously. 'Have you found Giorgione?'

'Yes, master.' Nani smiled. 'Have you ever known me to fail?'

'Let's go and find a bite to eat and you can tell me all about it.'

The avogadore and his gondolier sat down among the elegant mid-day crowds at a table in the Caffè alle Piante d'Oro, under the porticoes, and Marco ordered wine and some appetisers. Even though Nani was dressed as a simple commoner, his good looks drew admiring glances from many of the society women.

'It wasn't actually that difficult,' Nani started. 'Very early this morning I did the rounds of all the bakers in the Ghetto. There aren't that many, and by poking my head into the workshops, with one excuse or another, I soon spotted the only assistant who didn't look like a Jew. I waited for him to knock off work and go home to sleep, and then I walked into the shop.'

'Let me guess,' interrupted Marco. 'There was a girl . . .'

'Yes, how did you know, padròn? A girl called Ester. She's very attractive, with dark brown hair and fiery eyes. I told her I was looking for work. She told me that they were fully staffed and that, anyway, only Jews could work in the Ghetto. I told her that that couldn't be true, because I'd seen a Christian assistant earlier. She smiled and said that he was Giorgione, but it was a special case and he'd been recommended by the patron's friend. He was a good boy, it seemed, she said, and he didn't want to be seen out and about. "And where does he live?" I asked. And she told me that he had a room on the top floor, above the baker's oven, and that he only ventured out very rarely.'

'Did you ask what hours he worked, by chance?'

'Of course. I thought you'd want to know whether he might have been out and about on the nights when the crimes were committed.'

'Nani, you're a genius! What did she say?'

'I pretended that I was interested in the job. So I asked, "Tell me, what are the working hours like?" And she replied, "It's tough work. We start at eight in the evening and we work straight through till six in the morning, seven days a week." "And what if someone has another commitment?" I asked. "They'll have to change jobs," she told me. "Bread is made every day here." Then I left her, saying she was right that the job wasn't for me. I don't think she suspected anything.'

Matteo was already sitting in Zen's office when Marco arrived. The old man had dusted off his jacket with the gilded braid and he was even wearing a wig and white silk stockings. He looked confused, and when he saw the avogadore he became even more upset.

'Why am I here?' he stammered when Marco and Daniele entered. 'Zen's secretary wouldn't tell me anything. You can't think that it was me who killed the master?'

Marco struggled to hide a smile at the thought of the trembling old man picking well-built young men as his victims and then strangling them. He sat down beside Matteo and rested a hand on his shoulder. 'Of course not, don't even think about it. We only want to ask you a few questions in private, out of earshot of any inquisitive eavesdroppers in Palazzo Corner. You know a lot about the family, Signor Matteo, and you might be able to help us understand what has happened.'

'But I wasn't there when the poor master was killed,' argued the old man, flattered by being addressed so formally by someone of the avogadore's standing. 'His gondolier, Beppino, was with him.' He wiped his forehead with an immaculately starched handkerchief.

'We know, but what we need is a better understanding of what things were like in the family and the comings and goings of the servants. For example,' continued Marco, 'the gondoliers. There seem to have been several over a short space of time, is that right? Could you tell us about them?'

'Yes, I can,' said Matteo, evidently reassured. 'You'll already know about Biagio Domenici, of course. A nasty piece of work. He was poor Signor Piero's gondolier until a year ago. Since then he's lived in his mother's tavern and the other night he, too, was killed by the murderer who is strangling people in Venice, just like Signor Piero and his other friend, that Marino Barbaro.' He stopped for a moment, lost in thought. 'But, Your Excellency, do you think it was Biagio who killed the other two? If so, who killed Biagio?'

'Let's stick to the subject,' interrupted Daniele. 'Tell me more about the gondoliers working for the Corner family.'

'Yes, well, let's see.' The old man tried to concentrate by letting his eyes rove around the bookshelves, crammed with heavy law books, that lined the office walls. 'A year ago, Beppino arrived to take his place, and he was with Signor Piero on the night of the crime. He's a good lad, but he left fairly soon after what happened.'

'Was he the only gondolier?'

'No, how could he have been? The Corner family are always out and about and one would not be enough. There's also Signor Dario's gondolier, a new man called Marietto, who's been with the household for about a month now. He seems to be a good man, but he gets tired very quickly and is always complaining when he works for several hours. Then again, Signor Dario is always out, especially at night.'

'And before him?'

'Let me think. Up till September Signor Dario used one of the old house servants as a gondolier, until he couldn't manage any longer and retired. After him, another older man arrived, but he was much stronger and had been in Constantinople. He only lasted a few weeks because he apparently found another job. That's when Marietto arrived.'

'And what about the ladies?'

'They had their own private gondolier until Signora Eleonora became pregnant and stopped going out as much. That man was about forty and his real name was Luigi but everyone called him Gigio. He had a good voice and would often sit by the fire in the kitchen playing a guitar and singing. When he was fired, everyone said that he set up a wandering company of players.'

'It's strange that there have been so many changes,' remarked Marco. 'We've heard that Signor Dario has a terrible temper . . .'

Matteo smiled broadly. Gossip was one of his favourite pastimes. 'A terrible temper? Yes, you could certainly say that. He flies into a rage at the slightest provocation and starts shouting and goes red in the face.'

'Did he shout at his brother?'

'Well, strange to say, they argued constantly before Signor Piero married. It was usually about money. Dario didn't have much, at least not by the standards of the Corner family, and he'd made some bad investment decisions with what he had. What's more, Piero scolded him when he complained that his brother spent all the money on gambling and women. What really annoyed Dario were his brother's three friends, because he said they were leeching the family's money.'

Marco remembered the quarrel that Francesca Corner's dressmaker had witnessed. 'And what happened after Piero Corner married?'

'After Piero married Signora Eleonora, their relations improved. Perhaps the young wife knew how to restrain both her husband and her brother-in-law. But also because Signor Dario . . .'

'Signor Dario?' Marco encouraged him to continue.

'Well, all of us in the kitchen commented on how he changed. He started to dress better, his manners improved . . . In short, we were all convinced that he'd fallen hopelessly in love with his sister-in-law.'

'Well, that really takes the biscuit!' exclaimed Daniele after Matteo had bid them farewell with a respectful and dignified exchange of courtesies. 'The coarse Dario Corner falls in love with his beautiful sister-in-law! Now that she's a widow and he's a rich man, he'll certainly be hoping for some recompense. What's more, he had the best motive of all to kill his brother: money and love. There's no shortage of clues, either. The threats, the fact that – judging by what Matteo said – Dario was often out in the evening and came home late, the sash found at the Locanda del Principe. But why would he have killed the other two?'

'That's the crux. Why run the risk? Perhaps because if he just killed his brother, he thought he might be too obvious a suspect? Did the two other deaths serve to muddy the waters?'

'Either that,' continued Daniele, 'or he had to eliminate the two men who'd have suspected him immediately and would have blackmailed him.'

'And this idea also lets Giorgione off the hook. Yet it's still Giorgione who has the strongest motive: he wanted to avenge his fiancée's death. But judging from what Nani told me about his job in the Ghetto, Giorgione wouldn't be able to leave the bakery at night. Although, who knows if Ester is right?'

'We're clearly not going to be able to solve any of this now,' ended Daniele. 'Tomorrow we'll go and arrest Paolo Labia and then we'll learn more.'

CHAPTER 26

At dawn on Tuesday 19 December, Pisani and his companions disembarked at Fusina, where horses were waiting for them.

The road to Mira was muddy and rougher than usual, and the cluster of horsemen – Pisani; Zen; Vanni Cingoli, the chancellor of the Avogaria; and four guards – made slow progress through the persistent drizzle. They were spattered with filth in spite of their heavy cloaks, and armed to the teeth with pistols and daggers.

The Serenissima had never succeeded in making the mainland roads safe to use, and it was not unusual for travellers to encounter brigands who made a living by robbing passers-by, which was why the guards were with them, because it would have been very undignified for an avogadore to be stripped of his belongings, let alone anything worse.

There were few others on the road: the occasional peasant's cart carrying winter produce to the market, or more rarely a merchant's caravan, also protected by heavily armed guards, a couple of magistrates on horseback and a travelling company of actors seated on a ramshackle carriage pulled by a nag.

Most of the time the road followed the right bank of the Brenta canal, which Marco had travelled only a few days earlier with Chiara. The fields lay fallow during the winter and were interspersed with farm buildings. Parks surrounded the villas which could be seen on both sides, overlooking the canal.

At Oriago the horsemen stopped at an inn in the marketplace, and having handed their mounts to the stable boy, they shook the worst of the rain off their heavy cloaks before entering. Ravenously hungry, they promptly ordered cured meats and cheese, accompanied by good red wine, which helped to bring some warmth back to their limbs.

'You, guards,' said Pisani. 'As you aren't allowed into patrician villas, wait in the porter's gatehouse, but be on your guard and don't let Labia escape. You, Daniele, you'll come in with me and act as the witness, while the chancellor minutes the questioning.' Marco smiled at Vanni Cingoli, who, after years of office work in the ducal palace, was already feeling the strain after the first stretch of the journey on horseback. 'We'll try to surprise Labia and get into the villa without him noticing. In this respect, at least, the weather is on our side, as we're unlikely to meet anyone in the garden in this rain.'

Back on the road, they rode through Valmarana, where there were several parks and villas, and the road became increasingly deserted. It was about eleven when they reached Mira. Here they crossed to the left bank of the Brenta, cantering along the embankment and past several farmhouses before coming to the elegant façade of Villa Labia, with its central three-arch window topped by spires and statues.

Marco and Daniele dismounted and walked into the gatehouse. Standing chatting before the fireplace were two armed guards, who looked surprised but quickly reached for their swords.

'Put down your weapons,' ordered Marco. 'My name's Pisani, avogadore of the Serenissima.' The two men recognised him and immediately stood to attention. 'Both of you will stay here quietly, in the company of my guards, and you'll do nothing to warn anyone of our arrival. I'm here on official business and, irrespective of any orders given by your master, I am now in command here, in the name of the Republic.'

The two guards remained standing stiffly to attention. 'Are there other armed guards in the main house?' asked Pisani.

'No,' replied the older man. 'There are just two of us, and we stay here all year round with the families. We live in the building behind the villa. Inside, there are just servants and the master's friends.'

'Good. You'll wait here until we've entered the building and then you'll look after our horses, which need to be dried and fed.'

In front of the villa, which seemed uninhabited apart from the open shutters on the first floor, there was a wide paved area, flanked by porticoes running towards the side wings of the building. Marco and Daniele, followed by Vanni Cingoli, who carried a leather bag, reached the main door and, hidden by one of the porticoes, slipped unseen into the hall.

They were immediately aware of the strains of beautiful dance music coming from the salon on the first floor. The three men climbed the elegant staircase and found themselves looking at an unexpected scene. The austere hall of the villa, heated by two large marble fireplaces and watched over by several portraits of severe-faced forebears of the Labia family, had been transformed into a theatre for a private party. Beside tables set with every imaginable sort of food and drink, two figures reclined on the velvet sofa. At first glance they looked like two well-built and heavily made-up young ladies, wearing towering wigs and gilded fabrics with plunging necklines. A third was energetically hammering out a minuet on the spinet, and in the centre of the room another couple, in lace corsets and wide skirts, were moving through the semblance of a dance.

Dressed in a lace shirt, Paolo Labia, who was small and thin, was all but enveloped in the cushions of an armchair while a strange creature, who appeared to be wearing nothing more than a red body stocking and a huge white wig, sat on his lap, feeding him grapes.

When the officials arrived, everyone froze in surprise and it became clear that the young ladies were in fact well-muscled young men. Labia was wearing a stomacher and breeches, but his made-up face and dusky eyes left no doubt about the nature of the party.

'Who are you?' stammered the young man, even though he had immediately recognised his visitors. 'What are you doing in my house?' The spinet fell silent.

'It's over, Labia. The time for reckoning has come.' Pisani's voice left no doubt about the nature of their visit.

'I . . . What reckoning? But, Avogadore Pisani, do you know who I am?' Paolo's face under the layers of paint was ashen.

'Dismiss your . . . friends.' Pisani had instinctively used the familiar form of address, as he would when addressing criminals.

At the wave of a hand, the young men, heads down, filed out of the room through a side door, their coloured skirts sweeping the floor. 'Call me if you need me, master,' the youngest one, dressed in the body stocking, said quietly. He couldn't have been more than sixteen.

Labia walked over to a window, furtively cleaning his face with a napkin dipped in water. He put on a jacket of pink wool. 'What's wrong, Avogadore Pisani?' Labia confronted Marco. 'Since when has a gentleman not been allowed to enjoy the pleasures of villeggiatura in his own house?'

'Villeggiatura in late December? Doesn't it strike you as a little out of season? And from what I've seen,' he continued, 'two crimes are being committed here: dressing in feminine clothing, which is proof of sodomy under Venetian law, and, far worse, the corruption of minors. That boy in the body stocking is still an adolescent.'

Paolo Labia drew himself up to his full height, throwing out his hollow chest and standing arrogantly in front of Pisani, spindly legs well apart.

'Take care how you talk to a Labia, Avogadore. My family is rich and powerful, like your own. What do you think you can do to me? Your accusations need to be proved!'

At this, Marco lost his temper. He seized the corner of the table-cloth on the nearest table and pulled it sharply, sending plates, glasses and bottles flying before they shattered on the floor. 'You dare to talk to me about families? Disgusting murderer! I'm not here about your miserable vices, I'm here to make you confess to your crimes!' The worried face of a young boy peeked around a door, but he withdrew as soon as he caught Marco's eye.

Daniele intervened. 'Sit down, Labia. We need to question you about a murder that happened eighteen months ago.'

Paolo looked agitated: it was what he had feared from the moment he'd seen them.

'You will tell us everything you saw and took part in, and the chancellor here will record your statement, which you will then sign. Once that is done, you will come with us to Venice.'

Labia reluctantly obeyed and the others also sat down around the table. Cingoli set out the bound volume used to record statements and his pens and inkwell. Marco looked around for a few clean glasses and a new carafe of wine, which he poured out for his companions. Then, feeling a little calmer, he started the interrogation.

'Paolo Labia, we are informed that on the evening of 23 May 1751, together with your friends Piero Corner, Marino Barbaro and Biagio Domenici, you took part in the kidnapping, rape and murder of a young girl, Marianna Biondini, whose body you then disposed of. You shall answer these charges before the law.'

'I? What are you talking about? Who is this Biondini girl? I didn't do anything,' Labia began in an attempt to defend himself.

'That's enough, Labia!' Pisani's fist hammered the table, shaking it. 'We already know everything! The girl's friend told us. She was present when Marianna was abducted and she can identify you. Lucrezia Scalfi has also confessed to overhearing you all talking at her house after you had committed the murder.'

'That whore . . .' muttered Labia. 'Well then,' he continued, with a renewed spark of arrogance, 'if you magistrates already know everything, why have you come to trouble me?'

Marco stood up abruptly, seized Labia by the lapel and slapped him across the face with such force that he fell to the floor, knocking over the chair, which broke into pieces. Daniele rushed to pick him up and, while the latter wiped his mouth with his handkerchief, shot a disapproving glance at Marco.

'Nicely done,' complained Labia, replacing his wig. 'You're three against one . . .' Then he looked furtively at Pisani and said, 'You wouldn't have done that if you'd interrogated me in Venice with my lawyer.' But the quiver in his voice belied his bluster.

'Listen carefully, Labia,' intervened Zen. 'It would be better for you to confess everything straight away. You've hidden away here because you know that it's not only the law that's waiting for you in Venice, but someone who's already killed your friends, and that you will be next.'

Labia's face was now ashen, and he lowered his gaze.

'If you confess, you'll be brought to Venice under our protection, and you'll stand trial. There is also the chance that the death sentence might be commuted to perpetual exile and you might save your life.'

'But if you insist on remaining silent,' Marco stated, 'given that I will be the one to draw up the charges, you can be certain that I will accuse you of every single indictment that the law allows.'

Labia was silent for quite some time, sitting in front of his accusers, his head in his hands. At last, he started to talk in a tired voice.

He told them how, on that infamous Sunday eighteen months earlier, all four of them had dined at the Corner palace and they had drunk heavily. In the afternoon they had grown bored and, it being a fine afternoon, they had decided to go to the fair, where there was always entertainment to be had. They had wandered around among the crowds for a while and Biagio had asked Piero to buy him a new dagger, a wonderful thing with a damascene scabbard. They'd eaten some fritters and had stopped to admire the acrobats, when Piero had suddenly exclaimed, 'Look who's here!', pointing at two girls, pretty young commoners, one of whom was wearing a scarlet cloak.

'Now we'll have fun,' Piero had shouted as he'd made his way towards them, elbowing his way through the crowd. The girls had also seen them and were trying to move away as quickly as possible.

'Who are they?' Biagio had asked his master.

'Oh, one of them is a seamstress who works for my mother,' Piero had explained. 'She's called Marianna Biondini and you'll have seen her around the house. She always pretends to be uninterested when she sees me, but let's see if she can get away from me now.'

'What do you want to do here, with all these people around?' Barbaro had asked.

'Just have a bit of fun.'

They had all started to follow the girls, calling out to them to see if they would reply. But the girls paid no attention and soon disappeared into the narrow streets behind Saint Mark's.

'How did you find them again?' asked Zen. The chancellor's pen scratched furiously across the paper.

'Purely by chance. We walked around the taverns for a while and had a few more drinks. It was already dark when we spotted the two girls saying goodbye to each other under the lamp post in Campo San Zaccaria.'

'Silence!' Piero had whispered, stepping back into the shadows. It was late and there was no one around.

The brunette headed off up a side street, leaving the other one, the Biondini girl, alone. In a flash all four of them had surrounded her. She tried to escape but found herself cornered against the wall.

'You can't slip away from me this time,' Piero had sneered, seizing hold of her by the waist.

She was terrified. She managed to utter the words, 'No! Help!' but her voice was too feeble to be heard.

Her unwillingness had excited them even more. Even Biagio had joined in and started to touch her. It was he who suggested, 'Not here. Let's take her to Piero's casino; it's not far.'

'Good idea,' Barbaro had agreed.

In a trice they had gagged her with a handkerchief and wrapped her in her cloak. Biagio threw her over his shoulder and the others helped.

'What did you do?' interrupted Pisani.

'Oh . . . I enjoyed watching. Girls don't interest me.'

Piero Corner had for some months leased a small apartment in Corte Rotta, only a short walk from San Zaccaria. It had three rooms and was well furnished, and he'd go there to gamble with friends or to be with any girls or married women he'd picked up.

Marianna struggled, but in a few minutes the group had reached the apartment without meeting a soul. The three friends dumped the girl on the floor in the middle of the room and unwound her cloak. Her eyes were wide with terror as she tried to tear off the gag and pull herself to her feet.

Corner had stopped her. 'If you're good and don't scream, I'll take it off, but if you continue to struggle then I'll bind your hands too.'

The poor girl sat motionless, but huge tears started to roll down her cheeks. 'I beseech you! What have I done to you? Let me go!' she had pleaded as soon as she could talk.

'No one wants to hurt you,' replied Barbaro, but he was laughing. 'You'll see what a party we'll have! Because you've already enjoyed other men, haven't you, pretty whore?'

She had crawled into a corner. 'No! I'm a well-brought up girl. I'm going to be married . . .' Her eyes looked in desperation from one man to the other.

'And you mean to say that you've never had it off with your beloved? We're patricians,' he'd joked. 'We're entitled to *jus primae noctis*. Come on, who's going to be first?'

'No, no, it's no fun that way. We're not animals.' Corner had started to give instructions. 'What we'll do now is drink a good bottle of Malvasia, then we'll play some dances. You, Labia, given that you're not one for the women, why don't you strike a tune on the guitar?'

Labia had started to play while the others drank heavily.

'And what did the girl do?' interrupted Marco, feeling his stomach heaving.

'She crouched in a corner and whined like a bitch.' Labia smirked at the memory.

Enraged, Marco lost control a second time. This time the slap threw Labia into the chancellor's arms and knocked the inkwell over, spilling ink on to the table.

'You filthy whoreson of a sodomite!' shouted the avogadore as Vanni Cingoli tried to mop up the spreading pool of ink with blotting paper. 'You're not even a man, and you were there watching, without helping her . . . You were enjoying yourself, weren't you, pervert? You're worse than the others!'

'It's easy, Signor Avogadore, to insult a pederast, isn't it?' Despite his agitation, Labia had managed to recover a shred of dignity. 'I know that my friends were depraved, but they were also the only ones who allowed me to join them. Do you think it's a pleasure being a sodomite? Everyone looks down on us, without asking whether it's our fault or nature's. We have no choice in the matter, but nor do we have the luxury of choosing our friends.'

Pisani calmed down. 'Go on,' he said in a low tone.

When they were completely drunk, they threw dice for the girl. Corner won, or they let him win.

'She's mine! I'm going first!' he had shouted in triumph. 'Form a procession!'

They had lifted up the girl and carried her to the bed. She wasn't crying now; she barely had the strength to defend herself, let alone struggle. Piero had closed the door. They were all silent. Ten minutes passed, then the silence was broken by a shrill scream. Piero emerged from the room, covered with blood. 'She really was a virgin,' he said.

Then Marino Barbaro went in, and he really took his time. Outside the room they could hear a series of cries that became increasingly weaker.

Then it was Biagio's turn. He'd only shut himself in the room for a couple of minutes when they heard a long, harrowing groan, followed by silence.

The time passed. At last Biagio came out. Hanging his head and hastily dressed, he pulled the door shut behind him. He seemed strangely ill at ease. 'I don't know what's happened,' he stammered, 'but she's not moving.'

They had all rushed into the room. Marianna lay on the bed in a pool of blood, her eyes wide, her face a mask of terror, deathly still.

'What have you done to her, you bloody fool?' Corner had shouted, holding Biagio by the collar.

'It wasn't me,' Biagio had remonstrated. 'I don't know what happened, but just when I was enjoying it, I heard a sound, like something ripping . . .'

'She's dead,' Barbaro remarked. 'You've given her an internal haemorrhage, or perhaps a heart attack. What are we going to do?'

Then Corner said, 'For Christ's sake! I can't think straight with all this blood everywhere. Let's get out of here.'

The poor girl had been dressed as best they could and wrapped in the scarlet cloak, then they had loaded her into a gondola, taking advantage of the darkness. The four of them had cleaned any traces of blood and had hidden the bloody linen among the waste of a nearby convent. The rest of the story was as it had been told by Lucrezia Scalfi. Labia merely confirmed that it was Biagio who had taken responsibility for disposing of the body.

Silence fell in the salon of Villa Labia. Even Paolo sat, head down, as if he'd only just understood the scale of the crime. The room was growing darker by the minute. The chancellor went to look for a flint to light the candles.

'There's one other thing,' murmured Pisani, almost talking to himself. 'Where is the body now? Where did Biagio take it?' And he hoped wholeheartedly that Labia knew.

Labia began to talk again. For a few days, Biagio hadn't appeared. Then one evening they'd all met at Corner's house and here he'd told them what had happened.

On the night of the crime, after leaving Lucrezia's house with the corpse still in the boat, Biagio had already decided where to go. In total darkness and dipping his oar in the water with the greatest caution, he had taken almost an hour to approach the Lido, not far from the fortress of San Niccolò, where a garrison was housed. He could hear them singing, and they were certainly half drunk because of the feast day, but he'd have been in terrible trouble if they'd seen him.

He'd moored the boat to a pole close to shore, near the Jewish cemetery. He'd then heaved himself on to the embankment and, moving swiftly like a cat, had reached the old wrought-iron gate. The chain that held it shut was merely looped around the rails and Biagio had soon opened it. He'd then hidden among the tombstones.

The cemetery hadn't been used for over a century and there was moss on all the stone sepulchres. Biagio had chosen one of the oldest and with a great effort had pushed the cover sideways just enough to create a space into which he could drop the corpse.

Then, as silently as he'd come and still to the sound of the soldiers' singing, he had collected Marianna's body from the gondola and had slid it into the old tomb until it had been swallowed into the darkness. Then he'd shut the tomb once again.

'Ingenious,' commented Daniele. 'But how will we ever find her? I hope we won't have to open up every tomb in the cemetery.'

'No,' added Paolo Labia. 'The tomb containing Marianna Biondini's body is the third one, in the fourth row on the right from the entrance.'

'So why did you run away from Venice after all this time?' Marco asked.

'You said it yourself, Your Excellency,' confessed Paolo, looking down. He had lost every shred of self-confidence and was visibly shaking. 'No one had the remotest idea that it was us. The police believed the story that the girl had run off for reasons of her own. We were completely safe, even if things were never the same again between us. In the end we saw a lot less of each other. But when I heard that Barbaro and Corner were dead, I was afraid. I immediately thought that someone must be taking revenge for the girl's death, even if it was so long ago . . . I knew that I would be safe here in the country. Then news of Biagio's death reached me. What I want to know is, who is hunting us down now that over a year has passed?'

CHAPTER 27

It was night when they arrived, cold and wet, in Venice. Once they reached the New Prisons, Pisani sent Daniele and the chancellor off home and the guards to get something to eat. He personally completed the procedure for detaining Labia in custody.

Despite the fact that his previous arrogance and bluster had long since dissipated, the young patrician had still insisted that he should be accompanied by two of his personal servants, who were now dressed in the family livery rather than in crinolines, and he hastily sent them to inform his family.

The whole procedure was completed with the utmost discretion. From the prisons, Pisani led the way across the covered bridge to the ducal palace, followed by two guards and the prisoner. They walked through numerous chambers and galleries, and eventually came to the office of Corrado Memmo, secretary to the inquisitors. Having been roused from his bed and having struggled into his formal robe, he seemed to be in poor spirits, and his mood certainly did not improve when he recognised the heir of the powerful Labia family.

'Your Excellency,' he stuttered, still half asleep. 'What do you want me to do?'

'I would have thought that was clear. Accommodate the prisoner, Paolo Labia, in a cell in the Piombi.'

Pisani added nothing further and the secretary did not dare to ask for explanations. He merely recorded the prisoner's name in the register and then summoned Pietruccio, the warden.

The procession headed off again, following Pietruccio, a lightly built and rather curved figure, who seemed to struggle under the heavy burden of an enormous bundle of keys. Their steps echoed through the cold, deserted corridors before they headed up endless flights of steps leading to the attics of the ducal palace.

Labia trailed along disconsolately. For the first time since that terrible night, he had started to realise the true gravity of the crime, and he was filled with shame and remorse. His sole consolation was that he was safe; whoever had killed the others could not harm him in the Piombi.

But even that small comfort disappeared when they got to the cell. In the light of a flickering candle end he saw a straw mattress and a rough crate and, lying on a blanket in the corner and snoring loudly, a filthy old man dressed in rags. The smell that emanated from him nearly choked Labia.

'Must I stay here?' he mumbled. 'And who is he?'

'We don't have single rooms in the Piombi,' said Marco. 'But I don't doubt that tomorrow someone will think it worth their while to offer you something more comfortable.'

When he awoke the next morning, Marco was greeted by a smiling Rosetta.

'Good morning, paròn,' she said, pouring him his coffee. 'Do you know, Signorina Chiara's medicine has worked wonders? Maso brought me some yesterday and my backache has vanished. That woman really is clever!'

The woman did seem to be moving around with greater ease, despite the heavy mist that hung over the garden. *So that's how Chiara has won over Rosetta*, thought Marco with satisfaction as he got ready for his day.

Having disembarked in the Piazzetta after giving instructions to Nani, Marco headed to the office. There was one thing he needed to do straight away. He asked Tiralli to summon the head of police, and when he arrived, Marco informed him of the latest developments.

'So one of the two cases is solved,' commented Messer Grando. 'We still need to know who killed the three young men . . .'

'I've not troubled you to come here to discuss the investigations.' Pisani seemed annoyed by the policeman's comments. 'I am very busy today and I need to ask you to do me two favours. First of all, I am relying on you to inform the inquisitors about Labia's arrest.' Pisani preferred to see the supreme magistrates after the meeting he was about to attend. 'Then, I would like you to recover the body of that poor girl, Marianna Biondini, which seems to have been buried in a sepulchre in the old Jewish cemetery on the Lido.' Marco gave the policeman the precise location of the tomb.

'Don't worry, Your Excellency. I will send a boat with four of my guards and I'll have them accompanied by two Capuchin monks. What should we do with the body?'

Pisani had already thought about this. 'Close it in a coffin. But make sure it's not one of those used for paupers. I'd like a solid, carved coffin; she deserves it, poor girl. Take the coffin to the cathedral of San Pietro in Castello and lay it in a side chapel. Don't tell anyone who it is. I want to inform the family myself.'

It was only once Messer Grando had left to carry out his orders that Marco felt the need to see how Labia was getting on, so he climbed up to the attic prisons.

'Your Excellency,' complained the young man as soon as Pietruccio opened the cell door with one of his enormous keys. 'I can't stay in here! That old man snored all night and he stinks like a sewer. This is not what I'm accustomed to.'

He was lying in a comfortable bed, surrounded by braziers and well provisioned with silver jugs and porcelain cups. The old man had also been fed and was looking at Labia with gratitude. The family had clearly intervened, thanks to their substantial financial resources, but, judging from what Pietruccio had said, none of them had turned up in person.

'Be patient and you'll grow used to it,' Marco reassured him, looking around with an ironic smile. In spite of the various luxury items that had now been provided, the cell still looked squalid.

'There was a rat here too!' Paolo continued. 'I heard it gnawing something in the corner, and I saw its red eyes in the dark.'

'You could try to train it; apparently they're highly intelligent animals,' said the avogadore as he walked off, laughing. To Labia's ears, it was a sinister sound.

The office of the secretary to the inquisitors, which Marco had to walk through on his way out of the palace, was more crowded than usual. At his appearance, all the black-gowned gentlemen drew aside, like a stage curtain, respectfully making way so Marco could approach their leader: Carlo Dandolo, the most renowned criminal lawyer in Venice, who had brought this crowd of employees with him from his office.

'Your Excellency, what an honour!'

The lawyer bowed deeply to Marco. He was rather stout and wore a velvet cloak and an elegant wig. While his mouth smiled, his searching dark eyes scrutinised Marco.

'I am here to defend young Labia,' he went on. Marco had realised this when he'd first seen him. 'I am sure there must be a misunderstanding. A young man from such a noble family cannot possibly have carried out the crime of which he stands accused.' The man stared at Marco somewhat furtively. 'I hope that the misunderstanding can be clarified before you prepare the case. My office is obviously at your complete disposal for any type of investigation—'

'My dear Dandolo,' interrupted Pisani. 'I am the first person to wish that the crime had not been committed. But rest assured, you know better than I that our Republic has recourse to the death penalty only in increasingly rare circumstances, and it does not use torture. If your client can demonstrate that he was not directly complicit in the crime, he may perhaps be exiled intact, and he'll have a chance to reflect on his errors far from Venice.'

With a nod, Marco turned and left the ducal palace, walking out into the cold, fresh air. It was midday but the fog still lay heavily over Saint Mark's Square. On the left, the outline of the bell tower looked like the mast of a drifting ship, and the shadowy outlines of the Procuratie were barely visible. From behind the misted windows of the caffès under the porticoes, Marco could just make out the glimmer of lights.

He opened the door into the Caffè del Arabo and was met by a wall of heat. There was a vacant table in the corner and he ordered a snack. He needed a break in order to focus on the interview that awaited him, especially because he did not know what the outcome would be.

The murder of Marianna Biondini had been solved, but Labia's arrest and confession had not helped to identify the man who had strangled the three men.

What was known about the shadowy figure who attacked by night and vanished without trace? Marco went over the known facts: he was tall, strong, perhaps he was lame, and he must have a wound somewhere on his body. He had either been in the Orient, or had known people there, but he must have been in Venice for a month or more in order to have had time to organise the crimes.

He was an intelligent man, thought the magistrate, savouring a plate of sardines in a rich sauce. And he didn't lack means. An idea was floating on the edge of Marco's mind, but he couldn't bring it into focus. He had the strange sensation of staring at the truth and not being able to see it.

The man must also have had relations with the Corner household, Marco thought. The sash that had been found in the garden of the locanda on the Giudecca was proof enough of that. But a sash might also have been stolen and left there on purpose.

A gondolier's sash. Who were the Corner family's gondoliers? Old Matteo had spoken of several. There had been Biagio, then that man called Beppino, who'd been with Corner on the night of the crime. Then came Marietto, who had worked for Dario for about a month. Could it have been him? Matteo had described him as weak and easily tired, but that might have been just a façade. If nothing else came up, Marco thought, he'd have to be questioned. Then last of all there was Gigio, who used to accompany the ladies of the house but who left to set up a company of travelling actors.

Marco took a generous sip of wine. Again he had the strange sensation that the truth was here in plain sight. Who else? Yes, there was that gondolier who'd been with Dario Corner for a couple of weeks, before Marietto. He'd left because he'd found another job. What was his name? Matteo hadn't said. He'd have to ask him again.

Was Dario Corner guilty? He certainly had the means, the stature and a motive, and what was more, he was in love with his sister-in-law. But the more Marco thought about him, the less sure he felt. He continued to have the feeling that he'd missed something.

Was it Giorgione? From what he'd been told, Giorgione was also tall and strong. He'd been in Constantinople, he knew the names of the men who'd killed Marianna, and he'd been back in the city for a few months . . . But Giorgione worked in the bakery all night.

The time had come to question him. If Nani had done his job well, Giorgione would be waiting in Daniele's office right now.

Nani was waiting for his master in front of the church in Campo San Moisè, trying to keep warm by hopping around on his long legs.

'Go on in, paròn,' he greeted Pisani. 'I've done as you told me and brought him here.'

The gondolier had gone to the Ghetto late that morning and had kept watch on Giorgione's window on the eighth floor, above the bakery. Two guards were hidden behind the corner, ready to intervene should the young man have made a break for it.

When Nani saw the shutters being opened, he went upstairs. 'Eight floors, paròn, what a climb!' He'd introduced himself with his usual show of honesty and had told Giorgione that he'd been sent by the Guild of Bakers. If Giorgione wanted the time he'd spent working in Constantinople to count towards his apprenticeship and to gain his mastership, then he should come immediately to the office of Avvocato Zen to sign the papers.

'He fell for it, paròn, as I was certain he would!'

'Of course he would, Nani. No one can match you when it comes to telling lies.'

'He dressed himself nicely, and even combed his hair to make himself look respectable, and then he followed me like a lamb. He's here now, waiting inside.'

'And the guards?'

'Oh, I told them they could go and then watched as they headed straight for the nearest tavern.'

Sitting quietly in Daniele's office, Giorgione had just finished drinking his coffee. He was handsome and no mistake, thought Marco. Tall and muscular, he had grey eyes and a full head of chestnut, almost red hair. A passionate sort, most probably.

'Avogadore Pisani,' Marco said, introducing himself. The young man jumped. 'I am here to talk about your fiancée's disappearance.'

'Marianna?' cried Giorgio, leaping to his feet in astonishment. 'So I'm not here to sign the guild papers? I should have realised. But why is the law getting involved after so long?' Then he fell silent and sat down again, his head in his hands. When he lifted it, his eyes were red.

He spoke in a low voice. 'I've always known how she died, and I also know who killed her. If you've asked me to come here, it must mean that you've reopened the case. I can tell you who her murderers are and I hope you can punish them accordingly.'

Pisani and Zen looked at each other. Either Sporti was the murderer and he was also an excellent actor, or he was the only person in Venice who'd not heard about the recent killings.

'Tell us what you know,' Pisani encouraged him.

'When Marianna disappeared, I couldn't stop looking for her and my family decided that I should leave before I got into trouble. She . . .' A tear ran down his face. 'She was my whole life. I found work on a ship sailing for the East. But before leaving, I made my sister, who was the last to have seen her alive, tell me everything. I know her well and I knew she was hiding something important.'

'And then?'

'Then she told me. Marianna was forcibly abducted by four young men. I'll never forget their names. They are Piero Corner, Paolo Labia, Biagio Domenici and Marino Barbaro, may God curse them in eternity. They carried her away wrapped in her cloak and she was never seen again. It's up to you,' he added, looking at Pisani again, 'to find the evidence and punish them as they deserve.'

Marco shot a glance at Daniele, who was on the verge of interrupting. 'What did you do in the East?'

'I don't know how that helps your inquiries, but I'll tell you, if you think it's important.'

Marco noted that Sporti was not as naïve as he seemed. The young man told them how he remembered very little of the first few weeks onboard. He carried out orders, ate and slept, but he was in a daze. He disembarked at Constantinople and on the very first evening, being ravenously hungry, he sought employment as a dockworker. There was no shortage of work there and he stayed for a few months.

Slowly he came to realise where he was and what he was doing. The memory of Marianna was still very painful, but the anger had started to fade. Then one day he had looked at his filthy, torn clothes and decided to clean himself up and see what other work he could find. In the Venetian quarter he had found a shop that needed a baker and had spent the remaining months there, until homesickness had brought him home. But being back in his old neighbourhood had stirred up such painful memories that he had had to leave the area, at least for a while, until he could really accept that Marianna was no longer there.

'Your Excellency,' he ended, turning to Pisani, 'I've told you everything; will you tell me what's happened and why you've asked me here?'

'Do you not know that three of Marianna's killers are dead?'

Giorgio's astonishment was genuine. 'Have they been executed? I didn't know.'

'How long is it since you've seen your parents?'

'Why do you need to know? It must be over a month. How did they die?'

'It appears there's a murderer on the loose who strangled them at night with a rope,' interrupted Daniele. 'Only Paolo Labia has survived.'

'A murderer? You think it's me?'

'No,' Pisani reassured him. 'We know that you work at night. But did you really not know anything about the murders? All Venice is talking about them.'

'But I work in the Ghetto,' said the youngster, 'where they have their own worries. What's more, I sleep in the day and never see anyone.'

As Giorgio spoke, Marco mentally checked what he'd said against the other information he'd amassed. Suddenly, like a bolt of lightning, a flash of intuition hit him and the different pieces of the puzzle fell into place.

The truth had always been staring him in the face, but it was not the outcome he wished for, and perhaps that was why he'd been unable to see it.

'One more thing, Giorgio,' he asked, watching him carefully. 'While you were in Constantinople, you didn't meet anyone, did you? You didn't tell your story to anyone?'

'Yes, once . . .' replied Giorgio without thinking. Then he hesitated. He fell silent for a while as if collecting his thoughts.

In the room there was complete silence.

'I . . .' he continued, sitting bolt upright and looking around as if seeking inspiration. Finally, his words came tumbling out: 'Once at the bakery, to one of my colleagues, another assistant working there, like myself . . . I said . . .'

'What?'

'I told him I'd come from Venice.' By now he'd regained his composure but he was as red as a lobster. 'And I said I'd left because my fiancée had died.'

Pisani knew he was lying.

CHAPTER 28

Frowning, Pisani rushed out of the office without a word as Daniele Zen and Giorgio Sporti watched in astonishment.

Lost in thought, Marco reached the gondola at the quay by San Moisè and ordered Nani to take him to the Arsenale. Night was falling and the young man had to concentrate on his course in order to avoid the other vessels. The fog was so thick that it shrouded the boat lanterns, forcing the gondoliers to signal their direction using a series of guttural cries.

Alvise Cappello was still in his office and was astonished when Marco, enveloped in a damp cloak and clearly agitated, asked to see some documents. When a clerk brought them into the office, he watched as Marco leafed through them with shaking hands.

'What is it, Marco?' asked Alvise. 'At least let me offer you a glass of Aleatico.' He didn't press him further because he knew him well enough to know that if he was in such a state, then there must be a good reason.

Pisani drained the glass in one as he turned over the pages and compared a couple of dates, then he snapped the register shut and left, barely remembering to salute his friend. He almost ran back to the gondola.

'And now,' he said to Nani, 'take me to Rio Sant'Anna.'

Nani rowed in silence. From Saint Mark's Basin he found it difficult to turn into Rio Sant'Anna, which seemed to have been swallowed by the fog.

He rowed down the canal for a short distance, then Marco indicated where to moor the gondola. 'Wait for me in the warmth,' he advised Nani, pointing to the flickering lights of a tavern. Then he vanished into the dark calle.

The door was open. Marco climbed the stairs, helped by the light of a candle stub placed at the top. No one looked down as he approached.

On the first floor, he saw a pair of flamboyant Turkish trousers and a turban lying on a bed. The room on the upper floor was lit only by the flames from the fireplace.

'I was waiting for you, Your Excellency.'

Menico Biondini, known as the Levantino, was alone. He was sitting at the table with a glass of wine, holding a rag doll dressed in bride-like white lace.

He stood up stiffly and lit a lamp with a flint. He was not wearing gloves and the firelight revealed a long red scar on his left hand.

'Sit down, Your Excellency.' He motioned towards a chair. He stared at Pisani. 'I knew you'd put two and two together.'

Marco took off his cloak and sat down with a sigh. He drank the wine that the man had poured and looked back at him. In this light, Menico seemed less imposing than he had on that first evening. His white hair contrasted with his sun-scorched face. His eyes, red and swollen, had deep lines under them. Looking at him, Marco felt his heart ache.

'You are here to arrest me,' continued the man. Marco had not yet even opened his mouth. 'What does it matter to me? Whatever happens now will happen. Until a few days ago, avenging my daughter's death seemed like a duty. But now, I'm not so sure. I feel empty . . .'

'Tell me how you heard about Marianna's death.'

'You see this?' He held out the rag doll with a sad smile. 'It was hers. Giorgio gave it to her as a marriage token.' He pulled himself together. 'You already know the first part of the story. I'd recently arrived in Syria on a cargo ship. It was summer when my sister wrote to tell me that Marianna was ill, then in the second letter . . . she said she'd not survived the illness. I thought I'd go out of my mind. That little girl was my reason for living. I wish you'd seen her. She looked like a lady, so blonde and refined. She was going to be married when I got home. I liked Giorgione, he was a hard worker and sharp. They'd have been happy together. They would have given me grandchildren. What else can a man wish for? And then' – Menico wiped away his tears – 'a damned illness carried her off.'

'Why didn't you come back to Venice immediately?'

'I couldn't face it. I needed to be alone. I wandered aimlessly around those parts, until I happened to arrive in Constantinople. Being there, among all those people and in the hubbub of a large city, well . . . it brought me to my senses. I decided the only way to keep going was to work myself into the ground. I'm an experienced shipwright and it wasn't hard to find work in a shipyard. Venetian craftsmen are highly sought after in that part of the world.'

'And then what happened?'

'I see you already know.'

Menico got up and walked around the table to rest the doll on the dresser and pour some more wine into the glasses.

Marco noticed that he was limping slightly. 'What's wrong with that foot?'

'This? Oh, nothing. I twisted my ankle a few evenings ago, climbing down a vine at a locanda on the Giudecca. You know quite well what I'm talking about.' He stared out of the window in silence for a moment. 'But you were asking me about Constantinople,' he went on. 'It happened this spring. There's a place in the bazaar, run by a man from Verona, and it's a meeting point for all of us from the Veneto, or Milan, or from these parts. I used to go every now and then, just to enjoy a bit of home cooking. The landlord has a large room with long low tables and benches, and it's always nice and quiet. That evening Giorgione walked in: he's unmistakable, with his red hair. I couldn't believe my eyes. He spotted me too. We embraced each other, not needing to speak, and then he sat down beside me and told me about his adventures. Then we talked about Marianna . . .'

He gave a deep sigh and held his head in his hands.

'I was still under the impression that she'd died from an illness,' he went on. 'He understood and realised that I was confused, so he didn't want to say any more. But in the end, I made him talk.'

His voice shook. 'I can't tell you the agony I suffered when I found out the truth . . . my little girl in the hands of those filthy perverts. I howled like a beast. The other customers surrounded me, and I felt I was suffocating. In the end, I calmed down and I demanded to know the names. Giorgione was forced to tell me, and at that point I tore off my crucifix and kissed it, making a solemn oath to avenge my daughter. Giorgio was horrified. He rushed out, as if to escape me, and I've not seen him since. Is he back in Venice too? Did he set you on my trail?'

Marco was shaken. 'No, Giorgione said nothing. He didn't even say that he'd met you. To tell you the truth, he didn't even know that Marianna's murderers had been killed.'

'Now tell me, Your Excellency . . .' Menico hesitated, keeping his eyes down. 'Given that you've heard all the witnesses, do you know whether my little girl suffered? I've spent years at sea, and I've heard the tales told by soldiers . . . and criminals. I know what happens when they get their hands on a woman. I can't bear to think of my Marianna in the hands of those animals . . .'

'She didn't suffer,' lied Marco. 'I was told that the poor girl died from suffocation when she was wrapped in her cloak and carried away. They didn't have time to touch her.' Pisani hoped that his lies would soften the father's pain, and indeed he did seem slightly relieved. 'But what about you?' he went on. 'What did you do after you learned what had happened?'

'I planned my revenge. I came back to Venice in September but didn't come home. My sister believes that I've only been back for a few days. I stayed at the Arsenale, in the houses on Fondamenta Nuove which are used for sailors in transit.'

'I know,' interrupted Marco. 'I just checked the ships' passenger lists and your name appears among those on board a galley that docked in Venice on 16 September. Then you lived in the Arsenale, and it was there that you met my gondolier.'

'Yes, the young man who asked me about the rope. It was mine, but I told him that it might have been Portuguese in order to delay the investigations. I still had a job to do.'

'Indeed. Even Alvise Cappello told me about someone who was known as the Levantino. He said that he'd not been back home since his daughter had departed. But for some reason I thought that Cappello was simply referring to a man whose daughter had been married. However, I had that conversation on 12 December, and at that stage I knew nothing about Marianna's disappearance. Both Barbaro and Corner were dead, and I was groping my way in the dark. But how did you manage it?'

The man sighed deeply. 'I may as well tell you. Now it's over, I no longer care whether I live or die. It wasn't that difficult. I started to follow all four of them, sometimes dressed as a Turk, and sometimes hidden by a cloak. With Barbaro, there was no problem. All I had to do was study the route he took at night when he paid a visit to his friend.'

'Lucrezia Scalfi.'

'That's her, yes. I looked for the darkest corner where I could lie in wait for him and then carry out the deed . . . He was the first. He hadn't a clue who I was, but he put up a fight. See this scar?' Menico held out his left hand. 'I've had to wear gloves ever since so I don't have to answer awkward questions.'

'And Corner?'

'That was more complicated. He was often with his wife, and I couldn't find the right moment. Then one day I went to the palace and they took me on as a gondolier for Dario, his brother. I'm quite handy with an oar, and for a few weeks I was able to study the comings and goings inside the house and Piero Corner's movements, which is when I discovered that he visited the Ridotto every Sunday evening. Initially, I was a bit reluctant because he'd just had a baby girl and he seemed happily married. But then I told myself that he hadn't stopped to think about my little girl, and so . . . When his turn came, Barbaro was already dead, and he was frightened and made sure that a servant came with him. But even so, I succeeded. In the end, he didn't resist much.'

So Menico was the mysterious gondolier, thought Marco, the one whose name he had forgotten to ask old Matteo about. He should have guessed when Matteo had mentioned Constantinople. Another detail then came to mind. 'Was that when you got hold of the sash with the Corner coat of arms?'

'Precisely. I used to wear it even after I left the job. Then I lost it when I fled the locanda on the Giudecca. You very nearly caught me then.'

'And it was you who visited old Signora Domenici and persuaded her to tell you where her son was hiding.'

'That whole family is rotten to the core. That repulsive old woman had drunk her fill of wine, and the only thing she cared about was money. Her eyes glittered with greed. But her son was another matter. I had a real fight with him . . . At that point, with two of them dead, he must have understood that I had him in my sights. I walked into the tavern wrapped in my cloak, and no one paid any attention because of the two tarts who were singing, half nude by then. I grabbed a jug of wine and went up. I hadn't a clue which room he was in, so it was luck that I knocked on the third door. I heard someone moving around inside and pretended to be a waiter. "Here's the wine!" I said. The door opened a fraction and it was him. I'd observed him carefully when I had followed all of them earlier. I shoved my way in, but he slipped out of my grasp and then we fought. It was as if I had superhuman strength, though, because I couldn't stop thinking of his filthy hands on my daughter's body. I knocked him out with a blow, and then he came to the same end as the others. Labia was the only one I didn't get . . .'

'Tell me something. You're an intelligent man; why did you use the same method for each murder? This allowed us to connect them and finally led us to you. If you'd killed each of your victims in a different way, perhaps making each murder look like an accident, we'd never have managed to solve them. You'll have heard the rumours that are doing the rounds, because no one knows about your daughter's death, and so the talk is of a murderer who kills for pleasure.'

Menico shook his head. 'To begin with I didn't think I'd use the same tactic and the same type of rope. Look, I've still got a piece here, which was destined for Labia.' He pointed to a coil lying at his feet.

Marco shivered, and for the first time realised how strange this situation was: an avogadore drinking and talking amicably with a killer in his own house.

'But when they arrested that poor man,' Menico went on, 'the one called Maso who had nothing to do with it, I was frightened that an innocent passer-by might be blamed for it. It was then that I started following the gossip, and I let Maso off the hook by killing Corner while he was still in prison. But, Your Excellency, what led you to suspect me, given that none of my relatives know that I've actually been in Venice for the past few months?'

Marco understood that he owed him an explanation. 'For days I, too, didn't think of you. I was convinced you'd only just come back, even if, when we met last Saturday, I should have realised from what you said that you knew Marianna was dead. But a few hours ago, while I was talking to Giorgio Sporti, I had a flash of insight. Constantinople was always cropping up in conversation, and Giorgio knew the truth but was so obviously innocent. So I asked myself who could he have confided in. What other man would have wanted to avenge Marianna? That's when I put two and two together. I asked Giorgio straight out who he had met in Constantinople. He, too, understood at that point, and he hesitated for a long time, and then told me a lie. He wanted to save you.'

Menico sat there with his head hanging. Pisani was also deep in thought.

It was the sailor who broke the silence. 'I'm in your hands,' he sighed. He seemed resigned, almost serene. 'I'm sorry for my sister, who I'll leave alone, but I'm ready to go to prison. But there's one more thing I have to ask you: find my little girl. My last wish is that she has a Christian burial and a tomb where at least her aunt can go and pray.'

Marco drained his glass to give himself courage. He walked over to the fire, holding his hands out to the warmth of the flames. His voice was a whisper. 'Menico, listen carefully. I've been thinking about this. You are a good man and you've suffered enough. I am a man of the law and I believe in justice, but I also believe that there is a more perfect justice than the one imposed by us humans. I know you are not a murderer: you saw those scoundrels walking free around Venice, unpunished by the law, and you took matters into your own hands. You also know full well that if they had stood trial, they would have deserved the death sentence. In short . . .' At this point Marco turned and started to pace up and down the room. 'I don't have the heart to arrest you. No one knows anything about you yet. I haven't confided in a soul.'

He stopped in front of Menico, who looked at him in astonishment.

'We haven't talked this evening. I've never set foot in this house. You must now pack up your belongings and leave. Take a boat. The weather is awful, but you're a sailor and you'll manage to reach Trieste, which is Austrian territory. No one will come looking for you there. Or you could escape on one of the Dalmatian boats departing from Riva degli Schiavoni. You'll only need a few ducats to pay for a passage. You have twenty-four hours. You mustn't say anything to your sister, and above all don't bid her farewell. In a few months you can write to her and ask her to join you so you can make a new life together in the East. Now, you must go. In twenty-four hours, I'll send the guards to arrest you, and by then you must have left Venice.'

Menico, deeply moved, found the strength to stammer, 'Why?'

'I've already told you: you've suffered an appalling injustice. I don't want you to pay again. You're not a murderer. I'm sure you'll find a way to atone for your sins.'

'And my little girl?'

It was time for Marco to reveal the final secret. 'We've found her.'

Menico broke down and sobbed.

'Her coffin is at this very moment lying in San Pietro, not far from here. You can pray for her before you leave.'

Is this true justice? wondered Marco as he climbed back into the gondola. *Have I done my duty, or have I just played God?*

He had always been convinced that law and justice could and should overlap, but he wasn't so sure now. In this strange case what was morally correct and what was legal had clashed, and he had followed his conscience.

Yet he felt as if a weight had been lifted off him. And he wanted to see Chiara.

CHAPTER 29

Light streamed out of the Gothic windows of Palazzo Pisani, creating dancing reflections on the waves of the Grand Canal, and the discordant sounds of instruments being tuned up echoed through the doorway. Gondolas thronged around the water gates as their gondoliers jostled to come alongside. Once the passengers had disembarked, they processed in their ballroom finery into the palace. Today was 26 December, Saint Stephen's Day, which marked the end of the liturgical celebrations for Christmas, and it was the date on which the Pisani family traditionally inaugurated Carnival with a magnificent evening reception.

Liveried footmen holding torches and candelabras lined the dramatic grand staircase, which had been designed by Tirali and was one of the most beautiful in Venice.

Chiara was both nervous and thrilled as she walked up those stairs in the company of Marco and Daniele. She was wearing a full-skirted gown of dark gold brocade which set off her blue eyes, and her hair was gathered into a cascade of curls. In the candlelight her pale skin gleamed more than usual as her willowy figure swept gracefully up each ramp. Her companions attracted equal admiration. Marco was wearing a long black jacket edged with silver, a taffeta waistcoat and, for once, a white wig. Daniele had chosen a bottle-green suit trimmed with gold. The other guests who were climbing the staircase beside them shot curious glances at the beautiful young woman on the arm of the avogadore.

Teodoro and Elena Pisani stood on the landing by the main hall to welcome their guests. When they caught sight of the approaching trio their faces lit up.

Chiara bowed slightly and, turning to Elena, whispered, 'Thank you, signora. Thank you for inviting me and for this.' She gestured to the magnificent ring that she wore on her left hand: a circle of golden roses surrounding a huge ruby, whose purity made it shine with extraordinary radiance.

'My child,' interrupted Elena, pulling the younger woman into her arms in a warm embrace, 'you can't imagine how happy I am to have you here.' The old senator smiled benevolently. 'As Marco will have told you' – and Elena looked at her son, her face a study of emotions – 'it's a family ring and belonged to my grandmother. No one deserves to wear it more than you.'

The ballroom shone as bright as day, illuminated by hundreds of candles that glittered in the Murano chandeliers and in the gilded wall sconces, creating shimmering reflections in the huge mirrors. Between the mirrors Chiara noted the famous Pisani family paintings: Veronese's *The Family of Darius before Alexander* and Piazzetta's more recent work, *The Death of Darius*.

A few dozen guests had already taken up their seats on the chairs set in front of the stage where the concert would be played. As the trio approached there was a buzz among the guests. Marco greeted his acquaintances, and Daniele guided Chiara to a seat in front of the orchestra.

'See that family on my right?' He gestured discreetly towards a tall, elegant woman with a stout husband and a rather unattractive girl wearing an emerald necklace. 'That's the Foscarini family and they're looking at you rather pointedly because for months they've been angling for an engagement between their daughter and Marco. Now that they've seen the famous Pisani ruby glinting on your finger, their hopes are dashed.'

It was true: both mother and daughter were staring at Chiara in open disdain.

All the guests had now arrived and the place was full. Elena and Teodoro Pisani walked to their chairs beside the stage and were promptly joined by their son, Giovanni, and his wife, Rossana, whose wide skirt did nothing to hide her pregnancy. They, too, had welcomed Chiara affectionately.

When the orchestra started to play the opening notes of Vivaldi's 'Primavera', the chatter immediately died down.

Sitting beside Chiara, Marco let his mind wander. In the past few days he had resolved a number of problems. As he had promised, the guards had been sent to Rio Sant'Anna to arrest Menico on 21 December, but they had found only his sister, who had just returned from the cathedral of San Pietro in Castello, where she had remained in vigil over Marianna's coffin until the funeral. Menico had vanished without saying a word to her and she hoped that he had not come to harm after the shock of learning about his daughter's death. She had seemed, and indeed she was, sincere.

Pisani had not mentioned his conversation with Menico to a soul, not even to Zen. He had admitted to his friend that he had guessed that the old sailor might be the murderer they had been seeking and he had also confessed that he'd gone to his house. Daniele had given him a fierce telling-off for such imprudence. But Marco had shrugged it off, saying that, though the door had been open, the house had been empty, even though the Turkish clothing and the coil of rope served as sufficient evidence to confirm his suspicions.

He'd recounted the same concoction of half-truths to Chiara, who had looked at him with understanding but not said a word.

The inquisitors had been pleased that the case had been resolved and they had finally presented the investigations to the Council of Ten. Labia would be quietly put on trial in due course and sentenced to exile. He was a figure who brought prestige neither to his family nor to the

Republic. For the time being he was still in the Piombi, where a series of manservants, barbers, wig-makers and tailors waited daily on his every need. He had even managed to have his fellow prisoner given a bath, shaved and provided with a new set of garments. A special servant had been employed to set traps all around the cell and had already caught a dozen or more rats. Marco smiled to himself at the thought.

When Vivaldi's concerto ended, a handful of servants mounted a wrought-iron grille across the stage to hide the next performers from the audience. It was the turn of the choir from the Conservatorio dei Mendicanti, mainly made up of orphan girls who were being brought up as nuns and taught by the best singing masters of the city. Their renown had spread across Europe and visitors flocked to Venice from abroad, but the girls never showed their faces and usually sang in the convent churches, hidden behind the metal grates. Only on very rare occasions, and for a considerable price, did the Conservatorio allow them to perform in public. There were those who said that the girls' beauty was out of this world, and others who swore that many were fat and ugly or disfigured by the pox. Whatever the truth, no one could argue with the fact that they sang like angels.

The choir launched into a multi-voice cantata by Benedetto Marcello and Marco again lost himself in thought.

One thing had been weighing on his conscience. He should have done it earlier, but before Christmas there had really been no reason why Annetta should continue to wait for him in her small apartment behind the church of San Rocco.

He had gone to see her two days earlier, and in the end no explanation had been necessary because she already knew and understood.

'I will miss you, Your Excellency,' she'd said, with tears in her eyes. 'But I knew that it would come to an end. You must go your own way and make yourself a family, and I never imagined that I would become a Pisani.'

Marco had been quite moved and felt almost ashamed as he gave her the papers which his bankers had drawn up earlier. She would be assured of an annual income that would be more than sufficient.

'I cannot accept,' she had said in a low voice. 'You never did so before, but now you're treating me like a . . . as a—'

'No, Annetta,' Marco had interrupted. 'It's precisely because you are not one of them that I want you always to be able to hold your head high without having to rely on others.'

In the end Annetta had accepted, but nonetheless Marco still felt guilty.

Yet now he had the good fortune of having Chiara in his life. He had gone to see her as soon as he could and just yesterday, on Christmas morning, he had offered her the family ring chosen by his mother. 'I am delighted that you've found a woman worthy of wearing it,' Signora Pisani had said as she pressed it into his hand.

On seeing the ring, Chiara had fallen silent. 'Does this mean we're engaged?' she had asked at last.

'Yes, Chiara,' he'd replied, somewhat taken aback by her lukewarm response. 'It's not a new ring because it belongs in the family. But my wife never wore it, if that's what's worrying you. I'd never do anything so crass.'

'No, that's not the problem. It's only that . . . you should have asked me first whether I agreed. I've not even met your parents yet . . .'

That was how Chiara thought: true to character and the most independent woman in Venice.

'Chiara,' he had replied, 'I love you. You love me. Will you be my fiancée?'

'Yes. But what's the hurry?'

'Because tomorrow evening at the ball, I want everyone to know that you are mine.'

'And what if they disapprove because I'm not an aristocrat?'

'When they catch sight of you, they'll be green with envy. The men of me, the women of you.'

Noticing that the audience had risen to their feet and were applauding, Marco shook himself from his thoughts and joined in. Once the applause had died down, Daniele spotted a beautiful widow with whom he was acquainted and headed towards her to pay his respects. Marco offered Chiara his arm and led her towards the dining room in the large reception hall of the upper floor. Here, the refreshments had been set out on an enormous central table laden with silver dishes filled with truffled pheasants and partridges, trays of finely sliced meats and pyramids of oysters whose mother-of-pearl shells lay temptingly open. A huge sturgeon on a gilded platter resting on a chafing dish formed the centrepiece. At one end was a selection of prized early vegetables and salads dressed with aromatic vinegars. On the left was the dessert table with fruits and ices of all kinds kept cold on beds of crushed ice. On the other side of the hall was the wine buffet serving champagne, an array of Burgundy, Malaga, Moscato and Malvasia, and to conclude, a selection of liqueurs and Rhenish wines.

The stewards circled nimbly between the tables, serving the guests. Among them Marco glimpsed his butler, Giuseppe, who would never have missed an opportunity to wear the family livery at the annual reception in Palazzo Pisani. Indeed, even Nani, who had accompanied them to the festivities, was lending a hand downstairs in the kitchens, even though he had been given the evening off. Marco was sure that at the appropriate moment Nani would find a door ajar through which he could peer to admire the dancing.

After dinner the guests trooped back downstairs amidst much chatter. Marco took the opportunity of singling out some of them. 'My parents invite the city's most illustrious families, but only on condition that my mother actually likes them,' he told Chiara. 'As you can see, those families include the Erizzos, the Trons, the Mocenigos, the Zorzis, the Bragadins and the Giustinians. Those men at the end of the hall, still eating their ices, are the Memmo brothers, Andrea, Bernardo and Lorenzo. The gossip is that they're involved in black magic and are friends of Casanova. My mother would never invite him, that's for certain. Behind me,' Marco went on in a whisper, 'is Condulmer, the principal shareholder of the Sant'Angelo theatre, and one of the inquisitors. Let's move on, though, because I don't want him to start talking about work.'

The dancing had started and the ballroom was a magnificent sight. In the flickering candlelight the ladies' wide skirts formed circles of crimson and violet damask, silver lace and golden brocade, all richly embroidered. They looked like exotic flowers whose centres were adorned with sparkling gems and pearls. Their male partners were similarly resplendent in gold-trimmed coats, and they beat time with their fine leather shoes embellished with precious buckles. The scents of violet and jasmine wafted across the hall, mixed with sweet undertones of chypre.

Our civilisation may be declining, thought Marco, *but into such splendid decadence!*

At that moment he felt a hand on his shoulder. He turned and found himself face to face with Dario Corner, who was soberly dressed in black.

'Can I talk to you for a moment?'

They withdrew into the bow of a window.

'You seem surprised to see me here,' Dario started. 'Your mother was gracious enough to send us the invitation, but we are all in mourning and I've only come briefly because I wanted to see you.'

'Tell me how I can help.'

'I don't want you to think badly of our family. My brother did something appalling and my mother is distraught. We've not even dared to tell my sister-in-law the truth. I have my faults, it's true, but I had no idea my brother could be capable of something like that. We used to fight, but I was fond of him.'

Marco scrutinised the man and saw the signs of deep sorrow in his eyes. He remembered how, without knowing it, Dario, too, had been on the list of possible suspects.

'But,' Corner went on, 'what really grieves me the most is that my brother had been a changed man in the past year or so and he'd stopped seeing that group. And just when he'd become a father, that wretch chose to take revenge. Of course, he had his own reasons . . . I don't know what to say.'

Marco clapped him affectionately on the shoulder.

'I only wanted to assure you, in spite of everything, how much I appreciate all you've done,' ended Dario.

'Come to visit us, Corner,' said Marco as he turned away. 'And support your sister-in-law.'

He returned to join Chiara and sat down next to her on a divan in the grand salon.

'Do you see that woman dressed in lace whose glass is being filled by the waiter?' he said, gesturing towards an elderly lady whose ugly appearance made her stand out. 'That's Rosalba Carriera, the famous painter. She doesn't see that well now, but she's painted the most beautiful pastel portraits and miniatures of royalty all over Europe. She doesn't go out much, and it's a miracle that she's here this evening. My mother must have used all her diplomatic skills. And that rather stout man over there, chatting in the midst of a circle of admirers, do you see him? He's the famous Carlo Goldoni. He doesn't need to be invited twice, especially when he knows the food will be excellent. He's a formidable conversationalist.'

'All of Venice is here!' exclaimed Chiara.

'No, not all, only the chosen. My mother doesn't only invite nobles and artists. Look at that gentleman at the table beside the wall.' He gestured towards a man who looked like a commoner. 'That's Segati, the rich fabric merchant; perhaps you know him already. And on his

right, that tall. thin character is one of our greatest intellectuals. He's
Giovanni Poleni, the famous mathematician and astrophysicist from
the University of Padua. On the other side of the room, surrounded by
that group of women, is Andrea Tron, perhaps the only aristocrat who's
also an excellent businessman. He owns a series of wool manufactories
on the mainland and is reclaiming parts of the lagoon. He speaks five
languages. But now let's go and dance.'

The orchestra was playing a pavane and Marco and Chiara joined
the other couples. Chiara danced with infinite grace and Marco noticed
how all the other men looked at her with interest every time she was
turned by them. For the first time, he felt a stab of jealousy.

In the interval between two dances, they were joined by an elderly
gentleman. Marco smiled as he introduced him to Chiara.

'Here you have the greatest artist of all time, Giovanbattista
Tiepolo.' The painter bowed dutifully. 'I much admired your paintings
in the ballroom at Palazzo Labia,' Marco went on. Then he turned to
Chiara and said, 'But you must admire the ceiling that Tiepolo painted
for us in the room next door.'

Tiepolo smiled with satisfaction. 'Thank you, Your Excellency. I
took the liberty of interrupting you because I wanted to say that I had
such difficulty finding the right model for Cleopatra. But if I had seen
your splendid lady at the time . . . I've just been watching you dance
together . . . if I may say so, I would have asked her to pose for me.'

Chiara smiled with embarrassment. 'I am very honoured, sir. And if
my fiancé would permit' – she smiled as she looked at Marco – 'I would
be happy to sit for a portrait.'

There, she'd said it! My fiancé! Pisani was overjoyed.

'Shall we go, my love?' he asked, after Tiepolo had withdrawn. 'It's
past midnight and, outside, Carnival has started.'

Bidding many of the guests farewell as they left, soon they were out on the Grand Canal. It was snowing and the heavy flakes had already formed a white blanket over the city, lending it an additional touch of magic.

They caught a ferry and, surrounded by a bustling crowd of strangers, they soon reached Saint Mark's Square, where the oriental domes of the basilica, the straight façades of the Procuratie and the soaring silhouette of the bell tower were all dusted in white.

In the square, crowds had gathered under the lamplight. Warmly wrapped in cloaks and wearing bautta masks, men and women ran around laughing and throwing snowballs. The coffee houses were open and full to bursting. Here and there, nobles and commoners danced *manfrine* and *furlane* to the sound of pipes and guitars, the men jumping up and down while the women spun around like tops.

Marco and Chiara joined in the fun and joined hands in a large circle of dancers, showering each other with snow. An old man stirred hot red wine in a cauldron over an improvised fire, sending a tantalising spiced scent into the air. They queued for a glass and drank it eagerly before, laughing, they headed back to dance.

Marco wrapped Chiara even more tightly in her cloak and pulled her into the shadow under the arches of the Procuratie Vecchie. He kissed her and she responded. They held each other in a close and increasingly intimate embrace as his hands caressed her.

'Shall we . . .?' Marco's voice was hoarse.

She followed him up the dark stairs to the mezzanine room that he used as a dressing room and in the half-light of the lanterns that shone over the square she lay in his arms on the sofa.

Much later, warm under the avogadore's ample cloak, they smiled at each other, ecstatic and content.

'What a wonderful thing love is,' murmured Chiara. 'You are the first.'

Marco burned afresh with passion as he looked at her. 'That's how it will always be, Chiara. Will you marry me?'

'Marry you? Yes, of course, but in the future.'

'No, I mean now, Chiara. Will you be my wife now?' He kissed her again passionately.

Her eyes sparkled with a hint of mischief. 'Of course, my love. But not now. We'll wait a while.'

'And how will we manage until then?' stuttered Marco, looking at her in dismay.

'Until then,' echoed Chiara, as a consolatory dimple appeared in her cheek, 'let us enjoy living in sin.'

LET'S SPEAK VENETIAN: A NOTE
FROM THE AUTHOR

The Venice described in the book is not the city you see today but a reconstruction of what it might have looked like in the eighteenth century. For example, the Terranova granaries no longer stand on Riva degli Schiavoni. Rio Sant'Anna in Castello was filled in by Napoleon and later became known as Via Garibaldi. The Arsenale, too, is described as it was three hundred years ago. However, unlike almost all other centuries-old cities, in many respects Venice has changed very little.

It is still divided, as it was then, into *sestrieri*, or districts: Cannaregio, San Marco and Castello on the island north of the Grand Canal; Dorsoduro, Santa Croce and San Polo to the south. On the outskirts we find the island of Giudecca and the Lido, and among the other islands in the lagoon, Murano and Burano.

The streets are called *calli* (the narrowest measures barely 53 centimetres wide). Some still keep the name of *rughe* or *rughette*. The earliest paved streets are known as *salizàde*, and the part of a street that runs along a canal, or *rio*, is termed a *fondamenta*. A *ramo* is a short stretch of a calle that connects two streets.

A *rio terà* is a small canal that has been filled in and turned into a street, and *riva* (pl. *rive*) are stretches along the canals or the basin that are used as wharves.

The *sotoporteghi* are covered passageways, running below private houses, that lead into some of the calli.

When giving a specific address, because the names of calli were often repeated, it was important to state the sestriere and the parish where a particular building was located, as well as the name of a nearby monument. Today, every building in the sestriere is numbered progressively.

There is only one piazza in Venice – that is Piazza San Marco, or Saint Mark's Square. All the others are *campi* or *campielli*. The word is derived from the fact that in the early centuries of the city's history these spaces were used to grow vegetables or, if they are slightly raised, as cemeteries.

The word *Ca'* means a palace, often a resplendent building, and it is a sign of the modesty of the Venetian aristocracy, which did not include counts or dukes appointed by royalty, but simply patricians, who all held equal status in the Republic.

Two of the less well known among the numerous Venetian magistracies are included in the novel. First, the *avogaria di Comùn*. Among their various duties, the *avogadori* instructed proceedings, rather like present-day procurators, and they acted as public prosecutors. One of them (there were three in office at any one time) always had to be present at sittings of the Senate. All of them had the right of intervention, that is to say, they could take action with regard to measures taken by other magistracies if they believed that they did not comply with the law. Lastly, they kept the *Libro d'Oro*, the book that formally recorded noble birth.

Second, the magistracy headed by Messer Grando, who held a position similar to our modern-day Italian *questori*, or head of police. This man was always a commoner. In the mid-eighteenth century the office was held by Matteo Varutti.

GLOSSARY

Accademia dei Nobili: Charitable institution that also cared for orphans from noble families.

Arsenale: Once the largest docks and shipyards in Europe, employing thousands of specialised workers.

avogadore di Comùn: One of three public prosecutors, or judges, charged with defending the interests of the Republic and investigating violations of justice.

bàilo: The official diplomatic representative of Venice in Constantinople.

barnabotto (pl. *barnabotti*): An impoverished Venetian patrician, with no money but a strong sense of entitlement.

bautta: Full-face mask, usually worn during the Carnival.

bissóna (pl. *bissóne*): A large Venetian boat, manned by six or eight oarsmen.

bragozzo (pl. *bragozzi*): Large fishing boat used in the Adriatic, with coloured sails.

burchiello: Passenger ferryboat on the Brenta canal.

burchio (pl. *burchi*): Flat-bottomed rowing boat used to carry passengers or goods.

calle (pl. *calli*): A narrow street between houses.

corno: The pointed hat worn by the Doge of Venice.

Fondaco dei Turchi: The trading warehouse and offices used by Turks on the Grand Canal.

jus primae noctis: A (fictitious) feudal custom, more commonly referred to as *droit du seigneur* in English, that stated that a lord had the right to have sex with a woman on the first night of her marriage before her husband.

La Salute: The church dedicated to Our Lady of Health, built after the terrible plague of 1576.

listòn: The evening walk in Saint Mark's Square where Venetians would show off their clothes and friends. It takes its name from the *listone*, the broad strip of marble running around the square.

locanda: A public premises serving food and providing accommodation. Some were exclusive, such as the Leon Bianco, while others were merely drinking dens.

padrona: Mistress, or landlady.

parón: Master, employer.

Patrono: The Master of the Arsenale, a patrician and high-ranking official.

Piombi: The Leads is the name given to the prison cells in the attics of the Doge's Palace, under the lead-covered roof.

Quarantie Criminale: The criminal court.

Ridotto: The state-owned gambling house, near the church of San Moisè. The stakes were high, thereby limiting access to the nobility. Face masks were compulsory.

soldo: Small coin, similar to a penny.

villeggiatura: The period, usually from summer to early autumn, when the Venetian nobility would retire to their mainland estates to escape the heat of the city.

ACKNOWLEDGMENTS

First of all, I have a debt to pay to my husband, Arnaldo, who, by buying me a property in Venice, in the same building in the sestiere of Castello that I've described as the house lived in by the Biondini family, allowed me to get to know the city so well and to use it as the setting for my stories.

Likewise, I shall always owe a debt of gratitude to Maria Paola Romeo of Grandi & Associati, who I met at a women's fiction festival in Matera. On that occasion she agreed to read my manuscripts and, ever since then, she has always provided encouragement. Today she is my outstanding agent.

It was also wonderful to work with Alessandra Tavella, content editor for Amazon Publishing, and I continue to appreciate her extraordinary professionalism, as well as her friendship.

My heartfelt thanks also go to my Venetian friends: to Valeria Numerico for instilling in me a feeling for the soul of her city, and to Antonia Sautter, a leading expert on eighteenth-century Venice and the brilliant founder of the Doge's Ball (Ballo del Doge), for her steadfast belief in me. I have her to thank for the personal experience of a ball at Palazzo Pisani, which inspired the last chapter.

Many others have contributed unknowingly to this book.

For the settings I have drawn extensively on the paintings by Pietro Longhi, Gabriele Bella and, above all, Canaletto. For relations between the characters and for the servants' characters, I was inspired by Goldoni. For the details of everyday life, I owe much to Casanova's *Memorie*.

Among today's historians of Venice, I must pay tribute to the invaluable help provided by Alvise Zorzi and Pompeo Molmenti, as well as René Guerdan and many others. Much of the detail of daily life for the lower classes in Venice was inspired by the excellent descriptions given by Egle Trincanato and Carla Coco.

Lastly, it would not be right not to mention the contribution offered by websites such as Bauta.it, Baroque.it and Venezia-nascosta.it and the book series published by Filippi for *Il Gazzettino*.

ABOUT THE AUTHOR

Maria Luisa Minarelli is a journalist and writer. She was born in Bologna, where she also graduated with a degree in history. Her work has appeared in *Storia illustrata* and *Historia*, and she has also written about health and tourism. Her first book, *Donne di denari* (Olivares), a study of female entrepreneurship through the centuries, appeared in 1989. A German translation has also been published. *A tavola con la storia* (Sansoni) came out in 1992 and looks at civilisations over the centuries and countries with a tradition of fine foods. Her first novel, the thriller *La donna dal quadrifoglio*, was published in 2008.

She lives in Milan with her husband and frequently spends time in Venice, a city she has always loved. She enjoys travelling and her interests include art and antiques. She is an avid reader, mostly at night, and she cannot live without her cats and the many plants which she grows herself.

ABOUT THE TRANSLATOR

Photo © 2018 Giorgio Granozio

History and languages have always played a large part in Lucinda's life. After living for years in Italy, she is now based in Scotland, where she combines her work as a translator with teaching a number of university courses relating to the history of early modern Italy. She has translated a wide range of books from Italian, many relating to Italian history and art.

Printed in Great Britain
by Amazon